I0823697

ALSO BY THE AUTHOR

The Collaborators

Ground Up: A Novel

Made in Russia: Unsung Icons of Soviet Design (editor)

Dressed Up for a Riot: Misadventures in Putin's Moscow

THE CORMORANT HUNT

A Novel

Michael Idov

SCRIBNER

NEW YORK AMSTERDAM/ANTWERP LONDON TORONTO SYDNEY/MELBOURNE NEW DELHI

Scribner
An Imprint of Simon & Schuster, LLC
1230 Avenue of the Americas
New York, NY 10020

First Scribner hardcover edition January 2026

Manufactured in the United States of America

10 9 8 7 6 5 4 3 2 1

Library of Congress Control Number: 2025946872

ISBN 978-1-6680-8228-7
ISBN 978-1-6680-8230-0 (ebook)

THE CORMORANT HUNT

PROLOGUE

March 3, 2022

The glitching satnav map in the dashboard put the border a hundred kilometers in front of them, but it had been saying so for an hour now. Katya Lisichenko opened her backpack, pulled out an accordion file folder, and for what had to be the fiftieth time that day, flicked through its tabs. Her travel passport with a fresh Schengen visa; a domestic one, a deeper oxblood red, registered to her mother's dacha outside Moscow; a bank statement with a healthy but not extravagant balance; two separate certificates clearing her name of any tax debts or traffic tickets; a printout of a hotel reservation in Tallinn. She knew every crease in every paper by heart, but had found that the act calmed her down. It felt like going through prayer beads. The prayer, in each case, was the same one: *Let me out, assholes.*

Katya had always thought of her hyper-organized mind as her best asset. After all, it had landed a girl from Izyum a job as the executive assistant to the president of KhromBank and kept her in that position for twelve years. Ironically, it was the same endless ability for compartmentalization that led her to stay in Russia far too long. She saw the gathering madness but kept explaining it away. Vicious anti-LGBT laws were just political showboating. Massing armies at the border was just a negotiation tactic. Sunk-cost fallacy, they called it in her trade: She had invested so much into getting that red passport, was so proud of having made it from a crumbling apartment block in Eastern Ukraine to the glass towers of Moscow that it made her ignore the increasingly obvious. *Come on,* she would say to the few Ukrainian friends she still had, *think rationally. What does he stand to gain by this?* As if logic still applied to the paranoid whims of an aging emperor.

So, efficient as she was with color-coded tabs, she was also late.

Her second homeland's tanks rolled into her first one on February 24. On March 2, the Russian government declared any antiwar sentiment, statement, or action illegal. The law was to take effect in twenty-four hours. March 3 was thus the deadline for shutting up or getting out.

Almost everyone in her social circle chose the latter. The urbanistas with the good visas flew to London or Berlin. The noncommittal rich made a beeline for Bali and Dubai. The rest scattered to places like Georgia, Turkey, Montenegro, Armenia, and Kazakhstan. Vacation spots became shelters. Countries haughty Muscovites knew only as sources of migrant labor were now destinations, and they were now the migrants.

By the evening of March 2, all flights out of Moscow for the next day were sold out. She tried trains—no luck. The state railways' site had either crashed or been taken down. At the last moment, a friend of a friend texted her about a dissident couple fleeing to Estonia by taxi. Katya's actual destination was Spain, but details like that no longer mattered. The only meaningful border left in her world was between Russia and not-Russia. She called the number and claimed the remaining passenger seat for $5,000.

The couple were in their late fifties, both journalists at the same opposition outlet, with the touching and slightly creepy vibe of superannuated high school sweethearts. Free Pen Foundation, an NGO Katya never heard of, had wangled them emergency humanitarian visas to

Norway. They brought along a heavy-breathing French bulldog, whose odds of being allowed across the border worried them more than their own. "There's no room in the trunk," the wife had mournfully warned Katya before taking her cash; it held three duffels stuffed with decades' worth of common property, mostly books.

Katya traveled light because she lived light. Apart from a few hundred thousand rubles in her checking account, which was largely a decoy for the border service, she had moved all her real money to crypto and was planning to reunite with it in Barcelona. Her rolltop backpack held two changes of clothes, a MacBook Air, three fully charged power banks, a pouch with her favorite cosmetics, and a single sentimental item: a plush IKEA shark from an old girlfriend. She wore no jewelry save a vintage wristwatch that could, in a pinch, buy her a mid-range sedan. The rest of Katya's possessions fit on her phone, which was cleansed of the freshly outlawed Instagram (she had deleted Facebook the previous year, after an unpleasant catfishing episode) and scrubbed of questionable texts. She was ready.

Only one factor remained beyond her control. It was the very real possibility that her job made her too valuable to let out of the country. In Soviet times, they called people like that refuseniks. Katya wasn't an idiot; she knew full well that KhromBank, among its many other services, had been a sluice for clandestine government funds, and its head, Gennady Demin, a likely veteran of one intelligence agency or another. Still, she had kept her nose clean, had never asked a question if she suspected she wouldn't like the answer, and had had no trouble traveling to Europe or the States even after the bank came under sanctions from both. But what if, once the war began, her boss's bosses decided she knew too much—which, let's be honest, she did?

There was no longer any point in guessing. She would find out soon enough.

The bulldog sniffled and snored. Old-growth conifers towered on both sides of the road, lower branches weighed down with snow; early March in northwest Russia was still the dead of winter. The taxi sped through the night, a little bubble of warmth in a black frozen expanse.

They had been in the car for close to seven hours now. The scent of the dog mixed with that of the driver. For the first half of the trip, the cabbie, a potbellied, round-faced man in a matted shearling vest over a flannel shirt, kept hitting on her. Back in her Moscow comfort zone, Katya would have curtly told him the truth, that she liked girls, and probably stared him in the face for a few extra seconds, daring him to say anything to that. Here and now, it wasn't worth the risk. When his right hand crawled off the gearbox and found its way to her knee, she simply covered her lap with the backpack.

The dissidents, to their credit, attempted a rescue. After a quick spousal whisper session, the man asked the driver to stop the car so they could all stretch out and let the dog take a piss. When they got back in, he sat in the front instead of Katya. The women and the bulldog shared the back seat.

This, weirdly, made things worse. While the driver's previous interests had been limited to Katya's legs, the arrival of a fellow male in his peripheral vision prompted him to start talking politics. His views were a classic mishmash of imported conspiracy theories, continuing antivax delirium, legitimate grievances, and good old-fashioned antisemitism. At that moment, he was in a manic phase, as if his home team had just made the World Cup finals. The war was everything he'd wanted. He didn't even wish Russia a quick victory; he was just happy that men were men again, and someone somewhere was getting killed. It was a version of the world that made more sense to him than the amorphous new age of what he kept calling "transhuman values."

The dissident heroically absorbed the whole monologue, mumbling *mm-hmm* every once in a while. There existed a nonzero chance that if the man behind the wheel were to find out his passengers' real views on the war, he would kick them out in the middle of a frozen forest and drive off, leaving them to die of hypothermia. As idle conversations with cabbies went, the stakes ran unusually high in this one.

"I mean, not all Americans are bad," the driver suddenly said. It seemed unrelated to whatever his previous sentence had been. Katya wasn't really listening.

"Sure," the man agreed. There was a slight satirical edge to his docility, meant strictly for the back seat.

"You know what American I like? Felix Burnham. Smartest man alive."

"Isn't he British?"

"Whatever. He should live here in Russia, like Gérard Depardieu. They don't appreciate him over there." Katya had no idea whom they were talking about. The woman had fallen asleep on her shoulder, hugging the dog. Snow whirled in the taxi's high beams like old TV static.

"The main thing is that the globalists don't own him," the driver continued, largely to himself. "They're pretty powerful here, too, you know."

Katya scratched the bulldog's ear. The dog yawned and licked her hand. She suddenly felt like crying and made every effort not to.

Phone signal came back just long enough to reload the map. The Estonian border was five kilometers out. "Get ready," said the man, turning around to gently shake his wife awake.

They weren't heading to the notorious Ivangorod-Narva bridge crossing, where fleeing Russians mixed uneasily with Ukrainian refugees and from where rumors of an all-night traffic jam and sadistic searches were already spreading online. The dissidents had gotten a tip from their sponsor organization that they'd be better off entering Estonia at the Shumilkino checkpoint, via a forest road normally used by long-haul truckers.

The village of Shumilkino was barely there—just a few gas stations and a tacky motel made to look like a cluster of traditional log cabins. Border crossing appeared to be its only business. The checkpoint itself stood straight ahead, a corrugated-steel Quonset hut with a rounded roof tall enough for a semi to pass through.

The taxi rolled to a stop. "All right, guys," said the driver. "Travel safe. Sorry for your loss." The trip's official legend was a funeral of an elderly relative in Narva.

"Oh shit," said the husband, squinting into the snow. Beyond the metal shed, the road abruptly turned into a narrow dirt track cut into the pine woods, with no lights on the other side. "How wide is the no-man's-land here?"

"Here?" The driver shrugged. "Two klicks. Maybe two and a half."

"I don't suppose you could take us to . . ." The man fell silent. He knew the answer.

"I don't do visas," said the driver. "Besides"—he pointed ahead—"this time next year, all of that is going to be Russia anyway." Katya craned her neck to see if he was joking, but didn't look too hard because she didn't want to know.

They got out of the car. The husband took two duffels, the wife a duffel and the dog, whom she put inside her parka. Katya volunteered to help, but the woman waved her away with her free hand. The taxi backed up, made a three-point turn from snowbank to snowbank, and vanished in the night.

Inside a small overheated enclosure in the middle of the shed sat two puzzled-looking women in green uniforms with FSB border service shoulder boards. "Wow, they just keep on coming tonight," one of them said to the other as the trio emerged waddling out of the dark. They didn't seem to be aware that their country was deep into a shooting war with another and busy instituting a terror regime at home.

"Aw, cute," said the second woman, making a kissy face at the bulldog. "Is it going to be okay like this?"

Are any of us? Katya almost said. She missed the fateful moment her passport got stamped. All her thoughts were on how they were going to walk two kilometers in -27 degrees Celsius.

"You may go." The guard yawned, a bit more discreetly than the dog.

"That's it? You don't need to see the rest of my . . . ?"

"That's it, lady." Katya caught, or imagined, a hint of sympathy.

They exited the shed on the far side and trudged on through the no-man's-land in complete darkness. The road wasn't, strictly speaking, a road—just frozen mud, molded by truck wheels into tall sharp ridges. Snowflakes, at this temperature, prickled and stung; each gust of wind felt like glass breaking in front of her face. Once every few minutes, an eighteen-wheeler roared past, a nightmare of lights and mass and bellowing horn. There was no shoulder to step aside, so each time they just sort of half sat, half fell into the hard snow.

An excruciating hour later, the group reached a white two-story cube with the word *PIIRIPUNKT* and the Estonian coat of arms on the side. Katya, the youngest and least laden, was well ahead by then, but slowed down and let the husband and wife go in first. Just being indoors felt like heaven. Whatever came next in her life, she was alive and in Europe, one formality away from freedom. Or at least a lack of immediate danger.

The dissidents got their entry stamps, hugged, and cried. Katya petted the dog one last time; the poor thing was still shaking from the cold.

"The foundation sent a van to pick us up," the man said. "If you need a ride to Tallinn, we can wait for you."

"Oh my god, thank you," said Katya. "It will just be a minute."

The couple picked up their duffels and went into a little glassed-in lounge area behind passport control. A flag of the European Union hung on the far wall; the husband began taking pictures of the wife in front of it, trying to position the circle of stars as her halo.

The Estonian officer, a young man with a strawberry-blond beard, swiped Katya's passport against a magnetic reader, typed something into his computer, and frowned. Then he hit and held the delete key. Swiped again. Typed again. She could tell from the keystrokes that it was her own last name, L-i-s-i-c-h-e-n-k-o.

"I'm sorry," he said without looking up. "This is really weird." He folded back both covers of her passport, held the photo page up toward the ceiling lamp, and checked it against the light for watermarks. Scratched the edge of the photo with a neatly trimmed fingernail.

"Is there a problem?" Katya asked with a dutiful smile.

The Estonian cleared his throat. "You could say that."

She thought she knew herself well, and was surprised to realize that if they sent her walking back, she would just step into the path of the next eighteen-wheeler.

"What is it?" Her voice was calm. "I'm sure it's solvable."

"Well," the officer said, then stopped. "I don't— I'm not even supposed to tell you. But it says here that you"—he paused again—"Yekaterina Viktorovna Lisichenko, born in Izyum, Ukraine, on June 5, 1984? Right?"

"Right."

"*Glory to Ukraine,* by the way."

"*Glory to heroes.* Why? What's the issue?"

The young man looked at her with genuine sympathy. "It says here you crossed into Estonia, at this very checkpoint, two days ago."

The husband and wife stood and watched from the other side of the soundproof plexiglass as the officer made a phone call, shrugging a lot as he talked; as their travel companion, so cool and composed the whole trip, suddenly yelled, then slammed her palm against the booth, and finally crumpled on the floor, her face instantly scarlet and her legs kicking uncontrollably; as another guard hurried toward her with a bottle of water, which she slapped out of his hand, an action that made yet another, far less friendly guard rush in; and as together they half led, half dragged her off into the doorway from which they had just spilled out—a door leading not to Europe proper, where the husband and wife and dog were now, but to some sort of ill-lit liminal realm between legal and illegal, liberty and bondage, safety and peril. But their own relief at having escaped was too overwhelming to focus on this unpleasantness for too long.

"Maybe she's a spy," said the wife.

"She didn't sound like it when we talked."

"Well, she wouldn't, would she. I'm sure the Estonians know who to let in and who not to. It's not our place to second-guess them."

The van sounded its horn outside, and they hurried to it, their vague concern about the incident they had just witnessed already melting.

CHAPTER ONE

EuroCity 171 Berlin–Prague
December 10, 2023

Alan Keegan prided himself on never questioning other cultures' ways, but the tea-in-a-glass thing mystified him. It's not like the Germans had no concept of hot beverages in cups. Had he ordered a coffee, it would have arrived in a perfectly respectable cup-and-saucer combo with the logo of the railway company on both. Yet Keegan was, tragicomically for a devout internationalist with grave misgivings about Britain and Britishness, an equally devout tea drinker. And so tea he had asked for, and tea he got, in an untouchably hot glass with no handle or holder, filled to the brim so the slightest shudder of the train threatened to splash it out into his lap.

"The goulash comes shortly," said the waiter in a somewhat ominous tone, setting the liquid time bomb in front of him. Keegan wasn't hungry, certainly not for railroad goulash, but had felt compelled to justify his third hour in the crowded café car by ordering some real food. The plan was to spend the whole trip here, as a precaution. Keegan's life brimmed with them. He had consigned himself to it the day FleaCollar, his amateur open-source intelligence portal, published the Harlow Dossier.

The award ceremony was in Prague; the organizers, generous but clueless, had sent him a first-class plane ticket out of London. The only luxury Keegan craved was the ability to move around without compulsively checking for a tail, and no amount of money would buy that now. He took the ticket, went to Heathrow three hours early, passed security, then doubled back through Arrivals and got a seat on another flight that left at the same time, this one from Gatwick and with a layover in Berlin. Having barely made that one, he forwent the second leg of the trip, got off in Berlin, briefly losing his way around the terrible new airport, and grabbed an illegal cab to the Hauptbahnhof, where he finally boarded this train with two tickets in two different classes and zero intent to use either one. Thus, goulash.

That the life of a global transparency icon (the award committee's words, not his) would be cloaked in so much subterfuge was ironic enough. What no one else, including the committee, seemed to realize was just how *expensive* it got.

At least he lucked out with the ride. The EuroCity to Prague was a rather calming four-hour affair. The tracks ran alongside the Elbe, following its gentle bends, through a bucolic hillscape called the Saxon Switzerland for its supposed similarity to the Jura. The river hadn't fully frozen over yet, but skirts of ice had already formed at the shore, reaching toward each other across the dark current. On the far side, a single row of fairy-tale houses nestled between the cliffs and the water. *Sehr Europäisch,* blood-drenched history and all.

Was a journalism prize worth the bother? Was he even a journalist? Previous winners of the Aletheia Award, named after the Greek goddess of truth, included corporate giant slayers, war-zone aces, people who had gone to hell and back for a story. Next to them, Keegan felt, he was just a coder who had lucked into a trove of world-class intel. Literally. Two years ago, a CIA officer named Ari Falk had showed up on his doorstep and handed it to him.

The contents of the dossier were admittedly explosive. Rex Harlow, a top-ranking Agency veteran, confessing on tape not just to an attempted rigging of the 1996 Russian elections, but to the murder of several people who got wind of it twenty-five years later. The fact that the tape ended with the confessor shooting himself in the head made it the darkest kind of media catnip, and the response was enormous. The White House even considered an apology to the Kremlin—until Russia's invasion of Ukraine rendered this and every other issue moot.

But all I did was upload the documents and hit publish. It was Ari Falk who was the unsung hero here, emphasis on *unsung.* Not to mention that the officer's main reason for leaking the dossier had been to flush out the operation's supposed mastermind: a man known only as Cormorant, to whom Harlow incoherently referred several times in the recording and whom FleaCollar's community of techno-sleuths proved unable to ID. Two years on, the prevailing wisdom held that Cormorant was Harlow himself.

As for Falk, he had gone off the grid, and not without Keegan's help. Although they had met only twice in person, Keegan considered the man a friend. Not giving him any credit for this career-making gift—indeed, making sure that no one ever would—felt strange. To others, it might look like the award-worthy integrity of a reporter protecting a source. *But it's all ultimately self-serving, isn't it?* he thought, staring at the river.

For as long as he could remember, Keegan hated being the center of attention. The mechanisms of fame and fandom, in his opinion, were a bane of the modern world, a deformed stump where organized religion used to be. He had built FleaCollar as a tribute to the ideal of decentralized intelligence, free of individual vanity, fear, and spite.

So of course at the age of forty-three he just had to go and become a bloody fucking celebrity.

The goulash arrived. The Elbe snaked away. Wind turbines filled the view, white on white snow, strobing past the windows at two hundred kilometers an hour. The train decelerated into a turn. As he had predicted, a glug of tea leaped clear of the glass, though inertia obligingly sent it away from Keegan, not at him: small mercies. He dabbed the spill and, using the same napkin, picked up the still-scalding glass and drank more than he wanted, just to prevent this from happening again.

It now seemed safe to take out and open his laptop, so he did. Keegan dreaded having to write an acceptance speech, but he was an awful extemporaneous speaker and knew it. He began to put down bullet points—*FleaCollar is a community of equals . . . In an era of disinformation and uncertainty, accurate data is vital to . . .* —and felt exhausted within a minute. Before he knew it, he had drifted off into his usual procrastination routine: checking the portal's tip line.

The encrypted inbox he had set up guaranteed writers full anonymity. This was a mixed blessing, as various cranks and adversaries delighted in spamming it with right-wing memes and photos of genitalia. *Here's a tip for you, all right.* Today, though, Keegan welcomed any distraction that meant he wouldn't have to think or write about himself for a while. He copied the box's contents onto a USB stick sight unseen, turned off all network connections, and switched to a custom profile that used a partitioned section of the laptop's drive. (Ideally, he'd have a second computer with him, fully air-gapped, but this would do.) He then ran a decryption program from another stick, saved the result on the third one, erased the first one, and re-logged in as himself. Five minutes, successfully wasted.

The emails were now legible—or rather, an email. The day's catch turned out to be a single item. It was almost as if the usual merry bunch of pranksters got scared of being seen next to it and went off to party elsewhere. Smart decision, too, because its subject line made Keegan break out in instant sweat.

He took off his glasses, trying to blink it out of existence, then put them back on. The line didn't disappear.

He reread it at least three times before coming to terms with the fact that it said what it said.

A Message for Ari Falk.

For several minutes, Keegan just sat there, his pulse outpacing the frantic two-step of the wheels over rail joints. The bowl of cold goulash stood in front of him, sealed under a lid of congealed fat.

How?! He had been so careful. The whistleblower's identity remained unknown to the public; there was nothing out there in the ether to connect the two of them, Keegan was sure of that. The list of the email's possible authors was thus very short. It could be either a backchannel communication from someone high up at the CIA or an opening move in a game of blackmail from Russian intelligence. One way to find out. Keegan glanced at the clock in the corner of the monitor—just under two hours left until the train's arrival—and went to work.

He began by analyzing the email's metadata for the myriad obvious risk factors and found none. Aside from the subject, which startled him every time he glimpsed it, the only thing the letter contained was the signature:

—Petra.

No tech genius would be able to cram malware into that.

The email had arrived an hour and a half ago from—no surprise here—a freshly minted dummy address. The first server to handle it hid behind a VPN, which may have stopped a less seasoned data warrior but not Keegan. Many encryption providers used the same three digits at the start of all addresses they generated; this one had come from Krtek, a popular but flimsy Czech service. A simple port-forwarding trick exposed the sender's real IP, and with it the server's location: 159A Vinogradska

Street in Prague. The world headquarters of Radio Free Europe, the storied U.S.-run media nonprofit. *Interesting.*

Just for the hell of it, Keegan searched for Radio Free Europe employees named Petra and found seven. The next part always made him feel a little dirty. After plugging their full names and job titles into every engine at his disposal, he had each Petra's home address and passport number. A quick trip to the dark web, a fraction of a bitcoin, and he saw which of them had registered the dummy email, with which provider, and when.

"Nice to meet you, *Petra Lorencová,*" Keegan muttered, more than a little pleased with himself.

The river returned. The first Czech hačeks appeared on roadside signage, announcing the city of Děčín. An empty brutalist structure jutted out over the water—a former crossing between East Germany and Czechoslovakia; the train didn't slow down as it whipped past it. For all the pastoral beauty outside the windows, few sights lifted Keegan's heart more than abandoned border architecture and empty passport-control booths. The only time he ever cried in a museum had been at Berlin's Checkpoint Charlie, over photos of people stuffing themselves into suitcases and Trabant engine blocks to get across the Wall to freedom.

One day, all checkpoints would be obsolete. One day, humanity would come to its senses, stop slashing at itself along the imagined lines of blood and soil, and concentrate on borrowing one another's best practices instead. Like, you know, serving tea in cups.

Fine, he mouthed to himself. *I'll bite.* At least now he had a real reason to go to Prague.

He fished around his rucksack, took out a clean phone he kept for just such occasions, and began to type a text message.

■ ■ ■

Petra Lorencová stood in the middle of the lobby, next to an A-frame sign informing the hotel's visitors that the Recent Advances in Food Analysis conference had been moved to the Donna Anna Room. Shorter than Keegan (which meant quite short), she formed something of an A-frame herself, with the firm stance of someone about to be asked to leave but not about to comply. Her graying hair ran in a frizzy cascade over her shoulders, giving her a hippieish look. The woman had on a mustard-yellow puffer jacket as per their text correspondence. She was trying to look engrossed in her phone as opposed to frantically scanning the crowd, which she still did but with her eyes only. Keegan, for his part, had tagged her immediately. Her entire figure radiated such profound unease that even in a full foyer, it somehow drew the eye.

"Hello," he said. It felt strange to talk to her in person after rummaging through her life over the last hours. Petra shot one more panicked glance at him, then turned to stare at the reception desk. She seemed determined to play out the movie trope wherein two people sidle up next to each other and talk while looking in the opposite directions. "How much time do you have?"

"Twenty minutes or so," she said without turning her head. Her English was accented but fluent, with some clear signs—*twonny*—of regular exposure to Americans.

"Good. Same. Let's take a walk."

Their meeting had predetermined Keegan's last-second choice of the hotel. He had skipped the lavish suite at the Andaz, furnished by the Aletheia Award committee, and booked a single at the Don Giovanni, a 1990s eyesore east of the city center. The hotel's theme, relentlessly reiterated, was Mozart via Miloš Forman's *Amadeus*. Stills from the movie hung in every hallway, and notes and clefs were stenciled on the walls of every room. The locals hated it with a passion.

On the plus side, it stood a mere two hundred yards from Radio

Free Europe's imposing headquarters complex. This would allow Keegan and Petra to cross paths without disrupting either of their routines: she on her lunch break from work, he on his way to the award ceremony. Unfortunately, this also meant he'd have to talk to her while wearing a tuxedo, which made it all feel like some kind of mean-spirited James Bond parody.

"All right," Keegan said once they exited the building, adopting a stern tone. "Who are you working for?"

"No one. I mean . . . the Radio."

"I know *that.* I also know you're forty-five, single, born in Kolin, have a cat named Sasha, drive a Škoda Octavia, and just let your Amazon Prime membership lapse," he added with an increasingly sadistic lilt. "What I *don't* know is how you've come to be aware of—" Keegan stopped himself. Saying that name out loud felt like a curse, in both senses.

"Ari Falk?" Petra asked innocently. He looked around, a panicked reflex. "I have no idea who that is. I was hoping you'd tell me."

Keegan stared at her until Petra elaborated. Out on the street, she allowed herself to relax a little, to the point of making occasional eye contact. "They told me to put it in the email."

"*They?*"

"Why don't we go to the graveyard," Petra said. The offer was less macabre than it sounded. Nový Židovský Hřbitov, Prague's largest Jewish cemetery, lay right behind the hotel and made for a pleasant if melancholy walk. Its main attraction was Franz Kafka's tomb, which guaranteed steady tourist traffic to get lost in.

"Sounds grand," said Keegan, closing his overcoat tighter over his throat to hide the last hint of bow tie. "So. Tell me what happened and who 'they' are. From the beginning."

"I thought they were *you.* And what happened was, two days ago, I received a wire for half a million koruna."

"Is that a lot?"

"For me, god yes. About twenty thousand euro. But I'm not a thief, so I went to the bank to return it. The bank lady printed out the, what do you call it, the receipt? And look."

Petra pulled out a folded piece of paper with the Raiffeisen Bank logo. Keegan peered at it over his glasses. The message occupied the memo field, making the best of the allotted three hundred characters:

> This is a gift. Pls don't feel obligated to do anything. However, you'd really help me by emailing contact@ fleacollar.org w/subject "A message for Ari Falk" and leaving your first name. Thank you and sorry to bother.
>
> PS make sure you write from a new account, and from a work computer. Use Krtek VPN.

Keegan tried to hide his humiliation. His little feat of on-the-go tradecraft turned out to be a game of connecting a few very large dots laid out for him. It was like the time his five-year-old "discovered" a dinosaur jaw in a museum sandbox and wouldn't stop talking about it for weeks. *Nice one, Alan. Masterful, truly. You absolute prat.*

They walked down a snow-dusted alley. Ornate neo-Renaissance crypts rose on one side of the road like a scale model of Florence; tall, severe gravestones crowded the other, like an even smaller New York. A sign with an arrow read *Dr. Franz Kafka 250m*, and they automatically followed it.

"So? Do I return the money to you?" Petra asked. "I don't want to be a part of anything bad. The only reason I agreed to meet was hoping you'd explain what's going on." She hesitated before the next part. "Plus, you seem like a good man, from what I read about you online."

Keegan winced, forcing himself to stop soaking in self-abasement. "Let's forget the money for a second. Forget even who's trying to get to me. Let's figure out why they're doing it through you."

"Okay."

"Have you ever heard the name Ari Falk in any other context? Falk? Ari Falk?" He kept repeating it like an idiot, not in the hopes of jogging her memory but because finally saying it, after two years, felt like scratching an itch he didn't know he'd had. "Or mine, for that matter. Did you know who I was before today? Not that anyone should, of course."

Petra shook her head no—vigorously to the first question, apologetically to the second. Keegan believed her. Here was someone completely, totally out of her depth. Which, for the moment, made two of them.

"What's your job at the Radio?"

"Officially, an administrator," Petra said. "Unofficially, it's what we call *holka pro všechno*. How do you say it? Friday girl."

"Girl Friday?"

"Yes." She laughed.

"Hmm." Keegan felt a theory forming. The weird windfall had landed in Petra's account two days ago, just after it was publicly announced he'd appear in Prague to collect his prize in person. If this was Langley, scrambling to make contact on a forty-eight-hour notice, it made sense they'd enlist someone like Petra as an unwitting intermediary. A news service originally started by the CIA in 1950, Radio Free Europe had long since shed its Agency associations and functioned as a regular nonprofit, but its employees still underwent government-style security checks. For anyone in need of a blind asset in Prague with unimpeachable ethics and a U.S. employment record, it was the best place to find one.

They strolled among the graves, falling in accidental lockstep. A tourist in a blue parka farther down the alley was taking a selfie that, judging from the phone's angle, could include the two of them in the background. Keegan didn't like this. Having developed a sudden interest in the tombstone of one Esther Silbermann, 1832–1897, he took Petra by the elbow and led her onto a side path.

"I have an idea," he said. "Can you check the inbox for that email you created?"

"Sure." Petra reached into her puffer jacket's inner pocket, produced a cheap Nokia, and looked at the screen. Her eyebrows flew up. "Wow," she said. "You're right. Someone just emailed me. No text, no name, just a video file."

Keegan felt a very small measure of relief. "Which means someone just emailed *me*. That's the drop. Which makes you the courier."

"So I *don't* have to return the money?"

"Looks like it," said Keegan. "Might as well restart that Prime account. Hell, go ad free."

She didn't smile. They had reached Kafka's grave, a squat gray six-sided obelisk under which the great absurdist lay next to his parents Hermann and Julie. It looked, appropriately, like a pencil worn down to a nub. A dozen or so tourists milled about, not knowing what to do once they'd seen and photographed it, which always took a shorter time than seemed respectable. The blue parka was present as well, leaning forward to inspect the Hebrew lettering on the obelisk's face.

"Well," said Keegan, "as good a place as any to say goodbye. Thank you, and I'm sorry that someone has used you like that. Just send me the password to that email account, and I'll be out of your hair." Her face indicated unfamiliarity with the idiom. "Means I won't bother you anymore. And if anyone ever does, please do get in touch."

He nodded and started back toward the main gate. After some hesitation, Petra followed.

"Wait," she called out. Keegan turned around.

"What's up?"

"It's not just 'someone' using me, Mr. Keegan. It's you, too. I don't enjoy people looking into my life like that. I think I need to go offline for a while."

"Fair enough." At once, Keegan felt acutely embarrassed of flaunting his knowledge of Petra's circumstance to her face. "My apologies."

"Also, just take this." In her outstretched hand was the Nokia. "It's not mine. I bought it yesterday. I don't want any of this stuff anywhere near me."

"Thank you. Again, you're right, and I'm very sorry." He grabbed the phone and shoved it into his overcoat, away from view.

His hand froze in the coat pocket.

The alley led to a columnated, copper-domed ceremonial hall one had no choice but to pass on the way in and out. Against the beige facade, a blue parka moved like a scarab on sand. Keegan reflexively glanced back to check if there were somehow two of them. There weren't.

Behind the graves, a brick wall stretched as far as the eye could see. "Is there another way out of here?" he asked. "A second exit?"

"There's a little gate on Izraelská," said Petra. "Sometimes it's open. Why?"

"Take me there." They cleared the nearest crypt, turned, and sauntered south, to where the cemetery directly abutted both the Radio Free Europe compound and Keegan's hotel. The slight downward slope lent each step an extra spring. "Don't look now. Is the guy in blue following us?"

She stole a glance back while tucking a stray strand of gray hair behind her ear. "Do you know him?"

"I do not. I think we should split up now." Keegan kept his gait steady and his voice calm. He was used to people shadowing him, some more skillfully than others.

"Hm. I was hoping you would." Petra took out her actual phone, a

Samsung on a beaded crossbody strap, to show him a photo. It was an innocent snap of a pastry-shop window, the sign *Erhartova Cukrárna* in an Art Deco font floating over a display of fresh croissants and cakes.

"What am I looking at?"

"This morning." She zoomed onto the space between *Erhartova* and *Cukrárna.* The blue parka loitered across the reflected street, among other bundled-up Praguers waiting for a tram on the other side.

In the time it took them to reach the little gate and to find it locked, Keegan had recalibrated his view of the situation yet again. If the tail had been on Petra, not him, then . . . Well, first of all, it was a timely reminder that he, Aletheia Award laureate-to-be Alan Keegan, wasn't the center of the universe. He had no time to ponder the other implications.

"How about this," Petra said, appraising the endless cemetery wall in front of them. "We climb over and go to my work. That place is a fortress. And you can call a cab from there."

He'd had her all wrong, he thought. The only one out of his depth was him. This woman thrived in a crisis.

Keegan took another look at the parka, still patrolling the now-distant alley, then at the wall. It was about eight feet high. Red clay tiles ran along the top. The gray cube of Radio Free Europe towered on the other side, a hard clot of American soft power.

He had to admit that the idea made sense. The Radio building had the security perimeter of an embassy. In fact, as a Congress-funded Cold War behemoth beaming news and counterpropaganda to twenty-three countries, it was one in all but name. (Its previous headquarters, on Wenceslas Square, had famously housed a tank on the premises.) Keegan's only objection was to the prospect of climbing a fence, something he hadn't tried since the age of nine, and never successfully.

"Help me." Petra jumped, grabbed onto an overhanging tile, and shimmied upward with unexpected vigor. Keegan, too embarrassed to touch a strange woman's buttocks, held her by the waist for a largely symbolic boost. He expected her to roll over to the other side once she had made it to the top; instead, Petra fearlessly straddled the wall, lay flat on her stomach, and offered him both arms. A few tourists stared from the path. There was no going back now. Beet-red, Keegan took off and folded his glasses, unbuttoned the constricting overcoat, gripped her wrists, and scrambled up, a blind tuxedo cat.

They tumbled onto Izraelská, a narrow street separating the cemetery from the Radio complex, and jogged past the bollards toward the bunker-like security booth on the other side. Petra unzipped her puffer and took out an ID on a lanyard. Keegan reached for his specs and felt a sharp edge and a loose lens: he had crushed them rolling over the wall between his own weight and Petra's Nokia, which he had forgotten was in the same pocket.

Given his minus-five vision, the world without glasses was a pleasant blur. Keegan oriented himself by the movements of the mustard-yellow blob in front of him. Petra's ID unlocked the vestibule's heavy outer door; inside was a dull, airport-like setup with two guards, a metal detector, and an X-ray belt. The gray of the guards' uniforms matched the walls, rendering their faces two floating pink beans as far as Keegan was concerned. Past the detector, another set of remote-operated glass doors opened onto the compound's inner courtyard.

"Jackets, keys, electronics on the belt," intoned one pink bean in native English.

"*Je se mnou*," Petra said breezily, which Keegan assumed meant "He's with me." The fuzzy shape of the second guard replied with something curt in Czech. At least some of the security here appeared to have been outsourced to the locals.

"Petra. Petra Lorencová," she shot back, sounding more surprised than incensed.

"Everything okay?" Keegan asked.

"Guy must be new. Ugh, fine, let me go get a guest pass." Petra stepped toward the metal detector, or rather, the mustard shape moved toward the square shape.

"Jackets, keys, electronics on the belt," the first guard repeated. With an aggrieved groan, she wriggled out of the puffer and shoved it into the X-ray machine, extinguishing the only bit of color in the entire room. Keegan was now staring at a sea of gray.

As he took off his own overcoat, only adding to the room's monochrome, something made him think of the man hounding them back in the cemetery. After a moment's befuddlement, Keegan realized that this something was the color blue.

Why was his parka blue?

To restate: Why would someone whose job was to blend into a gray landscape of a gray city in a gray weather in a gray time of year wear anything other than gray?

Unless, of course, the job was *not* to blend in. Unless the job was to be noticed. To persist and unnerve. To herd them farther and farther down the snowy cemetery alley.

Into the safest logical place nearby.

"Hey," Keegan said in the general direction of Petra, lost to the grayness. "Let's just forget it. I, uh, I can get to the ceremony from here."

As if in response, the Czech guard reached under the belly of the X-ray machine, removed something angular and black with a distinct Velcro rip, lifted it and aimed it at the English speaker.

The gunshot, in this four-cornered kill box, for that's where he now knew they stood, was deafening.

Frozen in place, helpless, Keegan watched Petra dash past the beeping frame and lunge toward the courtyard exit. Two more shots rang off the walls and ceiling, sound waves cresting and clashing everywhere, metal singing high and clear.

The last thing he saw before his own turn came was color return to the room: a brilliant slash of red across the glass of the doors.

■ ■ ■

Three miles away, under the exquisite Art Nouveau skylight of the Smetana Hall, the Aletheia Award ceremony was under way. The host, a French actress, had dispensed with the lighthearted opening section of the speech and was in the process of segueing into the serious part, about the role of free press as a check on political power, when a man in a radio headset walked out of the wings and whispered into her ear at length. As she stepped gracefully off-mic, listened, gasped, and clasped both hands to her mouth, a few discreet snickers could still be heard in the audience from those who thought it was part of a comedy bit. The last of these died out when she returned to the microphone already crying.

In the very back of the room—in what would have been the cheapest seats had the event not been free and invitation-only—a white-haired man in a tuxedo got up. He sidled down the row and into the aisle, muttering excuses in decent Czech, and exited the hall in a hurry, hindered only by his advanced years. Given the developing chaos onstage, no heads turned in his wake.

■ ■ ■

McLean, Virginia
December 10, 2023

Jim Otterbeck stared down his shirt front, at the red dot in an ocher ring of oil, physically feeling the discovery ruin what was left of his mood. The origin of the blotch wasn't much of a puzzle: The Langley cafeteria had served a pappardelle lunch special earlier. Which meant he'd been walking around like this—well, sitting at his workstation like this—for a good five hours now. *Bleep my life.*

It didn't matter that the spot's total circumference was about the size of a microdot, or the dot over the *i* in the word *microdot.* To Jim, this was another defeat in a daily struggle with the material world. He liked things but felt he couldn't be trusted with them. Whenever he bought himself anything nice, like a pair of Alden penny loafers, he'd overfocus on not scuffing them; then, having inevitably done so, obsess over the imperfection. By the time both shoes were beaten up enough to relax about it, he hated them. If there was one human quality he'd sell his eternal soul to possess, it would be what the Italians called sprezzatura, the talent for moving through life without getting every detail just so.

A few of the guys he knew at Cornell, and later at the Agency, had it. They'd effortlessly wear a wristwatch over the cuff or tie a tie so that the narrow blade hung lower than the wide. Unimaginable! How did they pull it off? *They could afford to, that's how, Jim.* To men like that, everything was a plaything. To the Otterbecks—he could almost hear his father's voice whenever he thought about this—clothes were a set of rules, signs of belonging, intramural message boards. And right now the message on Jim Otterbeck's board, written in tomato, was that Jim Otterbeck was an effing slob.

At least it was nearly the end of the day. In Jim's current line of work, all-nighters at the office were few and far between. Once a Moscow Station officer under official cover as a third secretary at the embassy—not bad for a twenty-eight-year-old, on either count—he had been marinating back stateside since early 2022, when the war in Ukraine frayed the U.S.-Russia ties to a thread. As the embassies emptied out, the time for mutually tolerated diplomat-spies was over. New data would have to be gathered via the wartime combo of illegals, double agents, and SIGINT.

Langley, for its part, didn't quite know what to do with this sudden mass homecoming of officers, and saddled the arrivals with whatever busywork it could. Jim, for instance, was assigned to a task force developing new ways to measure Russian public sentiment: In a country that jailed you for calling the war a war, opinion polls were no longer useful.

Apart from Jim, the force consisted of five geeks nattering on about discursive patterning and blended data flows. Some of what they did was actually quite clever. For instance, absent official war casualty numbers from the Kremlin, the group monitored the rise in ads for funeral homes. The worst part was that the brass expected Jim to alchemize their findings into "predictive models," which meant humoring inane questions like "Which sectors of the Russian society are closest to revolt?" The short and correct answer was *none*, but short and correct answers were not how government careers got made.

Six o'clock. Jim closed a half-written document entitled *Tracking Effects of Sanctions on Regional Impoverishment Trends*. It was marked due by EOD, and the D was at an E, but oh well. He yawned, stretched, walked to the north windows and stared out onto the endless parking lot paved with sensible sedans, one of which was his. He then went to the bathroom and fought a spirited battle with the sauce spot, failing to get it out but rendering the center of his shirt transparent. Two men in adjoining stalls were trading brutal jokes across the partition, about Alan Keegan biting it in Prague.

When he came back for his jacket, the desk phone was blinking red, as if mocking his efforts. He pushed the button.

"Jim, you still here? Oh, good. Deputy Director Tamaskar's office. DD wants to see you right away."

Fudge.

After spiraling for a few seconds, he remembered he had a tennis sweater in his gym bag. He put it on over the shirt and under the jacket. It was too hot, and the wet shirt fabric pressed against his body, but at least these problems were sort of canceling each other out.

Asha Tamaskar, a star analyst from Counterterrorism, had moved into Rex Harlow's abruptly vacated seventh-floor office a little over two years ago. Her ascent to head of Covert Activities appeared to cap a frantic search for a person *least* like Harlow in every possible metric, which was fair enough. Still in Moscow at the time, Jim hadn't been there to offer his congratulations. He did know her a little from her analyst days. In fact they were close enough in age—Asha had only ten years on him—to have even bumped into each other at a party or two. Ever since his return, however, Jim had had exactly one encounter with her, a stilted elevator chat.

The only thing in the office left over from Harlow's days was a massive desk of bird's-eye maple. The rest looked stylishly bare, calling to mind nothing so much as an Apple Store: no books, no papers, no clutter, just a square gray sofa and a few devices with the same family photo as the screensaver. The unmistakable message of the space was *not your father's CIA,* which in Otterbeck's case could and should be taken literally. He was legacy, a third-gen spook.

"Hi," said Tamaskar, getting up and walking around the desk to shake Jim's hand. "Nice sweater." It was impossible to gauge the percentage of sarcasm in that sentence.

"Thank you."

"You wanna sit down?" She headed toward the sofa, leading by example. Asha Tamaskar wore her hair in the kind of short bob that actually bobbed as she walked. She had on a crisp white top, tucked somewhat carelessly into a gray pencil skirt: sprezzatura.

"Care to guess what this is about?" she asked once they sat, peering at him over a pair of tortoiseshell glasses. Jim had no idea. He didn't report to her directly and was pretty sure she had never read any of his task force's papers.

"Alan Keegan?" he ventured, just to say something.

"Hmm. What makes you think so?"

Jim shrugged. "It's just . . . the latest thing to hit the wires, that's all."

"Well," said Tamaskar, "not *just.* Keegan's the reason I'm sitting in this office, isn't he? Had he not published the dossier, they'd have simply replaced Harlow with another Harlow. Someone from Massachusetts, not Maharashtra." The last sentence felt a bit too slick to be off-the-cuff. She must have used it in every job interview.

"Do you approve of what he did, then?" asked Jim and immediately regretted it. It came out far too accusatory for a chat with a higher-up.

"I may or I may not, but I recognize it was his job. See, I think of guys like him or Bellingcat or whatever as media, not intelligence. Any newspaper would have published it. Plus, he paid the price, didn't he?" Tamaskar took a pause. "Who *gave* him the intel is another story."

"Of course. You're right. So, are we investigating that crazy Prague thing?"

The deputy director looked at him with something like surprise, cocking her head a few degrees. "No. Why would we? Like I just said, Keegan wasn't IC. And the number of people he pissed off in his lifetime, I mean . . . sheesh, take your pick."

"I just thought—" Jim began, then stopped himself. What was it with him today? Was it the pasta-sauce spot? The overdue impoverishment paper? There was a Ukrainian saying he liked for its merry fatalism. It went something like "The shed's on fire, so burn the house." Is this what was happening here, self-sabotage? The shirt's ruined, so why not ruin the career, too?

"Please do continue." Tamaskar studied him with an unreadable smile.

"I just thought," Jim repeated, "that we might want to cover our behinds so the world knows it wasn't us. Though, honestly, I'd understand if it was," he added.

"Is that what you think we do? Revenge killings of people who accuse us of revenge killings? Bit redundant, no?" The smile remained in place; she was toying with him now.

"I don't, of course. But, uh, some people still think of Radio Free Europe as our domain."

"The shooter was Czech. A security contractor, third day on the job. He took out two of their staffers, too."

"I know all that. But you have to admit we've lost some moral high ground lately."

Tamaskar got up from the sofa and began to pace—casually, not neurotically. The office was large enough to get a good saunter on before one had to turn around and go back. "Yeah, well," she said, "to half the world, we'll always be capitalism's bumbling enforcement arm. It's not our job to argue otherwise. Though some in this building would disagree. What do you think of the ads, by the way?"

Jim knew exactly the ads she meant. A month or so earlier, the Agency's social media team had released a somewhat puzzling series of public service announcements in Russian, filmed in the style of a Cold War thriller and seemingly aimed at Moscow's intelligence community, exhorting "honest officers" to switch sides. He concentrated hard before answering. She had graciously handed him a chance to drive this conversation out of the ditch, and he was going to take it.

"It depends on the objective," he said. "Is the goal here first level, to actually recruit assets; second level, to keep the enemy paranoid about defections in its ranks; or third level?"

"What's the third level?" asked Tamaskar, sounding intrigued.

"To make an ad so clumsy and desperate that the enemy *stops* worrying about defections."

She stopped and snorted, then laughed out loud, revealing perfect teeth. "You guys. Always looking for twists. I'll let you in on a secret. It's just a shitty fucking ad."

Jim flinched a little, as he did every time a woman swore in front of him, but thought he hid it pretty well.

He had not. "You're LDS, right?"

"Uh, yes. Why?" Otterbeck's religion was far from an outlier at Langley—the CIA employed thousands of Mormons, as did the FBI and the diplomatic corps. The church's calm forthrightness, aversion to vice, and baked-in American exceptionalism meshed well with the Agency values, and its vast missionary program conveniently provided young men and women with foreign experience far beyond your standard Eurotrip. Jim, for instance, had learned his Russian on a two-year volunteer posting to the Saratov stake.

"No reason. Cool. And your dad is Agency, too, correct?"

"As was my grandfather. Served under George H.W."

"Wow." Tamaskar nodded. "Respect. My folks are both dentists. I'm a *huuuge* disappointment, as you can imagine."

What was this? An interview? An audition? Jim had a distinct sense of being felt out for something, though he couldn't understand what. The deputy director, meanwhile, continued with the non sequiturs. "Got anyone in London? Any friends from the church?"

"I don't think so."

"Anyone who'd, say, recognize you on the street?"

"No one," he said, less intrigued than impatient. "I still feel like this is about Keegan somehow."

"Yes and no," replied Tamaskar and abruptly sat down at her, or rather Harlow's, desk, indicating that the chitchat was over. "All right, Jim, I'm ready to read you in now. What you're about to hear is operational info, so just by hearing it, you're part of the op whether you like it or not. The man who gave the dossier to Keegan was a case officer in this very department, named Ari Falk."

Jim got up from the sofa. "Wow. Oh. I—"

"You met him in Moscow in '21," Tamaskar interrupted, though not really, as he had no clue what he was going to say after that. "I read your report."

"Was it known? This whole time?"

"Of course. But it's complicated. I mean, I'm sure you heard the tape. Harlow *was* a pretty bad dude. Things needed to quiet down."

"And now?"

"And now," Tamaskar said, "I want you to go and find Falk for us."

Jim opened his mouth, closed it, thought about keeping it that way, didn't. "Why me?"

"Honest answer? Because you hated him even then. It was pretty obvious from the report. And I think you hate him just enough to see this through." She met his gaze and held it. "As do I. Which is why I don't want someone on this who might think Falk 'had a point'"—she delivered the last three words in a silly croon, accompanied by air quotes—"or 'did his civic duty' or 'punished himself enough.' I need a patriot, Jim. But a patriot with a similar skillset and mindset, one who can think like him and move like him. Close in age; I'm not giving this to some boomer buzzcut, either. Ivy League. Ex–Moscow Station. A bit of an outsider. I mean, if you really think about it, Otterbeck, it's you or it's no one. You're practically twins—"

"We're nothing alike," protested Jim.

"Good." Tamaskar pounced. "Prove it." *Was anything this woman said* not *a trap?*

"But I do know the type," he added. "The too-cool-for-school type. No values, no loyalty."

Behind the glasses, a satisfied twinkle. "Amen. Falk's been in the wind for two years. It's time to bring his traitorous ass in. Quietly."

"Yes, ma'am."

The only question still hanging in the air was *Why now?*, so Tamaskar preempted it. "And once you have," she added with a sly smile, "well, shit. Let's see if he had anything to do with that good man Keegan's murder. Maybe he got jealous of all the money and prizes. Wanted his cut. As good a motive as any."

Now and only now, to his endless embarrassment, did he get the full picture. "You mean . . ."

"We *applaud* transparency," said Tamaskar. "But we're not too hot on high treason."

She put out her hand over the old maple desk, and Jim shook it.

■ ■ ■

Tbilisi, Georgia
December 11, 2023

The paper strip next to the doorbell read დენიელ უოტსი. Daniel Watts had put it up himself the day he rented the apartment. He knew just enough Georgian to write his own name, or rather, the name he had been given forty-eight hours earlier. Transliterated back, it would look something like *Deniel Uotsi*. He could have easily used Latin letters instead—most of the building's other tenants did—but this was a sign of respect to his new homeland. At least outwardly. The actual unstated goal was to avoid foreign visitors.

Watts locked the door, checked the real and the decoy camera trained on it, took the stairs seven stories down—he hated elevators—and emerged into the cold Tbilisi morning. It was eight a.m. on a Monday, but the city still looked half asleep. A stray dog with a yellow ear tag sprawled across the porch, blocking the exit. He cleared his throat. It looked at him mournfully, yawned, got up, and trotted off.

The building, a generic glassy medium-rise, stood on Ilia Chavchavadze Avenue, in a modern but charmless part of town. Watts had picked the neighborhood for precisely that reason. People in his situation tended to doom themselves by being colorful: renting a historic villa, tooling around in a luxury car, picking a clever alias. The latter affliction was surprisingly widespread even among professionals who ought to know better. Imagine dying because you thought it would be droll to call yourself an anagram of your real name.

The other, costlier temptations weren't an issue. The only money Watts had at his disposal came from cautious dips in and out of crypto day trading. He made just enough to afford the rent, which had skyrocketed with the mass arrival of Russian war objectors, and local food, still cheap and famously fantastic.

He didn't have a breakfast routine. In fact, Daniel Watts didn't have any routines. He wasn't a morning lark or a night owl, a vegan or a carnivore, a teetotaler or a sot. He belonged to no gym, frequented no club, and changed dentists after every cleaning. The only pattern of his life in Tbilisi was a studious absence of patterns, as if, at the first hint of predictability, the ground would open and swallow him whole.

Today, for example, Watts opted to have his first meal at a café across the river, forty minutes away by foot. There was a similar one much closer, owned by a Russian immigrant couple, but he steered clear of it. Russian cafés drew an all-Russian clientele. This was a recent phenomenon: The same liberal Muscovites who'd once summered in Georgia to soak up the local color, upon moving here as wartime refugees immediately opened tony coffeehouses and coworking spaces "just like in Moscow" to shield themselves from it. No self-respecting Tbilisi native would set foot in one. Neither would Watts, but for a different reason.

He crossed a bridge over the Kura. Out in the open, gusts of freezing wind slapped him in the face. Despite the subtropical latitude, Tbilisi in December might as well have been Stockholm. Watts shoved his hands into his jacket pockets and walked faster, along the bridge's granite balustrade, the whole span of which bore fresh graffiti reading *Fuck Russians*. A popular refrain. Someone had crossed out the last two letters, reorienting the sentiment toward the country and away from its people. Someone else had then stubbornly added *and Russians*. Watts sympathized with both sides of this Socratic dialogue. Individual civilians were blameless, especially those who choose to uproot their lives rather than pay taxes into a madman's war chest. But how was a city supposed to handle a flood of refugees *more* prosperous than the locals? Wasn't that, too, an invasion of sorts?

Tbilisi was lovely. It was also a powder keg.

He found himself in Vorontsov, an older, shabbier neighborhood in the throes of gentrification. The backstreet he took still carried scars of Soviet-era poverty, with a local twist: Every other house boasted an amateur alteration of some sort, ranging from sheet-metal balconies to whole extra floors cantilevering over the sidewalk. Georgia had always been the place where rules and regulations came to die—even during the harshest Communist years, it teemed with private wineries and secret factories. The same spirit extended to its architecture. If someone living in a second-floor apartment wanted an extra bedroom, they'd just smash a hole in the facade and add one, on stilts. Younger, EU-oriented Georgians saw this as ugly and backward. Watts found it uplifting. Nothing like tyranny losing out to human nature.

The door to the café, when he found it, had a Ukrainian flag taped up in solidarity, and a printout that read, in English and Russian:

Russia is a terrorist state
Glory to Ukraine
If you disagree with the above
You are NOT WELCOME here

Watts pulled the handle, thus implicitly agreeing with the above. The place was still almost empty; it had just opened for the day. A screen above the bar, installed into a gilded rococo frame, showed BBC News on mute. He sat at the counter and took out his laptop to move some funds around.

The barista, an Amy Winehouse look-alike with a tattoo of an artichoke on her left biceps, eyed him for a beat longer than necessary and said something in her native tongue. This happened a lot. With his dark angular features, darker under-eye circles, and stubble on the verge of graduating to a beard, Watts often passed for a local until he opened his mouth.

"Sorry, I don't speak Georgian," he said in Georgian, contradicting himself a bit. "I'm not Russian," he added, seeing her face harden.

She switched to English. "Where are you from, then?"

"Canada. Toronto."

"Cool." She leaned on the counter. "What's your name?"

"Daniel. What's yours?"

"Nanuka."

"Nice to meet you, Nanuka," Watts said in an uninterested voice. He wasn't uninterested. What he was, and would remain, was careful. He ordered black coffee and eggs with mamalyga, a Georgian take on grits, and tried to study fluctuations between three equally doomed altcoins but soon found himself playing Life Is Strange 2 instead.

"So. What do you do, Daniel?" Nanuka had leaned over the counter, rocking on her elbows and brazenly peering over the top of his computer.

He tabbed out of the game. "It's really boring."

"I'm really bored."

"I, uh, trade crypto."

"Oh. *That.*" The spark in the barista's eyes went out. She splashed more coffee into his cup, a diplomatic gesture, because the flirtation was over, but turning and walking away would have been too harsh. This was the intended reaction. Every aspect of Watts's life was precision-tooled to prompt as few follow-ups as possible.

Still, this didn't mean his male vanity wasn't hurt.

"Look, I know what it sounds like," he suddenly said, veering off script. "I know it's basically a pump and dump at this point. But I'm just riding it. I'm not trying to get anyone else to invest or anything."

Nanuka chuckled, reengaging. "What's a pump and dump? Sounds dirty."

"Well, it's when—" Watts stopped. "I'm sorry." On the screen above the bar, a BBC anchor had just finished updating the audience on the latest nonevent in the U.S. primaries. A photo of a smiling man in wire-rimmed glasses filled the screen. The chyron read *British Journalist Among Three Dead in Prague.*

His immediate instinct was to ask Nanuka to turn the sound on, but that might have been too memorable an act. He had already erred by chatting more than needed. So instead Watts just returned to his laptop and opened *The New York Times*. The barista, incredulous, waited a few seconds, shrugged, and went off to another customer.

After a few seconds of scrolling, he found the story. It wasn't among the day's top items. In a world going mad in a thousand ways at once, why would it be?

Alan Keegan, founder of FleaCollar, an open-source intelligence portal, has died today in what appears to have been a premeditated attack that also took the lives of—

Watts stabilized his breath. It took all his training to keep his hand and voice steady as he closed the lid of the laptop and asked Nanuka for the check. She nodded, thoroughly convinced now that something was off with this guy. He tried not to look up at the TV as he paid.

Which was harder than he'd expected, because the next face on the screen was his own.

This time, Nanuka herself reached for the remote under the bar and nudged up the volume.

". . . tral Intelligence Agency has revealed the name of the person responsible for one of the largest leaks in its history." The anchor's plummy Received Pronunciation filled the café. The chyron across her chest had changed to *CIA Whistleblower Named.*

"The author of the so-called Harlow Dossier has been identified as Ari Falk, a case officer employed by the Agency from 2006 to 2021. Upon publication, the documents caused significant embarrassment to the U.S. intelligence community and led to a series of high-level shake-ups. Despite legal and political pressure, Alan Keegan never shared the name of his source. With Keegan's death earlier today, this unexpected disclosure suggests that the CIA might see Falk, at the very least, as a person of interest in the case."

By the time the barista turned to look back, mouth agape, reluctant Canadian crypto trader Daniel Watts was gone in every way possible.

Ari Falk ran down the street and back to the bridge, not feeling the cold, soles pounding the Vorontsov cobblestone. Once he got to the river, he didn't cross, turning left on the embankment instead; there was nothing in Watts's apartment worth picking up. A few passersby stared at the strange man jogging in jeans, but he was well past caring.

Thirty minutes later, out of breath, he careened down a flight of worn stone steps into an ancient bathhouse on Abano Street. A local institution since the Silk Road days, it rented lockers by the month to its most devoted clients. Inside Falk's sat a weekender duffel with a change of clothes, five thousand euro in damp bills, a shaving kit, and a CZ 75 pistol in a plastic bag.

Having retrieved the duffel, Falk booked a personal suite—no food, no drink, no massage, no guests—and locked himself in. At the center of the room stood a small pool or a large tub, fed directly by the sulfur spring running underneath and alongside the building. Odorous steam rose off the surface of the water. The only source of light was an arrowslit window in the domed ceiling; condensation swirled in the sunbeam, gathered on the tiles, and dripped back into the pool with a metronomic click.

His last real friend was dead. His former bosses were hard at work framing him for it.

Falk opened the bag. For several seconds, his hand hovered over the handgun.

Then he wiped a small clear swath in the wall mirror and reached for the shaving kit.

CHAPTER TWO

London
December 11, 2023

For the first time in two years, Jim Otterbeck woke up in an excellent mood. Even the cramped economy seat and the microwaved croissant for breakfast did nothing to change it. He was back in the field, on a top secret errand for the DD/CA herself, cruising toward London at 570 mph. Even better, every mile had the added benefit of leaving the Langley workstation and the impoverishment trends in the Urals farther behind. Once again, the life he considered a birthright was his.

Jim didn't second-guess the mission—he never did—but he was smart enough to sense that Tamaskar's tacit wish to hang the Prague murders on Ari Falk had been her own idea, a bit of overreach likely not cleared with the top brass. In his book, that was a positive. It meant that if he succeeded, she'd owe him a massive debt. The key to a long career, Otterbeck Senior liked to repeat, was to find the most powerful person in every room and help them stay that way. He never actually said *person* or *them*, of course; but if Asha Tamaskar was what new power looked like, Jim was fine with that.

All he needed to do now was play his cards right. If this worked out, who knew? His grandfather had been put in charge of the Agency's East Asia division at the age of thirty-seven. His father had run Special Activities in Bosnia at thirty-three. Chief of station at thirty was not *that* much of a stretch.

And if it all went to hell, he'd be clean. She made him do it.

"So? What's our first play?" Tamaskar had asked the previous night, once he finished the eighty-screen top secret file containing Falk's biography, psych eval, and last known movements. She had stopped by his desk on her way out to watch him read it; had his cubicle-mates not gone home by then, this would have seriously raised his status around the department.

"London, of course. You have him entering the UK at Heathrow on August 28, 2021. If MI5 are forthcoming, we can start tracing from a known location."

"Yes, yes, that goes without saying." Now he was glad there was no one around to overhear. "What's the *play*?"

It was always better to take a wild guess than to choke. "Publicity? Leak his name. Right now, tonight, so the two things link up in the public mind. Keegan's death will be all over the news tomorrow. So should Falk's face. The media will make the connection for us. A tattletale gets killed and the CIA is burning his source—*gee, I wonder why?*"

"Smart. It will help get the Brits on our side. If they see us willing to go after our own, they'll feel it's safe to pitch in." Tamaskar had grinned. "You're quite the schemer, aren't you?"

"Not at all, ma'am. There's a practical benefit. Two years is a long time. Wherever Falk is, he's probably lived there for a while. And he's not a physical-labor type, you know? We're not gonna find him on an oil rig somewhere. I mean, the guy knows how to shoot a gun, but . . ."—Jim had pointed to the file, still up on the screen—"he's got a literature degree and a bad tendon. What I'm saying is, he's likelier to blend into an urban environment. With eyes on him. New acquaintances. Girls. This will get him running scared, leaving witnesses. With any luck, he might even try crossing a border."

"Shit, I'm convinced. Let me run this by Burt." Burt was the Agency's acting director Burt Spaleta, a dour State Department lifer installed in the wake of the Harlow catastrophe; his predecessor had resigned, citing a convenient affair. Jim couldn't believe his offhand suggestion was going straight to the top.

His countenance must have reflected this awe somehow, because Tamaskar had chuckled and patted him on the shoulder, a quick double slap that meant both *attaboy* and *enough out of you*. "All right. You're flying out of Dulles at ten. Your London contact's name is Stuart Akinyemi."

The plane breached the lowest cloud's underside and almost immediately alit on the tarmac. Horizontal rain lashed the windows. The flight, assisted by the five-hour time difference between DC and London, had deposited Jim into the middle of the next day; with the plane still taxiing, he grabbed his phone, flipped on a British eSIM, and waited for the signal.

Yes! Just as he hoped, the news had broken while he was in the air. The world's leading media organizations were busy blasting Falk's name and face across oceans and borders, enthusiastically and for free. Jim couldn't help but smile as he imagined the traitor's horror at being called out on every single device with a screen. The sweat, the fear, strangers' heads swiveling in his wake. Fat fingers pointing from all angles, like in some silent German movie. There was still justice in the world, and he, Jim Otterbeck, was instrumental in meting it out. In a way, the mission was already a success.

Lost in the news scroll, he almost missed Akinyemi. The MI5 contact stood against a WHSmith bookstore display, leafing through a fat paperback of *The Three-Body Problem*. He was a tall, long-limbed gent in a navy trench coat over a suit with lapels as sharp and thin as crossed sabers; as he always did around superior dressers, Jim felt instantly uncomfortable in his presence.

"Mr. Akinyemi," he said. There was, a bit disappointingly, no need for passwords or call signs. Neither of them was undercover.

The agent closed the book and shoved it in a pocket, where it miraculously disappeared without ruining the coat's silhouette. "Just Stuart, please. Welcome to London." They shook hands while Akinyemi took stock of Jim's rumpled travel outfit. "No baggage?"

Jim didn't answer, distracted by a TV screen behind his shoulder. A picture of Keegan had just come on, followed by a uniquely unflattering file photo of Falk. Jim had picked it out himself.

Akinyemi glanced back and chuckled. "Feels mental to have it all play out in the open, doesn't it?"

"Feels great, actually. It was my idea."

The Brit mimed congratulations and fell silent, in a somewhat caustic key, for the next hour. They took a fast ride on the Heathrow Express to Paddington, a cramped and sweaty one on the Circle Line to Victoria, and emerged into Pimlico, a small residential grid pinned between rail tracks and the Thames. The MI5 had offered to handle Jim's accommodations, a gesture he initially read as an apology for letting Falk vanish on their watch. He was expecting a sad midrange hotel of the kind Londoners somehow manage to cram, Tardis-like, into regular row houses. Instead, the white stucco-fronted maisonette on Alderney Street to which Akinyemi led him would be all his own. The largesse was, if anything, worrisome: Either his hosts were feeling *really* guilty, or—likelier—about to give him zero assistance in the matter and treat the whole thing as a social visit.

"You know, we've had Falk stay here before he went, uh, solo," Akinyemi said, unlocking the door. The inside of the house smelled like books, with a vinegary subscent of a recent and thorough cleanup. "Nothing operationally useful, but I thought you'd appreciate a chance to mind-meld with your quarry, as it were." He wandered off to the kitchen. "Coffee?"

"No thank you," yelled Jim from the foyer. The MI5 agent may have been joking, but his remark shifted something in the air. Jim looked at the worn parquet, the wallpaper pattern of drooping lilies, and imagined Falk moving through the same space. Making the same notes. Plotting.

"Oh, that's right, you don't care for caffeine," said Akinyemi, back with a steaming cup. "My apologies."

"None needed. And it's not strictly true. We drink Coke and things like that. It's more about the temperature."

"Fascinating." Akinyemi took a sip. "So what do you do in the mornings? If I may ask."

"Work," said Jim with gunmetal in his voice, a touch more than planned.

The Brit nodded. "Right. In that case." He gestured with his coffee toward the stairs, letting Jim go first.

The maisonette's entire second floor was a sitting room, with a round table fit for the Potsdam Conference and a fireplace sealed shut five coats of paint ago. Silvery daguerreotypes crowded the mantelpiece, suggesting a rich family history in both senses. A closer look revealed no connection between the photos: They must have come from a flea-market haul. The tabletop held a computer with two monitors, a printout of a partial London map Jim recognized by a distinctive bight of the Thames, and a sad spread of bottled water and cold cuts.

Once again, Jim tried to observe the room as Falk, half hoping for some kind of magic idea trigger, but just ended up observing himself observing.

"You're positively sure you don't want to get settled in first?" Akinyemi set the cup down next to the map, the thunk breaking his reverie. "Shower and all that?"

"I am."

"You seem a bit distracted."

"I'm not."

"Very well. So, here is what we have prepared for you regarding Ari Falk's last known moments in London. I do have to warn you, Jim, it's not much."

Knew it. Jim gestured for him to go on. The Brit angled one of the monitors toward him and pressed play.

CCTV footage, shot from a twelve-foot height. The time stamp read August 28, 2021. A thin figure in an oversize hoodie, walking with a light but visible limp. The hood hid the top part of the face, but Jim recognized Falk at once. It was the impatient air, the way he swung his arms; not even the hobble, real or affected, could mask that.

"This is Clapham High Street, eight-fifty. Does he always drag his foot like that?" Akinyemi asked. "He didn't when I saw him, I don't think."

"No. Must be a fresh injury. His file mentions a repaired Achilles tendon, but it's the other foot."

Akinyemi left the video on a loop and pulled up another. "Queenstown Road, nine twenty-five." The same figure, now walking faster, almost jogging, the limp more pronounced as a result. Akinyemi took a pen, circled both locations on the map, then put a small tidy cross between the two. "Care to guess what this is?"

"Just tell me."

"The late Mr. Keegan's London residence. The dossier came out the following day. It stands to reason he handed it over in person."

"Is there no CCTV on Keegan's block?" Jim squinted at the map.

"There is. Believe it or not, it malfunctioned that evening."

Jim sighed. "Falk is many things but not an idiot. So where do you lose him for good?"

"Right here." Akinyemi pointed to the Queenstown Road footage. In the middle distance, where the street began to curve, an ill-lit railway overpass crossed the shot; as Falk walked toward it, its shadow claimed his figure in three steps—head and shoulders, torso, feet. By the presumed step four, Jim was staring at a block of black pixels as definitive as a censor's bar across redacted text. "He never comes out the other end."

The clip began anew, Falk limping into the darkness piecemeal. Head and shoulders, torso, feet, gone.

"This is just a start, of course," said Akinyemi, evidently sensing Jim's chagrin. "We had, what, eight hours to prepare? Keep in mind that we learned about Falk minutes before the rest of the world did. And it's frankly a miracle that even these bits survived. CCTV footage isn't exactly stored forever, you know. Had you bothered to tell us back in 2021—"

"If it makes you feel better, Stuart," said Jim, "I only found out yesterday myself."

"It does, a little. And since we're being frank . . ." Akinyemi paused to search for words. "I find the idea of retracing his movements from two years ago a little odd. He's out there *now*, isn't he? Don't your and your, um, sister organization's SIGINT capabilities remove the need for this kind of admittedly charming detective work?"

Jim felt a surge of anger, not on his own behalf but on the Agency's. To buy some time and calm down, he took and ate a piece of salami. It was unexpectedly garlicky, so he reached for a bottle of water next; the pause stretched out to distinctly comic dimensions as he struggled with the cap.

"Let's say I agree," he finally said. "So, did you check for more recent communications between Falk and Keegan? Anything from this year? This week?"

"What do you mean?"

Jim loudly exhaled, spreading exasperation and garlic. "Aren't you investigating Keegan's murder?"

The question seemed to take Akinyemi aback. "That's a—that's a bit of a change of topic, isn't it?"

He'd had enough of the obfuscation. Perhaps slapping his cards on the table was the way to go. At the very least, it would provoke the Brit into showing his.

"Not necessarily, Stuart. Not from where we stand."

Now it was Akinyemi's turn to take a long pause. When the agent came back from processing this new data, he sounded chipper in the way that usually masks fury—or, rather, telegraphs it by pretending to mask it.

"If your brief," he said, "involves anything other than looking for officer Falk's whereabouts, then this is something best discussed between your bosses and mine. I don't like being left in the dark. Though, if anything, it's *blindingly* clear what you're doing."

"What am I doing?"

Akinyemi grimaced. "Now to answer your stated question and not the implied one. We are not investigating Alan Keegan's death, because he was not a foreign agent and didn't die on our soil. You may want to ask the Czechs."

"Gee, thanks."

"That said," the MI5 agent suddenly added, raising his voice a bit, "speaking as someone who has met Ari Falk and is not exactly the president of his fan club . . . I find your insinuations not just clumsy but ludicrous."

"Oh yeah? Why's that?"

"Because," said Akinyemi, "we already *know* who murdered Alan Keegan. Prague announced it an hour ago. Some local ultranationalist knob, done ten years for killing two Roma in North Bohemia. Thought Radio Free Europe was a Soros machine for making Slavic men impotent with its satellite dishes or something. You know," he dryly added, "the usual."

"And you just take it on faith? You don't even interrogate the shooter?"

"I'm afraid we're all out of Ouija boards. The other guard got him before dying." Akinyemi wandered off to the window and stared outside, as if too peeved to look at Jim directly. "Look, you may believe whatever you need to believe to suit your preexisting objectives. You lot are *great* at that. Saddam has WMDs, the Russians yearn for freedom, Falk killed Keegan. Whatever. Just keep us out of it this time, will you?"

Jim abhorred direct confrontation, but the perspective of coming back to Langley empty-handed was worse. The smirk on DD Tamaskar's face. The long walk back to the cubicle. At home, his father's pitying look. He never fully understood what the phrase *screw your courage to the sticking place* meant, but he felt himself doing something like that as he strode toward Akinyemi across the room, hands in pockets, eyes locked on the opponent.

"Oh, I wish I could," Jim said. "Keep you out of it, that is. But you're the ones who got yourselves in, 'innit? You're the ones who let him waltz into the country to hand the dossier to Keegan. The country he, by the way, never officially left."

"What do you mean?" He could feel Akinyemi getting nervous. This was the right tack.

"The cover passport Falk had, in the name of Thomas Richards? August 28, 2021, was its last recorded use. So, yes, the charitable reading, *Stuart*, is that he wangled a new one while in your care. The less charitable one is that Falk is still in the UK."

The agent opened his mouth to protest. In response, Jim went in for what he hoped was the kill. "And let me tell you, once we start looking for him here, the entire force of the CIA will be brought to bear on this. I don't think you realize how much of a priority this case is for the director. So if I turn around right now and report that you've been less than one hundred percent helpful? Honestly, it's not a huge leap from there to checking if the two of you weren't in cahoots."

"Wait, wait, wait." Something was happening with Akinyemi's face. He blinked, squinted, bit his lower lip. For a split second, Jim thought he had overdone it with the threats and broken his British counterpart beyond repair.

The next moment, he realized the man was trying to stifle laughter.

"Wait," Akinyemi repeated, exhaling slowly and carefully. A lone chuckle still snuck through; he covered it with a cough. "Will you please . . . just . . . stop . . . talking? What's the name he traveled under, again?"

"Thomas Richards. Why?"

The agent unceremoniously walked past Jim, sat down at the table, and began to look something up on the computer. "Ta-da! Finally, some use from Brexit. A year and a half ago, a drug runner tried to cross the Chunnel on a U.S. Frankenpassport with traces of that name in the MRZ."

Jim understood about half of what Akinyemi had just said, but his heart did a somersault nonetheless. He rushed toward the screen. "Please tell me you have him."

"We do. He's doing five to eight at Brixton."

Staring back at Jim from the border-police mug shot was the face of a career criminal in his late fifties, puffy with vice. The name under it said *Jerome Odezenne, b. 1965.*

"Sorry, what does this guy have to do with Falk?"

"You know how Frankenpassports are made, right? All the visual and biometric data can be overwritten, but the microcontroller transport key—" Akinyemi caught the look on Jim's face and elected to cut the lecture short. "Someone used parts of the Richards passport to build this one. Again, if you cared to share this with us earlier, we'd have looked it up for you in a matter of seconds."

Stung as Jim felt, his initial excitement didn't fully abate. It took him a moment to realize why: This wasn't a dead end. It was a lead. The only problem was, the next words out of his mouth would technically be a breach of Agency protocol.

Then again, he really, really wanted results.

"This is great," he said. "This means Falk was broke."

Akinyemi furrowed his brow. "Please explain."

Now it was Jim's turn to lay down some expertise. "His passport was a quickie CIA job, 2013 issue. Each station had a stack. The newer ones have much better security features. But these are still fungible, to a point. So he must have sold it for parts to the same person he bought the new one from." Another wave of elation swept over him. "If so, all you need to do is have Odezenne say who got him that passport. Then we bust the seller."

Akinyemi made an impressed face. Jim had no idea the sniffy Brit's approval would mean anything to him, but to his embarrassment, it did.

The agent took out his phone and typed for a bit. "Now we wait," he said, putting the device down on the table.

"How long, do you think?"

"*Less than two years,* Jim." The conviviality vanished as fast as it had appeared.

An hour and a half oozed by. Akinyemi stayed at the table reading *The Three-Body Problem*, Jim perched on a plush settee in the room's far corner. Despite the sleep he had gotten on the plane, he felt jet lag creep in. The edges of objects blurred and doubled. The light outside changed imperceptibly; midday sun, harsh and bluish, poured through the freshly washed glass. Akinyemi got up and drew the heavy blinds, plunging the room into murk. It didn't help. To stay awake, Jim decided to engage his surly colleague in some small talk.

"Good book?"

"Quite."

The talk was so small, this was all of it for another hour. He went a floor up and took a shower that didn't energize him one bit, changed into a travel-creased suit, and returned to the room. If the Brit even noticed his absence or his new clothes, he didn't comment on either.

Finally, Akinyemi's phone chimed.

"What? What is it?" Jim opened his eyes, which he didn't remember closing, and sprung from the settee, half asleep and manic all at once. It felt like what he imagined extreme alcoholic inebriation to be like. The MI5 agent was already studying the message.

"Aw, *fuck*," he said.

"Bad news?"

"Terrible." Akinyemi got his coat and gestured for Jim to do the same. "It looks like you and I are going to have to spend the rest of the afternoon together, too."

■ ■ ■

Kakheti, Georgia
December 11, 2023

The leg kept finding surprising new ways to hurt. One moment the pain would settle in the calf, no different from the aftermath of a good workout; the next, form an electric bracelet around the ankle. Right now it had decided to ride the sciatic nerve all the way to the inner thigh. Falk sat down on the bed and executed a ruthless therapy routine that, to an outside observer, would look like a self-administered charley horse. Got up, walked a tight circle around the hotel room. The ache abated. Now he could focus on being absolutely fucking terrified.

Nothing to remind you that you're an animal like being hunted. In the last twenty-four hours, Falk found himself more acutely aware of his body than he'd felt since puberty, and separate from it at the same time. The thing that *was* Ari Falk—his memories, likes, beliefs muddled by experience—was stuck inside a meat-and-bone container *labeled* Ari Falk, and labeled so very, very publicly.

Tbilisi was no longer an option. His face was everywhere. By the time he emerged from the sulfur baths on Abano Street, even the print media had caught up. (Lest there remain any doubt that the CIA itself was behind the leak, the ugly photo on every newspaper cover had come from his personnel file.) "Daniel Watts" had been blown to atoms. There was being on the run and being on the *run*. Falk was now the latter.

At least the impromptu makeover he had given himself in the spa took some urgency out of the issue. The only tool at his disposal had been a razor, so any change had to come via subtraction. Falk had shaved his head and slightly reshaped his eyebrows. He debated the pros and cons of using a medical mask, then ruled against it: The still-recent pandemic might have given people an excuse to hide their faces, but so few in Georgia clung to the Covid-era protocols that by wearing a mask, you risked coming across as *more* memorable rather than less. Instead, he went to the communal part of the spa and stole a pair of someone's fogged-up glasses, which turned out to have a mercifully weak prescription. He then left, bald and bespectacled, without paying, so as not to premiere his new look to the receptionist. Let them bill Watts.

Tbilisi had already begun to dabble in facial-recognition CCTV, in preparation for the coming unrest around the next elections and the Russian presence in town. (Ironically, the government was buying the cameras and software from a Russian supplier.) This meant his visibility on the street had to be kept to an absolute minimum. From the doors of the spa, Falk had dashed straight to the curb, where a swarm of cash cabs preyed on tourists from nearby hotels, picked the shittiest-looking Lada 2105, and made the driver deeply unhappy by naming a place an hour and a half away in Kakheti.

Falk looked through the keyhole to make sure no one stood by the door, shoved the gun in his waistband, and walked out into the cold sunset. He seemed to be the hotel's only guest. The establishment itself was a ramshackle inn adjacent to a dormant winery, each of the two functions an afterthought to the other. Its eight bare rooms opened onto a grassy courtyard formed by the ruin of a medieval farmhouse; the same ruin's stonework provided bits and pieces of every room's front wall. Other than that, its only attraction was the fact that it didn't bother to check guests' passports.

Framing the entrance to the yard were two qvevri—giant terra-cotta pots the Georgians had used for fermenting wine since the Neolithic era.

An old woman in a Chicago Bulls cap sat beside one and baked shoti, a local bread, deftly affixing arcs of dough to the wall of a tandoor. Delete the cap, and nothing in this picture would have been out of place five thousand years ago. She waved him over and, not taking a no for an answer, handed him a piece.

Falk sat down on a fragment of an ancient wall and ate the hot bread. It was the first thing he'd had since the morning's eggs, served by Nanuka with a side of BBC News. His naked scalp prickled; the shaved spot between his eyebrows burned like a nascent third eye. The peaks of the Caucasus rose at the far end of the valley, coral against the violet sky. A fleeting sense of something close to calm visited him. He tried to bank it for the future somehow, or at least memorize what it felt like on the cellular level. Had he had a single moment of true peace since 2021? Perhaps he should have hidden out in the country to begin with. Taught himself to work the tandoor or make cloudy skin-contact wine. Not that things would end any differently.

Two years earlier, Falk had traded his safety, his fifteen-year career as a CIA case officer, and every human connection for the embarrassingly simple objective of saving one person from another. An innocent woman deserved to be left in peace and a dangerous man didn't. He had succeeded in the first half of the task and failed in the second. His own consequent survival was an incidental, almost dismaying corollary to that failure.

According to Harlow, who had no reason to lie in his last minutes, the dangerous man in question was someone nicknamed Cormorant. A man old enough to have already been in a position of wealth and power thirty years ago, spry enough to remain there still. An American, but with easy access to Russian and Turkish private military contractors. Not CIA, but also not *not* CIA. Someone with a keen interest in reshaping world history to his still-murky specifications and the wherewithal to slaughter anyone standing in the way. That's all Falk knew of the enemy. He had relied on Alan Keegan and his cybersleuths to suss out the rest.

Instead, a frozen conflict. No one had come after Falk or Keegan, but no one had come after Cormorant, either. The Agency, judging from the news, had done some cosmetic personnel reshuffling and called it a day. It appeared that by burying the truth alongside the bullet in his brain, Rex Harlow had indeed saved everyone involved.

So what changed? What made the CIA blow up this fragile equilibrium and burn Falk before the entire world?

Whenever dealing with the unknown, Falk adhered to the Occam's razor principle, better known in the intelligence community as *horses, not zebras*: The simplest answer is most often the right one. To this, he had added a small modification of his own: The simplest answer is the right one, but only once you ask the right question.

The question, in this case, was *Why now?*

The answer was Keegan's death. Sudden, tragic, unignorable. An assassination in broad daylight, on the closest possible thing to U.S. territory: the Radio Free Europe grounds.

Who would be most interested in framing me for it?

That's easy. The responsible party. The very fact of picking Falk for the scapegoat—and not one of the many actual enemies Keegan had amassed over the years—gave up the motive. The only thing connecting the two of them was the dossier. Thus Keegan likely died for publishing it.

But then we're back to square one: Why now?

The courtyard entrance darkened, putting an end to his inner back-and-forth just as it was about to loop around. At this time of day, the shadow preceded the body by a good stone's throw. Falk stared at his shoes, trying to angle his head away from the newcomers even as he studied them in his peripheral vision. Two men close in age, late twenties. Designer beanies on both; fifteen years earlier, one would have referred to them as hipsters. Either tourists trying not to look like tourists or non-tourists trying to look like tourists and doing a bad job of it. He would strongly prefer the former.

The CZ 75 sat jammed between his belt and his sacrum, covered by the canvas Carhartt coat. Falk wasn't a lightning-quick draw, and definitely not from the seated position. He unzipped the jacket and made a show of scratching his lower back. Inelegant, but it would be easier to grab the gun this way than to fumble for it from the outside.

Then again, he thought, what's the point? What's the desired outcome? Put two more bodies into the ground, and that's if no one clips the old lady in the cross fire? Survive another day as an international fugitive? To what end?

"*Gamarjoba*," said one of the men to the baker, and got a piece of bread for his trouble. His companion took a surreptitious snapshot of the interaction. "How much?"

From the accent, but more so from the way he made a single Georgian word sound like a favor to the natives, Falk had him pegged as a Russian. The baker shook her head: no need to pay. The man pantomimed a folded-hands *thank you*, like they were in Bali. Then he broke off a piece of the shoti and fed it to the one who had taken the photo.

Within a second or so, Falk cycled through relief and comic indignation at his own relief: Hey, who's to say a same-sex couple couldn't *also* be an assassin team. But the old Occam's razor suggested the far likelier scenario of two Russians on the run from their motherland's newly fascist anti-gay legislation, war, and military draft. Fellow fugitives, in their own way. Used to a good life, judging from the clothes; flat broke, judging from the choice of hotel. No one with money would stay here voluntarily.

The men walked past, the photo taker glancing at him with some alarm. Falk had to remind himself that with a fully shaved head, he came across more like a local thug than his usual self. He took out and put on the stolen glasses, setting the world in softer focus but hopefully softening his own look as well. The couple proceeded to their room, two doors to the right of Falk's.

Strangely, the momentary scare had its benefits. He knew what not to do now. *Fuck survival at all costs. Fuck the Snowden scenario.* In a rush of lucidity, Falk realized he was done running. That part ended now, in this weedy ruin in the middle of Kakheti. Whatever his next move, it wouldn't be a panicked scramble.

If Ari Falk, the animal and the soul, was still here, all it meant was that he had one last remaining duty. Not to himself or to the Agency or to the people of his or any other country. To his murdered friend. Yes, that corny and that simple.

The only way not to go down as Keegan's killer was to find out who killed Keegan.

And as soon as he formed this thought, a course of action presented itself. It almost made Falk laugh; in fact, he must have let out an actual chuckle, because the old woman turned and glanced at him through the blue air vibrating above the oven. He responded with a quick thumbs-up.

He knew what to do. The only remaining mystery was how. An official border crossing was out of the question. One could, of course, always buy a map and hire a guide on the dark web. The choice of land borders was Armenia, Turkey, Azerbaijan, and if one was feeling suicidal, Russia.

Still riding the clarity high, Falk went back to his room, cleaned it far more thoroughly than any maid despite having stayed there for only an hour, picked up the go bag, slung it over his shoulder, and was almost past the qvevri pots when another idea occurred to him. He doubled back. At the door to the Russian couple's room, he slowed his steps, rehearsed the opening phrase in his head, steadied his breath, and knocked.

CHAPTER THREE

Kent, England
December 11, 2023

They took the Deal Road exit, leading to the eponymous coastal town. The Kent countryside stayed green even in mid-December, though a frigid wind from the Channel left little doubt what time of year it was. Akinyemi drove a black mid-seventies MGB two-seater, as sleek as his Boateng suit and so small he was practically wearing it, too. Once again, Jim Otterbeck marveled at the Brits' ability to make their common line of work look glam. Maybe it had to do with the difference in role models. *They had James Bond and Emma Peel. We had Jack Ryan and Jason Bourne, a workaholic and an amnesiac.*

The fact that Akinyemi took his own car had operational significance as well. Their out-of-town excursion, according to the tense phone exchange that preceded it, would be a strictly off-the-clock visit. In fact, the MI5 agent was now on holiday, retroactive to the previous week. Stylistic differences aside, managerial ass-covering was a universal language.

"How's your British accent?" Akinyemi suddenly asked, downshifting.

"Why?"

"Just thinking ahead. Deb might clam up a bit when she hears you.

Or, you know, sees me. But I suppose only one of us can do anything about it."

"Oh," Jim said. "I see."

Akinyemi gave a philosophical shrug. "Back in her day, the Service looked a little different."

Jim's speech had in fact always been on the chameleonic side, owing more to personality than to tradecraft. It was just safer to talk like everyone else around you. With his parents, he sounded like his parents. At Langley, he defaulted to a kind of generalized East Coast elocution of his superiors; Asha Tamaskar spoke like that, too. And yes, even a short visit to London was usually enough to pull his vowels somewhere into the middle of the Atlantic, where they stayed for a week or two. A girlfriend had once referred to it as his "Niles Crane voice," which stung because Jim suspected it was less about the accent and more about him looking like a young David Hyde Pierce. But he had never attempted a full-tilt impersonation.

"'Name's Jim Otterbeck,'" he said, with a clipped *o* and heavily affricated *t*'s. "'Jim Otterbeck, how are you?' Too caricatured?"

"No, it's perfect. You sound like a pretentious twat trying to speak above his station. Keep going."

"'Um . . . So, uh, Deb, how long have you been teaching horseback riding?'"

"Oof. Just *horse* riding, please. I don't know why you lot feel the need to specify which part of the horse one rides."

"Maybe it's a bad idea," Jim said in his normal voice.

"Yeah." Akinyemi steered onto a dirt track going up a gentle hill. The roadster's engine voiced its displeasure. "Maybe."

A muddy bridle path ran parallel to the road. They cleared the hillcrest and saw the farm, sprawled over thirty or so acres of moorland: two long stables facing each other, a jigsaw puzzle of pens and arenas, a round manege under a soft circus roof. The sign over a decorative entrance gate read *Northbourne Riding Centre. Classes & Full Livery. Families Welcome.*

"Well, there it is," said Akinyemi, sounding glum. "The retirement every spy thinks they're going to get. Maybe one in a thousand does. Which is just as well, because I'd rather fucking kill myself."

The outburst startled Jim. Nothing about his host had yet suggested this kind of candor.

"So walk me through this," Jim said before the mask snapped on again. "How does an ex-MI6 support officer end up selling fake passports?"

Akinyemi shrugged. "Because someone always will. Better this way than the other."

The car crept down a gravel path, toward an ugly pebble-dash house that looked molded from the same gravel. A piece of rock loudly struck the undercarriage. The agent winced.

"It's not just forgery," he added. "They say, pre-internet, she used to be the queen of dead doubles. Dead Double Deb."

"Dead doubles?"

"You start by trawling cemeteries all over the Commonwealth for infant graves. Tax offices, parish records. Grim business. Find someone who died as a child, no living relatives, common surname. Request a duplicate birth certificate—"

"Ah." Jim nodded. "*Day of the Jackal.*"

"Yes, but think longer term. A good legend grows at the literal rate of human life. By the time Deb retired, she had raised hundreds of these homunculi. It would have been a titanic waste. They quite literally don't make them like they used to."

"So you allowed her to take the business private. A retirement package."

"Well, not us. The Secret Service. But yes. With the understanding that, if the client's a threat, she'll flag them."

"And she thought Falk wasn't? You just left it at some old bat's discretion?"

"Watch it," said Akinyemi. "You're still a guest here. And so am I." The MGB rolled to a stop. He killed the engine and got out. "Ah, there she is."

They followed a harshly amplified Cockney voice to a pen behind the house, where a riding lesson was under way. Four horses and a pony, with girls aged roughly five to fifteen in the saddles. Two older teenage boys led the beginners' horses by the reins; the three intermediates—including the very confident five-year-old—rode solo. The parents milled behind the fence, taking photos and videos of their own reflected prosperity.

Deb herself, a short woman of the elastic age definable only as "getting on," sat in the corner of the pen on a foldout chair half sunk into the mud, megaphone to her lips like an old-time film director. An unending, impressively multilingual stream of advice and corrections hung in the manure-scented air.

"Stretch down the back of your legs. Heels down, toes up. Violet, let your bottom go wibbly-wobbly. Let your legs hang down below you. There. Ursula, *streck die Beine. Sehr gut. Keine Angst vor Fehlern—das Pferd weiß, was zu tun ist.* Liv, imagine there's a broomstick up your shirt. Let your whole body lean forward a bit. Dasha, *ne boisya natyagivat' udila. Emu ne bol'no, ya obeschayu.* Poppy, I know, I know, darling, half seat is very tiring. You can just do the rising trot. Very good. *Molodec. Gut gemacht.* Well ridden."

Jim and Akinyemi hung back behind the parents. At no point had Deb so much as glanced at either of them—and yet as soon as the hour was over and the megaphone back on a wall hook, she waddled toward them directly and with purpose.

"Gentlemen." Up close, her face had an almost marbled texture, every blood vessel taxed by the breeze from without and booze from within. "Let's talk inside."

The house was a mess in a way that required not just carelessness but dedicated effort. Stacks of books moldered in corners. Akinyemi took off his coat but hesitated to put it anywhere. "Oh, good," he muttered, observing the thick layer of white canine fur on every surface, "a Build Your Own Dog workshop." The pet in question, an unbrushed Maltipoo, minced out of the bedroom, sniffed his shoes, and went back.

"Care for a nip?" Deb was already rummaging in the putative kitchen area. She had taken off her wellies but kept on the mud-encrusted fleece with the Association of British Riding Schools logo.

"No thank you," said Jim in his best Received Pronunciation.

She fixed him with a fast-blinking stare. "A sep, are you?"

"I . . ." Jim helplessly looked at his companion, who shrugged. "I assure you I'm not a separatist of any kind."

"Sep. Septic tank. Yank," said Akinyemi sotto voce. "You can lose the RP now."

"And you," Deb turned her attention to the MI5 agent. "Nigeria, is it?"

"Surrey, actually." Akinyemi stepped forward, coat in hands. "Look, Deborah, as pleasant as this is, we're not planning to take up too much of your time. Jim is with the cousins. Me, I think you know. We need a peek at your ledger for August 2021."

"I'm not an idiot," said Deb. She found a glass, feigned rinsing it, and poured herself a Scotch. "I still watch the news on occasion. You're here for the Jewish fellow. Out of curiosity, though, how did you—?"

"Jerome Odezenne."

Deb nodded and downed the drink. "That was shoddy work. But what can you do. The original stock's depleted. One has to use every part of the pig, so to speak." She winked at Akinyemi. "Especially when the client's a stingy cunt."

"Did Falk get a Frankenpassport, too?" Jim asked.

"Oh no, no." Deb sat down at a desk, or rather a heap of trash in the general shape of one. After shoving aside a stack of ancient magazines and a single roller skate, she produced an East Kent A–Z Street Atlas for the year 1989 and consulted a loose page stuck into it. It began to dawn on Jim, perhaps belatedly, that her Collyer Brothers act was at least in part tradecraft. "Gave him one of my babies. One of the very last ones."

"He paid well, then?"

"Not at all. His friend did, the dead one. Keegan." Another hole in Asha Tamaskar's preferred narrative, but they were so close to victory it no longer mattered.

"Great," said Jim. "All we need is the name you gave him, and we'll be out of your hair."

The last part was a promise to himself as much as to Deb. He couldn't wait to get back outside. By design or not, the place was giving him the creeps. Jim's eyes were beginning to itch and water, and he wasn't even allergic to dogs. The woman, however, had already lost all interest in him and pivoted to Akinyemi.

"I haven't heard an offer yet," she said.

"Come on. They're letting you do what you do. What else can there possibly—"

"I don't know." Deb squinted at the younger man, cocking her head. "The Yanks seem awfully bothered. Don't tell me there's nothing in it for you, either."

"Deborah." Akinyemi was now in his furious-calm mode. "An Englishman is dead. Some say a hero. Perhaps not to you or me, but to many. Falk may have the answers. There is such a thing as duty."

"Well, that's rich," Deb mumbled, pouring herself more Scotch and dispatching it in one unbroken motion. "Being lectured on my Englishness now—"

"By . . . ? Finish that sentence."

"Oh, you'd love that. Send me to sensitivity training, why don't you."

"All right," said Jim, stepping in between them, and loudly sniffled. His allergies were running rampant; there must have been black mold or something in the house. "Stuart, are the families still out there?"

Akinyemi glanced over his shoulder, through the rhombic glass panel in the front door. "Yeah. Why?"

"Good." Jim headed out. "You guys keep chatting, I'm going to go stretch my legs and let them know Northbourne Riding Centre is run by an alcoholic criminal. A couple of those moms looked pretty quick with their phones. I'm sure it'll be on TikTok before I finish speaking."

Deb just raised her eyebrows and looked at Akinyemi for a response. Jim's idiotic bluff had done its job: they were now, finally, compatriots.

"Uh, Jim," the agent stammered, "that's . . . not how we go about things."

"Well aware. Luckily, I'm not you."

"There's a lot of, uh, local factors at work here."

"Are there?" He turned and faced Akinyemi, without even bothering to look at Deb. "You see, Stuart, you don't seem to understand something I bet she does. And it's only the most important thing to understand about us. *Literally none of us cares what happens to any of you.*"

The speech would have landed stronger had he not sneezed at the end of it. Even so, combined with another step toward the door, it worked.

"Watts," said Deb in a strangulated croak. Jim and Akinyemi turned their heads in unison.

"What?"

"Oh, do sod off. Daniel Jason Watts, born in Toronto, Canadian passport number—"

■ ■ ■

Václav Havel Airport, Prague
December 12, 2023

The first alert came from the decoy camera on the landing, as it was meant to. Falk stole a quick, owlish over-the-glasses look around himself and opened the app. Technically, you weren't allowed to use mobile phones in the line to passport control, but almost every airport in the world had given up on enforcing that rule.

Free Wi-Fi struggled with the video file, but even the lowest-resolution version was enough to get the gist of what was happening back in Tbilisi. Two burly men in ski masks, one already at work picking the lock of the apartment, the other scanning the walls and ceiling for the very thing he was about to find. The masked face pushed in closer, distended by the fish-eye lens into something out of a nineties rap video. The image shook as gloved fingers pried the camera loose from the ceiling pipes between which it conspicuously hid, then contracted to a dot and died. *Thank you for your service.*

The men weren't locals. Every Georgian who looked like this would either be gainfully employed in someone's security detail or volunteering against Russia in the Georgian Legion, and, more important, be sporting a serious beard. His money was on the Sacs—the Agency's inevitable slang for its Special Activities Center. For a moment, Falk felt perversely pleased he was a valuable enough target to warrant a paramilitary strike team.

The visit from the goon squad meant that the Agency had already connected him to the Watts passport—at least ten hours ago, too, factoring in the time it would take the Sacs to show up in Tbilisi. Good for them. The question now was whether a notice with this name, and not just his face, had also gone out to the world's airports. Unlike an instant, global flash bulletin the movies tended to depict, this was a laborious interagency process that often took up to a day. Falk placed Watts's odds of clearing passport control at fifty-fifty. A fun thing to contemplate when you're fourth in line to the booth.

Meanwhile on Chavchavadze Avenue, the second, real camera kicked in next. It hid on the opposite side of the landing, masquerading as the neighbors' defunct buzzer. Unlike the decoy, which had come from Ali-Express and cost $20, this one had a sharper picture and an automatic motion-tracking zoom. The video loaded, treating Falk to a medium close-up of a Sac triumphantly unlocking the door. Unbeknownst to the goon, the act of turning the lock spurred to life three more cameras inside the apartment. For the next few minutes, or however long it would take the men to find and collect them all, he'd have a multi-angle, sitcom-style coverage of his former life being torn apart.

Somewhere under all the dissociative glee, Falk felt a sharp pang of sorrow for Keegan. Not only had that glorious nerd consulted him on this security setup, but he would have been precisely the kind of person to get a kick out of watching it in action.

But Alan Keegan was dead, perhaps at the hands of the very men Falk was watching on his screen. This fact justified every mad risk he was taking now. It's why he was in Prague, about to do what he was about to do.

The line moved. A clutch of Eurotripping backpackers bounded past control, jazzed to be hitting one of Europe's most notorious playgrounds. *Make good decisions, boys.* Falk took another step toward the booth, Schrödinger's cat slinking into the box. The masked party unfolding in his phone provided a suitable distraction, so he went back to it.

The next clip rolled in. It had come from a remote camera piggybacking on a webcam in a supposedly sleeping laptop. The movement that had triggered it turned out to be someone else entering the apartment: a slim, dimly familiar male figure without a balaclava. The man strode into the center of the living room, taking in the scene. Large eyes, narrow face, a curious air of pride and propriety at once. He was wearing a suit and tie under a quilted shell jacket: not exactly tactical gear.

"How many cameras have you found?" he asked the Sacs, his voice tinny and compressed over the bad mic. "Assume there's twice as many." Then he walked toward the laptop and closed the lid.

It was in the last moment before the image flickered out that Falk finally placed the guy. Jim Otterbeck, Moscow Station. They had crossed paths exactly once. A singularly unpleasant character, but in a way that reminded Falk of some of his own worst qualities as a rookie case officer. An interesting choice to head up the search; puzzling, even. Then again, Falk thought, two years is a long time. Maybe his star has really risen in the interim.

The Sacs, seen in silhouette from a kitchen cam, were busily bagging up his electronics. Otterbeck opted for a less obvious tack. He slowly paced the apartment, arms splayed out, touching nothing. It looked like he was trying to get a general feel for the space or commune with the remnants of Falk's aura.

Since he wouldn't stop moving from room to room, new clips kept slotting into the app's video grid. Two of them turned out to end in an abrupt smash-to-black, as Otterbeck discovered and dismantled their sources. *Not an idiot, then.* Falk's surveillance of the apartment was now down to a single camera, the best and most expensive one, no larger than a pearl and operating out of the keyhole in a locking desk drawer.

Otterbeck circled the desk, pulled out the drawer itself, and shook its contents onto the bed, inadvertently making the viewer dizzy; he then set it aside and called over the Sacs. That was the plan. The papers inside the drawer were a random mix of utility bills and takeout menus, but they should siphon off the searchers' focus for a while.

It was Falk's turn at the booth. He hid the phone, handed over the passport, and steeled himself for what was or wasn't coming.

"*Dobrý den*," he said, one of the few phrases he knew in Czech. The language wasn't close at all to Russian, which he did speak, but this particular greeting was.

"Purpose of the trip?" The Czech officer, a middle-aged woman, wasn't having it.

"Visiting a friend."

She opened the document. "Hmm. You look different here."

"Yeah, sorry, I shaved my head." Falk gave her an awkward smile and touched the rim of his glasses. "And my vision's gone to shit since I had the photo taken. I will get a new one as soon as I—"

She stamped the passport, if only to shut him up.

Falk was all the way to the luggage belts when his phone buzzed with a new alert from the sole remaining camera. In the video itself, a different phone was buzzing, a neat recursion. Otterbeck, seen only as a pair of legs on the drawer cam, picked up.

"Yes," he said. "Yes. We're there right now." He paused to listen. "I see. On it. Have the locals been alerted? Great."

He must have shoved the phone back into his pocket, since the hem of his jacket moved.

"Gentlemen," he called out to the unseen Sacs. "We're done here." Even on the lo-fi recording, Falk caught a slight echo of an English accent in his speech. It definitely hadn't been there in Moscow. "That was DD Tamaskar. Guess where the Watts passport just pinged."

Falk exited the app and deleted it. By the time he lifted his head from the phone, both corridors leading to the arrivals hall, the green and the red, were being cordoned off; at least six uniformed officers moved upstream through the groaning bottleneck.

■ ■ ■

Jim was the first off the plane. He sprinted down the jet bridge, flashed his ID to the Czech police already waiting at the doors, and ran into the terminal, leaving them no choice but to follow. Having flown from London to Tbilisi and from Tbilisi to Prague in the same day, both times via Istanbul, he was done with the finer points of international security service etiquette. Right now, adrenaline was the only thing keeping his body from shutting down altogether.

As usual, he didn't question the op. Considering that he had managed to have Falk located and captured within forty-eight hours of taking up the assignment, however, this *would* have been a nice moment for Tamaskar to break out an Agency jet. After all, Special Activities had taken one, direct from Virginia, the moment the Langley analysts traced the name "Daniel Jason Watts" to that rental apartment on Chavchavadze Avenue. Yet the deputy director had apologetically insisted that he fly to Prague commercial. Clearing a CIA aircraft to land in the middle of a European capital, she explained, was a political ask that would necessitate looping the Czechs in and sharing credit. "Unless, of course, you're okay with them claiming they caught him for us."

"I most certainly am not."

"Didn't think so." Jim was thus to quietly collect Falk from border-control custody and deliver him to a safe house on Lucemburská, from where the Sacs would exfil both of them within a few hours. Full credit was worth a little sleep deprivation.

His one real regret was not being able to end things on a better note with Stuart Akinyemi. The dapper MI5 agent, who for all his hauteur had proved indispensable, never fully got over Jim's little speech at Deb's; their entire ride back to Heathrow had unfolded in stony silence.

Oh well. I'll mention him in my report.

One of the Czech uniforms had jogged ahead of Jim and was now showing the way. They turned into a narrow staff-only passage connecting the international zone with Arrivals and took the stairs down into the bowels of the maintenance area. Through the left wall, Jim could hear the thrum of the baggage belts. Every once in a while, a gate would rattle open and a train of three or four loaded carts crossed left to right, blocking the hallway; each of these mini-delays felt like torture. An intoxicating sense of finality gripped him. In the back of his mind, he was already retelling the story of this day to his father.

It would be interesting to know why, of all places he could have tried to run, Falk headed straight to Prague. Back to the scene of the crime? Last place anyone would look? Perhaps he'd get the answer out of him on the way to the safe house. That would be the real cherry on top.

One step at a time. You've already won. Relax.

The border-control holding facility, which took up a small suite of rooms at the hallway's far end, looked more like a tax-free office than a jail. To Jim's alarm, a dozen people were already milling around its entrance. Some were cops, some airport employees, some unmistakably press: Three or four stood with their phones out in a semicircle around a shy-looking young man in a beanie, interviewing him or taking a statement. This must have been what Tamaskar had warned him about: The Czechs were already taking credit.

"This is a matter of national security," Jim hissed, slowing down to a brisk walk. "Get the media out of here."

The uniforms pretended not to hear. Instead, they just politely shooed everyone away from the door, clearing the way for him to enter. Jim had nothing left to do but mumble, "Amateur hour," give the reporters a withering glare as he passed, and step inside.

The room was overheated and overlit. In a metal chair facing the far wall, wrists cuffed behind his back, head shaved, sat Falk. Two border-control officers—a man and a woman—stood off to the side whispering urgently to each other. As Jim walked in, followed by the uniforms, they stopped and raised their heads as if caught doing something untoward.

Another second later, the man in the chair slowly turned his.

"Excuse me," Jim said after a long pause. "Is there a restroom nearby?"

The woman silently pointed to a side door.

By the time he was done vomiting, swished some Prague water around his mouth, cleaned himself up, and reemerged, the very chemical composition of the room had been altered. The Czechs stared at him with a mixture of amusement and pity, the handcuffed man—who was decidedly not Falk—with abject fear.

"What's your name?" Jim asked him, to ask something.

"Roman Avdeev," the man replied with a husky Russian accent. "I'm very sorry."

Jim turned to the border-control duo. In response, the woman handed him a navy blue Canadian passport.

He opened it to the photo page. Daniel Jason Watts. One of Deb's babies. The workmanship was excellent. The man in the picture was unmistakably Falk.

"We detained him right away," said the male officer. "I mean, he looked nothing like the photo. So when your people called, we actually had him here already."

"How—"

"Says he found the passport on the plane."

"Found and *decided to use*? What the—excuse my language, but what the hell? And why is there press in the hallway?"

"Yeah." The male officer cleared his throat and rocked on his heels a bit. "That's where it gets complicated. He's a Russian national. His husband has entered the country legally. That's him outside, giving interviews."

"What's complicated about that?"

"Let me repeat." The officer's English was very good, but he was enjoying the opportunity to flex it a little too much for Jim's already dire state of mind and body. "He's a *Russian* national. His *husband* is outside. Giving *interviews.*"

Had Jim not just spent a sleepless day and night crisscrossing the continent, he would have gotten it sooner. The Kremlin's draconian new laws meant Russian same-sex couples were now eligible to request political asylum immediately after arriving anywhere in the EU. The actual legalization process was, more often than not, an uphill battle. But sending an applicant back right away, with the media present, meant a guaranteed international scandal.

He could feel Falk's mind working behind this. One part clever, two parts insane seemed to be his signature recipe.

"What's your real name, again?" Jim asked in Russian.

The man in the chair, whose head had drooped to his chest in the meantime, stirred. His eyes darted from Jim to the Czechs and back.

"Avdeev, Roman Artemovich," he said. "I speak English."

"Did this guy put you up to it?" Jim showed him the Watts passport.

"No. Found in plane, in bathroom."

"Bullcrap."

"So are you taking him or what?" asked the male officer. "I can't just keep, uh, keeping him in here."

Jim ignored the question. "And did you geniuses bother to check if anyone has used *his* name to enter the country? A-v-d-e-e-v," he acidly spelled in the direction of the female officer.

"Oh. I . . . I will now."

"*Please.*"

She darted next door. Even before Jim heard a keyboard tapping, he knew what was coming next. The overhead lights seemed to dim. He felt like sitting down, but the only chair in the room was occupied by poor Avdeev.

Several seconds, or perhaps an hour, later, reality gleefully confirmed his darkest presentiment. The woman returned with a hangdog expression, pawing a printout. "We, uh, do have an Avdeev in the system," she said. "Same flight."

She handed him the document. A scan of a Russian transborder passport issued in 2015, outdated design, barely biometric, with a black-and-white photo of a much younger Avdeev. Next to it, a smeared, streaky picture taken by a camera at the border booth. A bald white male in glasses. The time stamp in the corner was from over ten hours ago.

Perhaps it was a crease in the paper or a flaw in the flow of ink, but Falk appeared to be winking.

Jim, expressionless, handed the printout back. "I'm afraid you'll be hearing more from us." He nodded at the chair. "Please . . . just let him go."

"Thank you," said Avdeev to the closing door.

Jim walked out into the hallway, where the scrum around Avdeev's husband had grown to include reporters with actual cameras and BBC, ČT24, and Current Time mic cubes. Dragging the back of his jacket along the chalky wall, he squeezed past them.

The outside greeted him with a fistful of fine snow in the face. At 5:30 p.m., wintertime Prague was fully dark. Christmas lights twinkled along the undulating canopy. Jim emerged from Arrivals in what was, for him, the rarest of states: completely lost as to what to do next.

The magnitude of his failure was only beginning to bear down on him. With a ten-hour head start, Falk could be anywhere in the EU. Most of the Schengen countries' land borders conducted no passport checks at all. The Czech Republic's location smack-dab in the middle of the continent meant that places as far-flung as Greece, Spain, and Finland were now all equally in play. If Falk was desperate enough, he could even cross from Slovakia into Ukraine and vanish in the wartime chaos. Perhaps that was the real reason he had picked Prague: as a hub for his next disappearing act.

The grown-up thing to do would be to call it in. After some pathetic dawdling, Jim did, via text. The last thing he wanted to hear was Asha Tamaskar's sardonic voice. Her response, as he had suspected, was a curt instruction to proceed to the address on Lucemburská and wait for the Sacs.

A minute later, as he watched an icon of a cartoon taxi creep toward him in the Bolt app, the second message arrived: "U did ur best."

The car pulled up, a snow-dusted Škoda Octavia. He got in. The radio was playing some godawful nineties dance hit, would-be Caribbean but with distinctly German diction. *Put me up, put me down, put my feet back on the ground.*

Jim was about to ask the driver to switch the stations when three things happened in very fast succession. The left passenger door swung open; someone plopped onto the seat next to him, laughing hysterically; and a metal cylinder pressed against his ribs through the jacket.

"Jim! Holy fuck!" a drunk voice boomed in his ear, though the breath accompanying it carried no trace of alcohol. "Let's go, let's go, vámonos!" This to the driver, who had glanced back in confusion. "Turn it up! Love that shit! This is a fuckin' party bus now! Right, Jimbo?" Falk threw his free arm around Jim's shoulders. The barrel pushed in harder. "Right?"

"Yes," said Jim. "It is a party bus."

The driver shook his head—*Americans, am I right?*—and took off. The song switched back to the insufferable chorus. *Ya ya ya Coco Jamboo, ya ya yeah.* Falk enthusiastically sang along for a few more bars, then phased out of the persona.

"What do you want?" Jim half whispered, looking down.

"Who's DD Tamaskar? Deputy director? Which department?"

"Yours. Covert Activities. Harlow's replacement."

"Call him."

"It's a her."

"Call her."

Jim gathered what was left of his wits. "I'm on my way to the safe house. We can make the call from there." *And if I stall long enough, the Sacs will have time to arrive.*

"Fine."

The Škoda sped through the dark. There were no city lights on Jim's side of the car; the road lay alongside some kind of nature preserve. Falk sat in silence, keeping him at invisible gunpoint. Every time they ran over a pothole, the barrel hit him in the ribs again.

"I understand the passport switch," said Jim. "Trip the alarms, see who comes running." All training manuals suggested talking to the captor as much as possible. They didn't specify what to do with a captor trained on the same manuals. "But how on earth did you bring in a weapon? Unless you're holding a stapler or something."

"In four parts. In checked luggage. You're welcome to look, slowly."

Jim did. The gun was a CZ, which seemed mildly ironic.

"Did you fly from Tbilisi?"

"Batumi."

"Smart." Jim nodded. "Casino town. They don't care."

The car neared the center. Bits and pieces of the famed skyline rose in front of them: the Gothic bauble of St. Vitus, lit from below, the ornate bridges girdling the Vltava. The radio kept blaring Europop hits, the chintzy sound in painful conflict with the timeless view.

"Are the Russian couple okay?" Falk suddenly asked.

"Yes. The Czechs are letting Avdeev go. In the grand scheme of things, you actually helped them."

The safe house was in the newer part of town, in a Communist-era slab near the Žižkov TV tower. Modernity was making some aspects of clandestine life surprisingly easy: a dozen Airbnb lockboxes hung on the bike rack by the building's entrance. Jim found the right one and retrieved the key. Out on the street and in the stairwell, Falk kept the gun in his jacket pocket. Once they reached the right floor, however, he produced it again.

"Sorry," he said, aiming. "But if there's anyone—anyone—inside . . . please understand I don't have very much to lose."

"I understand," said Jim.

"We go in. You call Tamaskar. We talk. I leave. You stay. Yes?"

"Yes."

Jim paused at the apartment door. *What if the Sacs arrived early? Open and duck? Try to grab the gun?* Neither scenario sounded like a good idea. Mostly he just felt tired. Having produced a record amount of adrenaline for the day, his body appeared to have chosen this moment to close up shop.

Falk pushed him forward, barrel to the nape. Jim was fumbling with the key when the round knob in front of him turned by itself. The door opened.

In retrospect, he owed the rest of his life to Falk's reflex control. Otherwise, his brains would have ended up all over the front of Asha Tamaskar's burgundy top.

"Officer Falk!" The deputy director leaned against the jamb and talked past, or rather through, Jim. "Love the new haircut. You've been a tough man to find. Good thing Officer Otterbeck proved to be such a dedicated bloodhound."

I'm right here, Jim almost said. As if responding to that thought, Tamaskar lay her hand on his shoulder and nudged him aside, putting herself in the path of Falk's shot instead.

“My name is Asha,” she said. “I’m alone.” For several seconds, they studied each other across the threshold. Then Falk lowered his gun.

“Thank you.” Tamaskar smiled. “Would you mind stepping in? We have a lot of ground to cover in a very short time. Jim, I’m going to have to have you wait out here for a bit.”

What about the Sac team? Jim wanted to ask before realizing the obvious.

No Sacs were ever going to show up. The official op ended in Tbilisi, if, indeed, it had ever begun.

At least this also explained his flying commercial.

“Now, Ari. May I call you Ari?” The faint, fading echo of this phrase was the last thing he heard from the depths of his humiliation, fetal on the bottom of an endlessly telescoping well, before the door of the safe house gently closed in his face.

■ ■ ■

Falk looked at her and couldn’t even begin to figure her out. Tortoiseshell glasses, same age as him or a little older, dressed like a paralegal at a good law firm. Maybe he was wrong. Maybe the changes the Harlow scandal had forced at the CIA were more than cosmetic.

Or maybe it was still the same clusterfuck of bureaucracy, cruelty, hubris, and overreach, just in a fun new millennial wrapper. He was about to find out.

The living room held a table, two chairs, and a dresser, all from IKEA and all still festooned with stickers marking each part for easier assembly. Whoever had been in charge of furnishing the apartment followed the venerable public-sector tradition of giving every task their absolute least. Falk and Tamaskar sat at the table, neither willing to start. Then Tamaskar murmured, “I’m sorry, this is really bugging me,” reached down, and peeled a sticker from the table leg closest to her. Falk didn't know if it was a genuine tic, a shrewd icebreaker, or both, but he did feel a little more at ease.

"So," he began. At this juncture, the act of speaking carried more value than whatever was being said. "DD/CA, huh. In some parallel universe I'd be reporting to you now."

"Funny, right?" Tamaskar replied in a flat tone. "I only have the job thanks to you."

Falk gestured at the door. "Seeing how you've kicked out poor Otterbeck, I'm going to assume this is all extremely off the record." She gave a curt nod yes. "In that case, first things first. Did you murder Keegan?"

"God no."

"Do you think I did?"

"Also no. But I did need a pretext to flush you out, and for that, I am deeply sorry. You see, in Langley, there's a bit of an omertà around the Harlow dossier. The consensus is that it was a good thing it came out. Not so good that we'd want to *celebrate* you or anything, but . . . you get it. Burt's sense is that your staying in the wind indefinitely is the optimal scenario for everyone."

"Burt Spaleta, the new guy."

"Yes. He's fine. A technocrat. A little toothless for some of the old guard. Obsessed with cleaning up our reputation. We have a Social Media team now, for some reason."

"Cool. Don't forget skateboards," said Falk. "I hear the kids are into skateboards. So, what do you want from me?"

"This. To have this talk."

Falk fidgeted in his chair. He was too tired for riddles. "I'm sure there were ways of getting in touch that didn't involve an international manhunt."

In response, Tamaskar silently lifted a travel bag onto her lap, took out a tablet, and set it in the center of the table with the screen facing Falk. Each of these simple gestures looked a tad too precise for comfort, as if she'd rehearsed the whole sequence before his arrival. Whatever she said next would be the thing she had come here to say.

"Ari, we know who killed your friend. And these people are just getting started." She tapped the tablet. The screen came alive. The preloaded photo, taken in the cold glare of an evidence locker, showed several objects laid out on a metal tabletop next to a ruler. A set of keys on a silly chain. A mangled pair of still-familiar glasses, flecked with red. A scuffed Nokia phone. A *nature morte* in every sense.

"The Brits found it on Keegan's body," Tamaskar said, zooming in on the phone. "They're embarrassed enough about Dead Double Deb to let me copy the contents."

"A burner," Falk said. Not much of an observation, but he was still processing Tamaskar's previous statement. *These people are just getting started? What people?*

"Obviously. Had one single email on it, with one file attached. But it's not his. It belonged to a woman named Petra Lorencová."

The name rang a bell. "One of the Radio Free Europe bystanders."

"We don't think she was a bystander. We think she was the primary target of a meticulously planned hit." It had never occurred to Falk that the object of the attack wasn't just Keegan. "By a man trying to contain *this*."

Tamaskar swiped to the next screen. A video began to autoplay on mute: a conference room as seen through a CCTV-camera fish-eye. A long table distorted into a smile, an acoustic ceiling bent into a canopy. Five figures, all men, all in business attire, languidly conversing over formal china. Two sat with their backs to the camera, three faced it. Though Falk didn't recognize anyone, the space, sterile at first glance, yielded a few clues.

"Russia?"

"What makes you say that?"

"European outlets, a valance over the curtain, tea on the table." She looked impressed, so he decided to go in for the kill. "But the people are Westerners, at least some of them."

Tamaskar stared at him. "Okay, how the fuck—"

"The tea service. It's the kind of self-exoticizing stuff they pull out in front of the visitors. An all-Russian group dressed like that would be drinking espressos."

The deputy director's mien curdled into irritation faster than Falk could stop himself. "All right, enough showing off. What do you want, your old job back?"

"Am I wrong?"

She sighed. "You're not. This is Hotel Angleterre, St. Petersburg. On the margins of this year's Economic Forum. And yes, three of the men are American."

Now it was Falk's turn to frown. Ever since the start of the Ukraine war, the St. Petersburg International Economic Forum, once a global fat-cat summit styled after Davos, had become the kind of place where the Chinese and Venezuelan delegations reluctantly rubbed shoulders with "business leaders" from various failed states, unrecognized people's republics, and the Taliban. U.S. media, once the belles of the ball, were banned from attending, and reputable companies wouldn't be caught dead within a hundred-mile radius.

"Officially, this is a panel on 'traditional values in higher education.' What it actually *is* is a Brink's truck full of rubles backing up a very particular driveway. I take it you're familiar with the men's rights movement," Tamaskar said, putting the slightest of sarcastic spins on each of the last three words.

Falk shrugged. "No one ever went broke telling guys that nothing is their fault."

"And you get a fractured society as a bonus, which is why Russia's been helping finance it for years." She put her finger on the screen, pointing someone out and pausing the video in one motion. "You know this dude?"

"I'm a little behind on my manosphere. Am I supposed to?"

Tamaskar sneered. "Honestly, I'd be concerned if you did. Name's Felix Burnham."

Falk looked down at the freeze-frame. The man trapped under Tamaskar's index finger was in his fifties, with a studied Clint Eastwood squint under a shock of graying hair. The moment caught him leaning forward in a swivel chair, left elbow on the armrest, right palm a smudge as he animatedly explained something to the others. Unlike the rest of the group in their high-corporate regimentals, he wore a tweed sport coat over a plaid shirt. Thick eyebrows, high forehead, refined and simian at once: half teacher, half hunter.

"You've heard of Andrew Tate. Burnham's the champagne version of that. An Oxford classics professor, at least until they kicked him out. Now he runs something called the Alpha Academy. Thousands of dollars for a playlist of YouTube lectures. For fifty grand a year, you get a newsletter. Double that, and they let you into a group chat with the man himself."

Alan would have loved this, Falk thought. Exposing puffed-up frauds was FleaCollar's bread and butter. He briefly wondered if Keegan even got to see the contents of the video.

"At first it looks like your classic pyramid scheme," Tamaskar continued. "The only way to reduce tuition is to recruit others. Once you reach the top tier, though, you can work it off by running errands for the boss. It's kind of brilliant: It incentivizes you to go *into* debt to get *out* of it, and by the time you can, you're so deep in the red you'll do anything."

"Errands," Falk repeated, readying himself for what was coming.

Tamaskar saw him tense up, nodded, took off her glasses, and began wiping the lenses with a little green cloth.

"The Prague shooter owed Alpha Academy a quarter of a million. Until a week ago. Someone paid it off the day he got his job as a security guard at Radio Free Europe."

So there it was. Falk looked at Burnham's face on the tablet screen, noticing—or imagining—things he hadn't at first. The cold glint in the eyes. The subtle disdain for the room and the company, betrayed by the imperious way his hand grabbed the armrest. *Being listened to* was this man's most, perhaps only, natural state.

"I can show you the paper trail," said Tamaskar, mistaking his silence for disbelief.

"No need. Is there audio on this thing?"

"Sure. It's not very helpful." Tamaskar nudged up the volume. The video played on, Burnham gesticulating fluidly as he talked. It was something about Dostoyevsky's gambling habits. The accent was the first thing to catch Falk's ear: British and Boston Brahmin by turns, with a very slight Mitteleuropean burr underpinning both. It put him in mind of Humbert Humbert in Kubrick's *Lolita*, though he had seen the film only once and didn't actually remember what James Mason sounded like in the role.

"Where's this piece of shit from?" Falk asked. He wouldn't be surprised to hear something like Milwaukee. Burnham's diction seemed as consciously self-styled as the tweed uniform and the hand movements.

"Where *isn't* he from. His real name is Philipp Brenner. Best we can tell, his family moved stateside from East Germany when he was in his teens. Went to the UK on a Rhodes scholarship, stayed on to teach."

Falk nodded, half listening. As convincing as the evidence was, something about this still didn't compute. "You're saying he had three people killed over this footage. But all it shows is him with his hand out to the

Russians. Not to be rude, but this kind of stuff barely dents reputations anymore. Especially on the right."

"Agreed," said Tamaskar. The glasses were back on, and so was the flat affect. "Here's the thing, though. You know what Burnham has been doing with the money? *Hiring*." Tamaskar took the tablet and searched for something before flipping it back toward Falk. "These are just a few people who started getting paid out of Alpha Academy accounts shortly after he got back from St. Petersburg."

Falk looked. A gallery of thick necks and dead eyes. "Security detail, I take it. He's scared. Which he ought to be."

"If only. Ari, they're all ex-agents. Spookshops and private military." She pointed at the photo of a human colossus with broken ears and a nose so upturned you could see both nostrils head on. A face coauthored and signed by violence. "This one is one of ours, Stan Vlasic. A former Special Activities blue badger. Let go for harassing a female analyst in 2019. I actually knew the girl." Tamaskar pinch-zoomed on the photos as she spoke, until each face crumbled into pixels under her fingers. "This one used to be Internal Security at the BND. 'Retired' with a sealed record. These two are ChVK Orlok. God knows what they did to get fired from that one."

"Okay, so elite muscle. The guy sure thinks highly enough of himself."

"It's a high-functioning psycho urban assault team, is what it is," said Tamaskar. "There's a demolition expert here, fuck's sake. *This* is what the Russian money is for. The man is putting together a purpose-built private army. We just don't know the purpose yet."

As often happened when a revelation was around the corner, Falk felt a little queasy. He got up and began to pace the faceless room, touching the walls for balance. "Jesus Christ."

"Thank you!" She slapped the table with both palms. "That's the reaction I was hoping for."

"No, I'm afraid it isn't." Falk broke out in laughter despite himself, a gasping, mirthless cackle he didn't even recognize as his own. "Jesus Christ, Asha," he repeated, cracking up again. "You think you can get me undercover with him! That's your big plan." Falk leaned back against a wall, waiting for the last giggles to subside. "And your idea of building a legend is strapping a giant neon sign to my back that says *rogue agent*, without even bothering to ask me first. Brava. Wow. Slow clap."

Tamaskar sat and waited for him to stop, patiently, but with an extra-icy countenance.

"Well?"

"If you want me to act impressed by your deduction skills again," she said, "I was actually expecting you to get there a couple of minutes ago."

"Go to hell. I'm not doing your job for you. Plus, it's obvious you're out on a limb. The seventh floor would never clear me for this. I'm a gray actor at best."

"Yes. And I was *also* hoping you'd realize why," Tamaskar said very quietly. "Why I'm meeting you here in secret. Why this operation, if it were to commence, would have to be hidden ten layers deep in my continuing fruitless search for you, elusive gray actor Ari Falk."

He didn't even notice as he sat back down. For a second, reality became porous. The room with its unused and unloved furnishings felt like a poor computer rendering. Falk was no longer sure he was there or, say, still lying in a hotel bed in Kakheti, delirious with fear and fatigue.

"Did you *really* think I put all of this together in the last forty-eight hours?" Tamaskar waved at the tablet. "I've been on Burnham for years. Young men's radicalization pipelines were my area as an analyst. We've made some inroads, but not with him. In fact, it is my firm conviction that he was always the first reader of every report I wrote. When I got promoted, one of my day-one orders was to finally move against him.

The Brits had a team in place. Stuart Akinyemi, your old buddy, made the mistake of mentioning the date to me over email. Burnham bolted to an undisclosed location ten hours before the raid. We still don't know where he operates from."

"I see," Falk said. "Shit."

"I used to assume someone was running him from inside the Agency, but it was above my clearance level. Well, now I'm cleared for every SAP there is, and somehow I know even *less*. Ari, this video"—she touched the screen— "this video is the only piece of uncontaminated intel on Burnham I ever got my hands on. And it already took three human lives."

The word *Cormorant* rattled on the tip of Falk's tongue, but he wouldn't give it new life by saying it out loud.

"All right," he said instead. "What would you have me do?"

"For now? Nothing. We never got you. You slipped away in Prague. With the shooter dead and publicly ID'd, you're off the hook on that one, too. The news cycle will move on. Most of Europe should be safe for you."

Tamaskar reached into her bag once again and handed him a fresh passport. "Maybe post a few anonymous rants online about how much you hate the CIA. Let me know if you need any help with those," she deadpanned.

Falk cracked the passport open. It still had the sour smell of new plastic. The name inside, Richard Daniels, was a portmanteau of his two previous covers: Thomas Richards and Daniel Watts.

"Sloppy on purpose," Tamaskar preemptively commented. "But not too glaring. You're a prize to them now. They should feel like it's *their* win when they find you."

He wasn't wild about being dangled as bait, much less in front of a creature whose size and ferocity neither of them fully understood yet. Still, it was worth it if it meant nailing Keegan's killer. And now that he had a better view of the scheme that had brought the two of them into this room, he couldn't help admiring its gall.

Except it still had a flaw. Falk felt it instinctively, almost synesthetically, as a dent or a gnarl in the surface of Tamaskar's plan, even before he knew exactly what it was.

"If we do our jobs right, Burnham's recruiters should be onto you within a month. Another two, maybe three, weeks to shadow and vet you. So I'd say expect overt contact in February or so. When that happens, all you need to do is ask for a sit-down with the man himself. That's it. Once I've located Burnham's camp, the Brits can take over from there. And Keegan won't have died for nothing," she added for Falk's benefit.

"Asha," he said, "you can stop selling. I'll do it."

The deputy director got up, took a black blazer from the back of the chair, and slung it over her travel bag. Falk realized, against his will and better judgment, that he was finding her attractive—had been, in fact, under all the layers of wariness and confusion, since the moment he stepped into the room. The discovery came as a surprise. He had never gone for the overachieving valedictorian type, not to mention someone almost a full foot shorter than him. Perhaps this was just another way his nervous system was dealing with stress.

"Well, I guess this is our first and last meeting for the foreseeable future," Tamaskar said, suddenly awkward, as if having somehow read his thoughts.

"Looks that way."

"Too bad. I would have liked to get to know you under less insane circumstances." They shook hands with ironic pomp, turning the tension into comedy.

"Hang on." Not a second too soon, Falk identified the gnarl. "Wait. You're leaving one *very* loose end. He's outside right now, probably composing a ten-page report to Spaleta as we speak."

Tamaskar laughed. "And whose fault is that?! My plan was to read you in one-on-one at the airport. But nooo, you had to be clever. So I'm afraid you brought this upon yourself, Ari."

He caught the glint in her eye. "No. God, please no. Not this guy."

"I know, right?!" Falk still found it jarring, and a little funny, to hear Harlow's replacement talk like that. "But there's no other play here. Don't worry, I'm only reading him in halfway. Up to the Felix Burnham of it all. The rest is just you and me."

She walked to the door, leaned out into the hallway, and made a beckoning gesture. Jim moped in. Falk would have felt bad for him if he weren't busy feeling worse for himself.

"Officer Otterbeck," Tamaskar announced brightly, "welcome to the *actual* op." The young agent panic-nodded and stalled in the center of the room, unsure where to look: at the boss who had deceived him or the adversary who had bested him. "Officer Falk, meet Officer Otterbeck, your field liaison."

CHAPTER FOUR

McLean, Virginia
March 25, 2024

If there was one thing Asha Tamaskar knew about Asha Tamaskar, it was this: She was a lifelong, inveterate, terminal System Girl. She loved structures and her place in them. (Sometimes she felt lucky to have grown up in the 1990s, the last era before these types of enthusiasms began to be seen through the medical lens.) Intelligence appealed to her as a superstructure, an invisible universe layered atop ours and keeping it on course. The idea of being a gear in its vast machine struck her not as depressing, the way it did some of her peers, but as ecstatic. She would never forget the feeling that had come over her as she stepped onto the Grounds for the first time: that civilization was more than just random outcomes of conflicting desires. Someone had a plan, and she was about to be in on a tiny part of it.

This unironic commitment to drudgery turned out to be a superpower of sorts. It made her rise through the analyst ranks at a much faster clip than most of her peers. In Tamaskar's first years at the CIA, she had hit a snag only once, when, at a cocktail-bar party celebrating yet another promotion, she downed three Sidecars in a row to overcome a natural discomfort with being feted. The drinks had evidently done too good a job, because Tamaskar surprised herself by positing that all the world's intelligence agencies existed to balance each other out, and the only way of achieving that balance was to ensure double-agent penetration of *every* service. She even dimly recalled trying to illustrate that point with a mathematical formula, which she proceeded to scribble on a coaster.

Needless to say, a barful of envious coworkers was not the ideal audience for this. Within hours, at least three of them had reported her ramblings upstairs—at least the little they thought they understood. One of those, Tamaskar later found out, was the cute economic analyst she had taken home that night.

Drunken thought experiments aside, the very idea of treason—which she visualized as a single cog induced to spin backward, gumming up the whole gearworks—made her physically ill. *Not on my watch.* The incident made her paranoid, paranoia made her vigilant, and vigilance looked a lot like ruthlessness; somehow, all this only enhanced her reputation. When it came to replacing Rex Harlow at the head of Covert Activities, the choice seemed like a no-brainer. The System Girl got the keys to the system.

So, uh, why are you doing this? The question, complete with Ari Falk's amused cadence, echoed in her head. It was the last one he had asked her in person, standing body to body in a too-small Prague elevator, moments before they headed off into opposite directions in the same swirling snow. Why side with a self-admittedly chaotic and unreliable ally against your own organization? Compared to the Olympus Mons of devilry in the Agency's past, covering for Felix Burnham amounted to barely a hill. Why pick it as the one to die on?

Whatever she had mumbled in response to him that night—it must have been some platitude about institutional integrity, she was dynamite at those—was a feint. The real reason was one Falk, or anyone else, had no business knowing.

It's because I would go insane if I didn't.

Officially, the operation was called Birdbath, and its brief was to keep searching for Falk after the near miss in Tbilisi. Jim Otterbeck's report, which Tamaskar had ghostwritten from his account before editing from hers, had the rogue officer popping onto the grid in Georgia on December 11, 2023, paying off a stranger to cross the Czech border with his passport, then vanishing back into the ether. The best kind of lie: a lightly abridged truth.

The op behind the op did not have a name. In fact, it didn't involve anything other than sitting and waiting for Burnham or his Russian financiers to make a move on Falk. There were no regular comms channels, no scheduled check-ins, no marching orders. Their only method of keeping in touch was simple to a fault: a closed loop between two Instagram accounts automatically spamming each other. (Falk, who had set this thing up, called it the Otterbot.) Most of the content they pushed into each other's junk folders was just that—random photos pulled from Google, porn ads, AI slop, etc.—but nestled within it were actual updates, marked by a specific pattern of emojis in the description. The last message of real significance had come in mid-February, nestled between a cat meme from 2007 and an AI picture of Jesus with shrimp for arms. It was a photo of a storefront window in Pisa, Italy. "Must be nice," Otterbeck had said, quietly seething as he confirmed receipt by pressing a little heart under it.

Since then, nothing.

The lull was, of course, to be expected, but it still unnerved her to no end. Falk was like a phantom limb: His absence had become a part of Tamaskar's days in a way his presence never could. Every conversation felt newly remarkable because none of them were about him. It was obsession by omission.

Maybe the plan was shit from the start, she thought. Maybe she had overdone it, made him too attractive to Burnham's organization, a goat so fat and slow that even a cursory glance could tell it was stuffed with explosives. Or else Burnham, having collected all the ex-spooks and mercs he needed for his mystery purposes, had simply stopped hiring.

The most plausible scenario, however, was that the operation had just wilted on the vine. Most did. If anything, this was the intelligence community's biggest trade secret: For every quiet success and loud failure, a hundred more operations ended in precisely nothing. A bold exploit that didn't backfire but produced zero intel. A long-cultivated native asset keeling over with a genuine stroke. A change of wind from across the Potomac. Spycraft was a field of empty traps, rusting open.

So it was almost a relief when, six weeks into Falk's Italian silence, the phone rang and a familiar baritone told her to stop by the office of the acting director.

"Hey, Asha. It's about Birdbath." The always-on cordiality filter made Spaleta's actual tone impossible to parse. The analysts back at her old job had a term for it, Deep State Nice. "Somewhat urgent."

The last part was hardly needed. Spaleta wasn't in the habit of phoning deputies unless something was literally or figuratively on fire.

The director's office suite was in the Original Headquarters Building, seamlessly yet still somewhat confusingly connected to the new one. Tamaskar felt herself age a year as she navigated the doors and hallways between the two. She saw a women's restroom, badged in, patted her face with a wet paper towel and her armpits with a wad of dry ones. The mirror offered a glimpse of a wild-eyed fawn in glasses. *Calm down. Calm the fuck down. Breathe.*

The boss greeted her on his feet—a man her own modest height, honestly balding, in rolled-up shirtsleeves. Tamaskar always found that the first name Burt fit him perfectly. The Spaletas were Croatian Italian, but his manner was pure Midwest.

"Thanks so much," he said, closing the door behind her. "Sorry to tear you away from work like that." His office, unlike hers, telegraphed the maximum allowable amount of personality. The back wall was plastered with framed ephemera—kids' drawings, signed pleasantries from the White House, and many posters for what she assumed was a rock band called Rush. Tamaskar's own taste in music ran toward the nineteenth-century Romantics.

"Always good to see you, Asha." Spaleta opted to keep standing, hands in pockets. "They keeping you busy at CovAc?" No one else had ever called it CovAc, but now he did, so they all did.

"Nothing I can't handle," she said with a smile.

"Good." Spaleta scratched his chin. "Look, this is going to sound very silly. As you know, I've always been more or less okay with a certain individual staying in the wind. Especially since the original breach was technically ours, not his. When it comes to whistleblowers, I say better lose one in the couch cushions than risk creating another folk hero."

"Pun not intended," Tamaskar blurted out. She must have been even more nervous than she realized. Spaleta frowned for a second, trying to figure out what she meant. When he did, the frown stayed on.

"Sorry," she said. "I do have an, um, a small task force still on him. Are you calling it off?"

"On the opposite. There's been some new chatter that's frankly making me rethink my position."

"Sir?"

Spaleta grabbed a collated printout off the table, a couple dozen pages thick and emblazoned with the TS stamp, and handed it to Tamaskar. "Turns out the Russians are looking for him, too. And their 'task force' appears to be a bit larger. Check this out."

She did. It was a report from the Operations Support Branch, written in impenetrable geek speak with numerous tables. Tamaskar caught the repeated word *WhisperGate*, which she dimly recalled was a piece of malware, but not much more.

"Yeah, I know," Spaleta said, watching her face. "Basically, we've been monitoring a hacker unit. Freelance, but mostly for the Kremlin. Over the last two days, they piggybacked on four different CCTV systems in four different cities and ran a photo of you-know-who on each one. Looks like they're trying to pin him to a location."

"Which cities?" Tamaskar asked innocently.

"London, Prague, Tbilisi . . ." Spaleta pronounced the name of Georgia's capital the State Department way, *Tub-lissy*. He paused, took the report back, and leafed through it looking for something. "Ah. And Pisa, Italy."

Tamaskar's heart leapt somewhere between her clavicles. She willed it back into place. Burnham had taken the bait, or at least bitten. After months of suspense, this is how she was finding out that her plan had worked: from the Agency's goddamn director.

"They didn't seriously think he'd still be in Georgia after the raid," she said just to fill the pause. "So, what do you think it all means, sir?"

"See," said Spaleta, "that's the silly part. I don't care what it means. If *they* want him, I want him first." He spread his hands apart in apology. "You know how the game is played."

"Of course. Makes sense." As usual, when she was cornered, her voice went clipped and flat.

"Look, Asha." The boss had misinterpreted the tension, charitably. "It's one hundred percent on me that there's been no results on our end. I was the one who set the priority on this at pretty much the floor level."

"Thank you, sir. You don't have to say that. I'm on it."

"No, no. This is not me telling you to dig deeper," said Spaleta. "This is me taking it off your hands, with an apology. Given the news"—he flicked at the printout—"Birdbath needs some actual muscle behind it. And I'm sure you have enough on your plate as it is."

"Who are you giving it to?" He stared at her a beat longer than she liked, so Tamaskar elaborated. "So I can forward our findings. Maybe a joint effort. We did toss his apartment in December—"

"A team best suited." One side benefit of Spaleta's Deep State Nice was that when the steel in his voice came out, it really came out. "And get that Ottenberg kid off it. Adults only."

She almost corrected him before realizing that the misnomer was part of the message. "Yes, sir. Glad you're doing this. It's time he came in." *Laying it on a little thick, but oh well.*

"I'm afraid it is a little past that time." There was no change to Spaleta's face or voice, but the room instantly felt a few degrees colder. "Good talk."

Back in her office, with the door closed and locked, Tamaskar collapsed into the ergonomic chair, stared at the maple desktop in front of her, and silently shook in short-term relief and long-term terror. Spaleta wasn't onto her, at least not yet. He wouldn't have briefed her at all if he were. But the only way the op worked now, hell, the only way Falk *lived,* was if Felix Burnham's people got to him before Special Activities (implied by the director's use of the words *actual muscle*) did.

And what if *Spaleta* was the one running Burnham? What if this was not two opposing forces converging on Pisa, but a coordinated pincer movement? What had she done to Falk?

Tamaskar found herself hyperfocusing on the surface of the desk, and didn't fight it. The thing used to be Harlow's, an antique from the OSS days. At the time of her promotion, Tamaskar had thought keeping it would be a clever nod to both continuity and growth. Not even the Agency's founder Wild Bill Donovan, in his dementia-ridden final days, would hallucinate a Desi woman behind this desk.

Now it taunted her. The knots in the maple—a patternless churn of curls and ripples—suddenly reminded her of those Magic Eye pictures that had been all the rage in her childhood, except with nothing but more chaos for reward. *This clandestine shit is hard enough*, the desk hissed, winking up at her with a thousand beady bird's-eyes. *Clandestine shit within clandestine shit? Yeah, that tends to end with you blowing your brains out.*

Just ask the last guy.

By the time she emerged from this trance, she had a new plan.

■ ■ ■

Pisa, Italy
March 26, 2024

Falk knew his Italian vacation was over when he saw the Goan for the third time. The first had been at the little flea market by the train station, where he pretended to shop for an antique mirror, followed by a chrome Reggiani floor lamp, followed by a silver cake server. She wasn't the Goan yet, only a discreet streak in each of those three reflective surfaces. Just in case, he had taken a surreptitious photo and sent it to Otterbeck.

The second sighting occurred a day later by Palazzo Blu, a modern art museum on the Lungarno Gambacorti. This time he was honestly walking home while she pretended to study the Keith Haring exhibition poster. Two was enough of a trend to stick her with the nickname: She had on a quilted patchwork jacket of the kind sold in Indian dollar stores next to patchouli oil and beach towels. Apart from the outfit, or rather costume, the Goan was almost aggressively clean-cut, with plucked eyebrows above her button nose and straight blond hair in a high ponytail. For her actual provenance, he'd wager Eastern Europe or Scandinavia.

Falk assumed the Goan would be too much of a pro to follow him home outright. Turns out she was enough of a pro to do it without him noticing. On her third and definitive appearance, the woman was found strolling the embankment kitty-corner from his house. He watched from behind a curtain, like a cartoon pervert, as she reached into her upcycled messenger bag (her getup this time was something rave-adjacent) and taped a small flyer to the lamppost in front of the entrance.

For a man on the run—or pretend-run, as was the case now—Pisa was a smarter pick than it might seem at first glance. The city had exactly one big attraction, the damned tower, which concentrated the tourist hordes in a single neighborhood and left the rest to the locals. To get lost here, you simply had to step in any direction outside its central square mile. The airport was so close you could run to it from the banks of the Arno on foot.

In fact, Pisa split the difference between hiding and plain sight so well that Falk had spent his first weeks in town worrying he had set the bar for his would-be wooers too high. After two years of obsessively covering his tracks, being sloppy on purpose—as Tamaskar had put it—felt strange and not at all relaxing. If anything, the constant calculation required to be just the *right* amount of sloppy drained the mental battery much faster than his overcautious life in Tbilisi.

Falk had rented his place, an Airbnb on Via Giuseppe Mazzini above a porcelain store, in the name of Richard Daniels. Unlike Watts the cagey Canadian, Daniels was a positively gregarious dude. He shopped at farmers' markets, went to the movies to burnish his Italian, ate street-kiosk cecina, and chatted with old men in bars. Then he came home and spent evenings writing anonymous online rants about the CIA. Daniels's special ire was reserved for the women and minorities supposedly ascendant within the Agency. (The backstory Falk had given himself was that he'd been driven off the deep end by the rise of Asha Tamaskar.)

The anonymity, online and off, was designed to be hard but not impossible to pierce. For every two or three posts' worth of pure venomous fantasy, one would get certain details of the trade right. To any insider reading this, it would telegraph that the poster had indeed been one of them at some point, just not nearly as high-ranking as he claimed. This part of the performance was aimed straight at Stan Vlasic, the pug-nosed giant and disgraced Sac. As Burnham's lieutenant with an actual Agency pedigree, Falk had reasoned, Vlasic would be the likeliest to vet him as a possible addition to the team.

He also watched Felix Burnham's Alpha Academy videos, though perhaps not as diligently as he should have. It was hard to stare at the man's beetle-browed face and listen to his plummy voice without thinking of Alan Keegan bleeding to death in a Prague hallway. It had taken Falk several weeks to make it through his harmless early Oxford lectures on Greek and Roman poetry. He got into the habit of falling asleep with the man's Teutonically tinged drone in his ears, letting the rhetoric wash over him. Burnham's greatest trick was performing the *idea* of intelligence while keeping his actual ideas extremely simple. He had perfected a manner that pandered while appearing to challenge: The viewer felt miraculously smarter for being able to follow his train of thought as it chugged from point A to, well, point A.

It was hard to imagine this dapper gent, who appeared to relish the sound of his own voice above all, turning from words to any kind of violent action. Still, the slippery, shape-shifting charisma of a born cult leader was there. Rex Harlow had once told Falk that the same qualities that made a man a spy in one environment made him a terrorist in another. "It's easier to act like they're aliens from outer space," he said. "But I've looked enough of these guys in the eye. When we're in the same room, what we're really looking at is botched versions of ourselves."

Days ticked by. The Airbnb consisted of a room and a half carved out of a much larger apartment, with a postcard panorama of the Arno compensating for the cramped quarters. Double mosquito netting over the windows flattened the view into a Renaissance tapestry. At sunset, the riverbank's granite, the terra-cotta roofs, and the stucco facades all turned the same shade of ocher; the glow reached to the back wall, igniting the dust in the air and inspecting every scuff on the ancient headboard like a stern landlady. As waiting rooms went, you could do worse.

The problem was not with the room but with the waiting. Until the Goan showed up, Falk's baseline state had been that of steadily rising antsiness. Every day without an approach retroactively whiffed of wasted time. Like a movie-star wannabe, he had come to town with one goal: to be discovered.

And now, finally, he was.

The Goan gave the flyer an extra slash of Scotch tape and took a step back to admire her handiwork. Falk stood and watched from two stories above, careful with his breath lest it sway the curtain. The netting and the narrow angle made it hard to be sure, but just before hopping on an e-scooter and rolling away, she may have shot a glance straight at his window.

He waited a few sensible minutes, collected the week's recycling, and headed downstairs. Hundreds of lampposts dotted the Lungarno at even intervals, but only the three or four facing his house had the flyer. *A personal invitation, then. How charmingly old-fashioned.* Falk took a pensive photo of the riverbank, making sure to position one of the posts casually off-center, disposed of the trash, and shuffled back up.

The leaflet announced a lecture or a debate concerning *la globalizzazione* and *l'imperialismo,* set to take place the next evening at a local Casa del Popolo and sponsored by a body called the Eco-Socialist Congress. The speakers hailed from Switzerland, Norway, Portugal, and the Basque Country. Among the subjects to be discussed: Gaza, Ukraine, Snowden, Assange, microplastics, the tyranny of Brussels, and the "controversial legacy" (*eredità controversa*) of Alan Keegan and FleaCollar. It must have taken the designer all their restraint not to add *Disgruntled Ex-CIA Officers Welcome*. Falk opened his laptop and fed the photo to the Otterbot. Then he went to work researching every party and organization named in the flyer.

The Eco-Socialist Congress repped an olio of causes under the unifying notion that capitalism had grown incompatible with planetary survival. That any of these hard-left firebrands would also carry water for Felix Burnham seemed unlikely—until, that is, Falk googled the photo of the organization's secretary-general and recognized him as one of the Western guests in the St. Petersburg video.

For a moment, he found himself missing the simpler times of, say, ten years ago. Social media and the Russian funding of every illiberal cause had made such mincemeat of old orthodoxies that even Falk, at thirty-eight, often felt hopelessly behind the curve. The left-right distinction, he kept having to remind himself, no longer applied. The only existential standoff now was between the people who wanted to replace institutions with better institutions and the people who wanted to replace institutions with themselves.

It was getting late, and he wanted to be sharp for tomorrow, but the mix of excitement and jitters made sleep impossible. Falk paced the room in his socks, did a three-minute plank, solved the *New York Times* crossword, Wordle, Connections, and Spelling Bee, and cleaned his gun. The night felt longer than the month preceding it. For the first time, he found himself wishing he had a direct comms channel with Asha Tamaskar; it would have been nice to off-load some of this restlessness on someone who understood the stakes.

Finally, he ordered himself into bed and put on an ancient episode of *The X-Files* he knew by heart. Then he closed his eyes and let it play out as a radio show, until Mulder's and Scully's voices blurred together and words stopped making sense.

■ ■ ■

McLean, Virginia
March 26, 2024

Stuart Akinyemi sounded surprised, but pleasantly so. A personal call from a CIA deputy director was well above his level—normally, she would be talking to MI5's First or Second Desk, from which his own was at least a dozen down. Tamaskar had been counting on this. She had even added an extra shock-and-awe element by using Otterbeck's ID to place the call. The frosty "Hello, *Jim*" that had greeted her before the mask came off indicated that the British agent was not a fan.

"It's about the Keegan case," she said, once Akinyemi had adjusted his tone from snark to guarded respect. "As you may recall, we took an interest a few months back."

"Right. I believe it's closed now on our end. Perhaps the Czech police—"

She saw where this was going and interrupted. "Sorry, I should have been more specific. It's about the material found on his burner phone. Have you made any progress on it before shutting things down?"

The idea had come to Tamaskar in the middle of yesterday's freak-out. With Birdbath out of her hands, she had no way of figuring out if Falk was about to be recruited or killed—but perhaps someone else could. Someone, on either Burnham's or the Russians' side, had already tried contacting Falk by sending him the fateful Hotel Angleterre video. She might have an ally on the inside. She just couldn't identify that ally, couldn't even have the video analyzed, without potentially tipping off Burnham to its existence.

"Yes and no," said Akinyemi. "Do you want the full report? I could have it sent to you via normal channels."

"Why don't you give me the gist right now," she said casually. "Hate being kept in suspense."

The agent paused. His discomfort was, though silent, somehow audible even over the phone.

"Stuart. If you guys picked up Burnham three years ago, we wouldn't be here now. You still owe me."

"Fine," he said. "I do have to warn you, it's not exactly earthshaking. The source of the video is not the hotel's security camera, as we originally thought. There's a TV in that meeting room that they wheel in and out for teleconferences. The camera angle and some artifacts in the file suggest that it was recorded through the Webex app on that TV."

"And no one in the room noticed?"

"Not if the person responsible dimmed the screen to zero and taped up the camera light. Sometimes the simplest tricks work best."

"And do we know them?" she asked. "The person responsible?"

"Well, it wouldn't be anyone *in* the video, would it. But the room was booked in the name of Orlan Finans."

"Yes, the Economic Forum cosponsors," Tamaskar said impatiently. "Their logo is literally on the brochure. When the Russians buy themselves some useful idiots, they tend to flaunt them. This gives us nothing."

"True. But, speaking theoretically . . ." Akinyemi slowed down, selecting his words. "If one were to peek into the Angleterre's booking system on that day . . . One would perhaps see the name of the person who reserved the room and logged into the app."

"So have you?"

"Of course not. As I said, entirely theoretical. And irrelevant to our investigation."

"Thank you," said Tamaskar. "Please don't share this with anyone."

"Well, I do need to log the call."

She turned her head away from the receiver and mouthed *motherfucker*. "Of course. And, just so we're on the same page, who was it that called you?"

"Jim Otterbeck," said Akinyemi, a bright young man indeed. "Hope this gets him in trouble."

Tamaskar hung up. This was good, or at least not terrible. She would never dare expose the video itself, but a request to hack a St. Petersburg hotel website might be just vague enough, and close enough to her Covert Activities purview, to slip by Burnham's eyes and ears at the Agency. After all, on the date in question, the Angleterre housed hundreds of other unsavories drawn in by the Economic Forum: from black-market oilmen and their morally flexible Oxbridge advisors (as Spaleta once quipped, "Every sanction compliance expert is a sanction avoidance expert") to a full Taliban delegation. *Frankly,* she thought, *we should have hacked it a year ago.*

Still, she was not about to take any chances. There had to be a right guy—and let's face it, it would be a guy—for the job. Someone low on the totem pole, skilled but easily intimidated, and in a precarious enough position to do what's asked of him and shut up.

A few hours later, she had found just the right nerd: Dave Patero, a thirty-four-year-old senior developer at the Agency's cyberwarfare division, which hid under the anodyne name Operations Support Branch. According to his heavily marked-up file, Patero was brilliant, irreplaceable, a true savant; he also had the misfortune of being married to Stacy Patero, a naturalized U.S. citizen born Anastasia Pakhomova in Kursk. Before 2022, this was not a deal-breaker. Then Russian troops streamed into Ukraine, and the developer's routine application for clearance renewal got stuck in the system. Firing the guy would not be a great look, and keeping him around the most sensitive ops in the world felt risky; the Agency ended up putting Patero in a bizarre holding pattern. Not just certain tasks but certain areas of his own building were now off-limits to him. For instance, every time he left his ninth-floor roost and headed to the second-floor cafeteria, he had to be escorted by a senior officer, because the path to the elevators led through a higher-clearance hallway. The fact that Patero had stuck with the job for almost two years despite this daily humiliation spoke very well of him.

It also meant Tamaskar would have to visit the Operations Support Branch in person, a prospect that didn't exactly thrill her. The powers that be had moved the whole outfit off-site in the hopes that a loosey-goosey, Silicon Valley vibe would attract the right kind of psychopath without spreading the insanity to the main campus. They succeeded beyond their wildest dreams. The OSB was now a breakaway fiefdom within the CIA, a hacker heaven with its own rules, populated by insufferable geeks who considered themselves God's gift to the Agency. Its employees wore shorts and T-shirts to work and were reported to cap their evenings with Nerf-gun fights in the office. She had never set foot inside.

"So! You're here to see our Navorski." The unit's supervisor was a tired-looking woman ten years Tamaskar's senior, with a vaguely antagonistic edge to her demeanor. Tamaskar couldn't tell if the hostility was aimed at her, for being younger yet higher-ranking, or just a general side effect of managing a room full of overgrown boys. The floor behind the supervisor's shoulders looked like a regular open-plan office, all cold lighting and colder AC. No foosball tables or beanbag chairs. Unusually for the Agency, however, muffled music wafted in: something very heavy but played at a low volume, which made it sound like night insects beating against a lamp.

Tamaskar frowned. "Navorski? That must be a mistake. I'm here for David Patero."

"Sorry. That's his nickname around here. That or the Cave Troll, but that one was too close to harassment." The woman led her down a row of cubicles. A few people glanced their way, without interest or recognition.

A boss from some inferior analog cloak-and-dagger department was not an authority to them. "Navorski, you know, Tom Hanks, from what's that movie? Guy lives in an airport terminal?"

"*The Terminal*?"

"Maybe." Tamaskar thought this was pretty funny, but the supervisor didn't react at all. "Well, there he is. Enjoy."

They had reached the end of the row; in front of them was a door to what she had assumed was a supply closet. The music had gotten louder. The older woman moved in conspiratorially and took Tamaskar by the elbow, exercising a certain middle-aged lady privilege. "You taking him off our hands?"

"No. This is a onetime thing. Sorry to disappoint."

She knocked, waited a bit, then let herself in. The source of the racket became deafeningly clear. Patero was blasting heavy metal from two desktop speakers, set to the left and right of his monitor array. On top of the left one stood a pewter figurine of the Xenomorph, vibrating with each bass-drum kick. The man himself—tall, large, and bald as a knee—lounged in a massive swivel chair, taking up most of the space between the walls. Tamaskar was a little surprised to see him wearing headphones.

"Hi, Dave," she said, squeezing between him and the desk; there was nowhere else to stand. The room must have indeed been a closet at some point. "What's with the cans?"

"Oh." Patero took the headphones off and flashed an unexpectedly disarming smile. "The music's for *them*." He pointed to the door. "I don't even like this shit."

"I see. Your popularity around the office is beginning to make sense."

"Look," said Patero, "you're seventh floor, so you must know my situation. The bastards did this to themselves."

"Fair enough," she said. "Now would you mind turning it off so we can talk?"

He reached forward with a groan and flicked a switch. The silence was as pristine as it gets only in the seconds after some terrible noise goes away. The whir of the hard-drive coolers was now the loudest thing in the room. Someone across the wall sarcastically applauded.

"Thank you." Tamaskar leaned against the edge of the desk, not knowing what else to do with her body. The pose ended up accidentally sexy, which she realized only when she saw a flicker of distinctly male attention in Patero's eyes; she hunched her shoulders and cleared her throat. "Look, this is a pretty straightforward exploit, but I need it ASAP and I'm told you're the best. I want to get into the bookings for Hotel Angleterre in St. Petersburg during last year's Economic Forum."

Patero's face tightened. "That's, uh, pretty irregular. Why aren't you going through Emma? Is this a test or something? I say yes, then SPS"—Security Protective Service, the Agency's internal cops—"barges in and hauls me away to some freaking black site? No thank you."

"No one's barging in here." Tamaskar looked around and couldn't help herself. "There's no room."

He chuckled. She leaned back, this time intentionally. "Look, you have my word. I outrank anyone who could possibly mess with you for this. And just so you know, this is ultimately about Alan Keegan."

This much seemed safe to give away, and she gambled on Patero's obvious rebel streak to help speed things along. It worked.

"Keegan was a damn hero," he muttered. "All right. Fuck it. If I do this, will you get my clearance renewed?"

"For our purposes," she said, "it's renewed already."

Patero nodded and went to work. Tamaskar watched him type for a while, which was about as exciting as watching someone do dishes. There was a reason, she thought, movies about hackers would always add frills to the act—a graphic interface, an ominous countdown, "access denied." After a few minutes, she went off to get a coffee in the kitchenette. By the time she got back, he was beaming ear to ear.

"What'd I miss?"

"Nothing," Patero said. "This was *insultingly* easy. They're using some supposedly sovereign homegrown system. You know what it is? Open-source booking software from India they literally downloaded off the internet. I was so bored I went to the state contract registry to see how much the developer charged the Kremlin. Three mil. Someone's got a nice dacha out of this."

"God bless corruption," Tamaskar said. "All right, now I need to see every booking on the following dates—"

"You can check it yourself." Patero got up, stretched, and yawned. "I want a coffee, too."

With him gone, she didn't have to keep up the pretense of looking at the entire hotel and all four days of the forum. The Angleterre had five meeting rooms; the one in the video was called the Malevich, after the Suprematist painter, and had an appropriately odd trapezoid shape. She checked its bookings for June 14, 2023. *Bingo.*

Orlan Finans, two hours. A special note asked for teleconferencing equipment—for a meeting with no remote participants.

Room reserved by . . . by . . .

No name. Just a contact number, Moscow area code, too many zeros to be a real person. The bank's main switchboard. *Fuck.*

Patero came back with some beige concoction radiating the sickly sweet smell of hazelnut syrup. "All good?"

"Since I feel like I haven't challenged you enough today," said Tamaskar, getting up, "would you mind looking into something else for me?"

"Honestly," said Patero, "this is the most excitement I've had in two years." He wriggled past her and back into his chair. "What is it?"

"Someone called the hotel from a bank called Orlan Finans. I need to know at which extension the call originated. Is this something you can do?"

Patero grinned. "Now you're talking."

An hour later, the coffee was long gone, but the hazelnut smell remained. Slowly mixing in with it was a distinct rising stench of sweat. Finally Patero pumped his fist, exhaled, and stretched back in the chair, which made it hit the back wall. "Jesus, these guys are not messing around. Military-grade perimeter."

"It's a military-grade bank," Tamaskar responded. "If you know what I mean."

"Figures. But I got it. The lucky caller is . . ." Patero drummed his fingers on the desk, "one Yekaterina Lisichenko, vice president of Acquisitions. A pretty weird thing to do for a VP, personally book meeting rooms."

"What else can you tell me about her?"

"Shh, way ahead of you." Patero typed furiously. "Double citizenship—ooh, Russia *and* Ukraine, spicy. A former exec at KhromBank. Orlan Finans absorbed it after they got sanctioned out of existence."

Tamaskar felt her pulse in her temples and, for some reason, her lower lip. KhromBank was mentioned in the dossier. It was the slush fund Harlow and the Russians used to finance their off-the-books adventures. Falk had visited it in Moscow in 2021. A direct connection.

Patero stopped typing and said, "Holy shit." The timing made it eerie, as if he could read her thoughts. "What is it?"

"Well," he drawled, "I don't know *who* this Lisichenko person is, but I sure know *where* she is. In prison. In Georgia. Not the peach one, the cheese-boat one."

Tamaskar looked at the screen. A mug shot stared back.

The inmate was in her late thirties, short-cropped hair, thin. A defiant lift of the chin put two triangles of shadow under her sharp cheekbones. The supposedly neutral gaze leveled into the camera was a master class in subtle derision. Smart and angry, the two things no regime can handle in a woman.

"What for?"

"Illegal border crossing." Patero highlighted a few curls of Georgian script, copied them into an online translator, and mouthed *wow*. "This is pretty badass, actually. She came in from Russia on foot. Through the Upper Lars overpass, on an expired Ukrainian passport."

"When was this?" Like she had many times over the last days, Tamaskar made her voice sound blasé while her heart pounded against her ribs. She already knew the answer. December—

"December 12. Georgian intelligence picked her up a few days later."

The dates didn't lie. The entire timeline unscrolled before Tamaskar's eyes with an almost painful clarity.

June 2023. Orlan Finans, a known front for Russian military intelligence, invites Felix Burnham to St. Petersburg and puts him on their payroll. For whatever reason—Tamaskar could think of a couple—Katya Lisichenko is not okay with her bank financing a neofascist men's rights guru. She bravely sets a trap, records the meeting, and banks the tape.

Early December. Alan Keegan is announced as the winner of the year's Aletheia Award, putting him in Prague for the ceremony. Lisichenko is one of the few people in the world who know that Ari Falk was Keegan's source: She had seen him at KhromBank in Moscow, collecting material for the dossier. She trusts him, and only him, to do the right thing with the video. So she reaches out to Keegan, trying to get the evidence to Falk. Burnham finds out, and Keegan and his courier die.

December 11. She, Asha Tamaskar, in her infinite fucking wisdom, blasts Falk's cover to smithereens, exposing his Georgian whereabouts to everyone—including Lisichenko.

December 12. Desperate, and likely shaken up by Keegan's death, Lisichenko heads to Georgia herself to meet Falk.

She looked at the mug shot again. Here, at long last, was an ally. An ally who needed and deserved saving.

"So, uh, what do you want me to do with all this?" Patero asked.

"Literally nothing," Tamaskar said, opening the door. "A dead end, I'm afraid. But hey, good work."

"Am I getting my clearance back?"

"I'll talk to your supervisor." She walked out into the relatively fresh air of the office. As she did, Dave Patero may or may not have muttered "bitch" under his breath; she wouldn't know, because a split second earlier, the heavy metal had come back at twice the volume.

CHAPTER FIVE

Pisa, Italy
March 27, 2024

The People's House stood on the outskirts of town, a concrete modernist slab built either right before or right after Mussolini. Falk had heard about these establishments. Roughly similar to the Soviet houses of culture, they had their origin in the earliest days of Italian Communism and were part lending library, part social club, and part lecture hall. He chained his bike to the rack by the entrance and walked in, catching a glimpse of himself in the vestibule mirror.

Three months had been enough for Falk's hair to return to its normal unruly state, making him more recognizable as the subject of last December's news stories. (It came back noticeably grayer than before.) The stories themselves, once Keegan's death got decoupled from the dossier scandal, had conveniently faded from public memory. Still, for anyone wanting to make a cold approach, he was an easy target. Nothing more complicated than "Haven't I seen you somewhere?" was required.

The Casa del Popolo's main hall had all the charm of a dilapidated dental clinic, albeit one with a bar in the corner. Cardboard boxes for a clothes drive lined one wall, ancient arcade machines another. Falk followed the flyers to the reading room in the back, where several dozen foldout chairs, about half of them occupied, stood in a semicircle around a podium knocked together from lacquered particleboard. A lecture was under way. The presenter, an intense man in a utility vest, had brought photos from Gaza and was beaming them onto a wall—and partly onto himself—from a portable projector. He spoke through his teeth in Swiss-accented English, punctuating each pause with an accusatory remote click that loaded the next terrible slide.

Falk took a seat in the back row, next to the projector, and was looking around in search of the Goan when she appeared at the podium, leading the applause for the speaker and welcoming the next one. She must have been one of the evening's organizers.

"Thank you, Ludovic. Heartbreaking," she said, in unexpected Italian. Falk's command of the language was just enough to understand the gist. "Our next presentation is going to be a little controversial. As you know, we always talk about intersectionality, the need to build wider coalitions. *Politics makes strange bedfellows*"—the Goan said the last part in English, and Falk could swear she glanced at him as she did—"and some of you will rightfully find some of this content reprehensible. Yet please know that more than one of you has forwarded me this, noting some platform similarities and saying it merits a look. So let's take that look."

The young woman commandeered the projector and performed the usual embarrassed ministrations until it cooperated with her laptop. The next thing Falk saw on the wall was Felix Burnham's face.

He almost jumped, which wasn't in itself catastrophic: The tweedy fascist's appearance has elicited similar responses from half the audience. Someone to Falk's right booed instantly. The Goan scanned the crowd with a stern look, mouthing *pazienza*.

The video had been mercifully cued up to the middle, as the first minutes of Burnham's lectures usually had him reading from Ovid or

Byron or Brodsky. The backdrop was blank, just a wall and a dais, purposefully denuded of time and place identifiers like all his secret-lair communiqués. Still, Falk recognized the clip at once. It was part of a premium-tier Alpha Academy series he had suffered through a month ago, entitled *The Murder of Quality*.

Tech industry people have a lovely term, enshittification. *It's when a concept or a product or an experience, imagined well and executed purely in its initial iteration, gets steadily worse due to the owners' greed. Well, gentlemen, we live in an enshittified world, and you can thank* our *owners for that.*

Burnham orated with a kind of faux spontaneity, using plenty of studied gestures and often running his fingers through his moussed graying hair. Compared to the competition, it was certainly a higher class of drivel, Falk thought for the hundredth time, but drivel nonetheless.

Authentic experience is being leached from our lives at every turn. Sounds and smells of our childhoods going extinct, the crack of the turbo engine replaced by the mosquito whine of the electric motor. Make no mistake! The ultimate goal of what they call "equity" and "sustainability" is, quite simply, to drain the world of flavor. To make you ashamed of desire. To make ambition a dirty word. To cancel joy.

"Nazi dog whistle," said the same person who booed earlier. A couple of others whooped and grunted their concurrence.

We are alienated, and not just from one another. Marx was onto something—don't boo!—Marx was onto something when he defined capitalism as workers cut off from the means of production. Except we are now cut off from the means of consumption, *too. We no longer own what we buy. We know nothing about the objects we use, because they like it that way. We have no say in the entertainment being streamed at us, because we're no longer the ones making it.*

This occasioned some grudging nods in the room. Keegan's murderer beamed incongruously, as if seeing the reaction in real time. He then continued, white-knuckling the podium with his left hand and chopping the air with his right:

And we're getting dumber, my god! We have outsourced our memory to the cloud. We fumble for words when they're not being spoon-fed to us by predictive text. We have forsaken the great Western canon, which trained our brains to remember, to synthesize, to combine and create new meanings, and replaced it with a children's treasury of insipid fairy tales about self-actualization. It sounds petty, yes, but it adds up: Our destiny is out of our hands, in myriad ways large and small.

"Oh, fuck you," exhaled a man in a military surplus jacket in front of Falk, getting up to leave. The Goan stopped the video.

"He's not totally wrong," someone responded in Italian. "He just blames the wrong powers."

The man turned around. "You're literally sitting here listening to fascist propaganda."

His interlocutor, an older gentleman with a well-tended goatee, stood up, too. "What I hear is ninety percent frustration with neoliberalism and ten percent red meat for teenage boys. One could learn from this."

"I'm sorry, I can't get past the misogyny."

"*You* can't get past the misogyny?" a woman acidly asked from the back. The surplus guy, abashed, beat a hasty retreat.

"See?" said the Goan, beaming. "We *can* discuss this. I move to add it to next week's agenda." She beckoned someone to come forward. "Our next speaker is a tireless fighter for digital privacy and against the surveillance state. Please welcome Mars Caturix."

Polite clapping ensued, with Falk joining in. A person in black rose from the front row and clambered up to the lectern. When they turned toward the crowd, the beam of the projector caught their unusual makeup—a camo-like pattern of flowing mercurial shapes around the eyes and forehead. Falk recognized it as a decorative riff on CV Dazzle, an old technique for foiling facial-recognition cameras. It looked rather cool.

"Mars will be taking a deep dive into the so-called open-source intelligence, and how it launders and advances deep-state narratives in the guise of independent research," the Goan said, switching to English again. Falk wondered if she did it for his benefit.

A second later, he wondered no more. As Mars began to speak, in a rapid-fire Italian dialect Falk had no hope of following, she walked to the back of the room and sat down right next to him.

"Thank you so much for coming," the Goan whispered. "It is truly an honor. I am such a huge fan."

"Glad to be here," Falk muttered back.

"I don't suppose you'd like to speak tonight? These people would die. You're a real live hero."

"I think I'd rather take it one step at a time."

"Too bad." She scrunched up her nose. Behind them, the Swiss lecturer was in the process of packing up his A/V rig. "But I understand. You don't know us well enough yet."

"Exactly."

"I'd be happy to change that." The Goan tilted her head toward his. "Do you want to have a drink after?"

"Telling me your name would be a good start," said Falk.

Up at the podium, Mars Caturix noticed the two of them whispering in the back and took a displeased pause before clearing their throat and saying, "*Continuiamo.*"

Her full name, as he learned two hours later over Campari sodas at the People's Bar, was Silje Jenssen. She was the only daughter of an Italian biochemist mother ("fully evil") and a Norwegian civil engineer father ("he at least kinda tried"). Her résumé of direct action included gluing herself to the highway blacktop near the Hague and pouring ketchup on a Botticelli in Berlin's Bode-Museum, for the environment.

Someone less experienced or more boorish might be forgiven for imagining Silje's role in the process as a mix of honey trap and greeting committee. Falk knew better. She was step one in a multistep vetting ritual, a day player whose only brief was to approach, identify, and hand off. Step two would be the Interrogator: someone with only a cursory knowledge of the big picture but unlimited agency when it came to character assessment and lie detection. Step three, provided he'd get that far, would be either the Principal—self-explanatory—or the Gofer, who would re-vet, prep, and deliver him to the Principal.

After months of lying in wait, Falk felt a sudden surge of impatience. There was something vaguely insulting about taking a career case officer, for whom wrangling assets used to be a daily job, and putting him through the same paces as he himself would, say, an Aeroflot executive with a bad cocaine habit. *Just get it over with.* He had a momentary vision of his hands around Felix Burnham's throat, which he imagined, in tactile detail, as well-moisturized, warm, and flabby.

Silje was now talking about Ukraine, unselfconsciously mirroring every Kremlin talking point. Falk nodded politely, sucked down the bittersweet dregs, and counted seconds until the handoff. He'd much rather discuss her superb shadowing skills from the other night. She must have received at least some instruction as a watcher, and from someone good. Perhaps even someone in Burnham's camp. Bringing any of it up, however, would have been overeager and crude. He might as well have shown up in a T-shirt that said *Take Me to Your Leader*. You didn't get to skip steps.

Sure enough, before she had a chance to really expand on her views of the latest Kyiv bombing (staged for the media, but also somehow justified), Silje was predictably joined by Uncle Christian, a raven-haired Italian of Falk's age who bore no physical or temperamental resemblance to her. Falk recognized him from earlier in the evening. He had yawned through the Burnham video and spent Mars Caturix's entire presentation playing Connect Three on his phone.

Silje and Christian performed a little "oh wow, hey, good to see you" skit, in Italian far too basic for either of them but pitched right at Falk's level of understanding. With that part over, the uncle proceeded to pull up a chair, plop down, wave to get the bartender's attention, draw a circle in the air over the empty glasses, and flash three fingers, all in one move. The bartender nodded.

"So you're the man, huh," he said, grinning at Falk. His front teeth were immaculate but unusually large, making him look a bit like a sidewalk-artist caricature of himself. "The man who almost took down the CIA."

"Not really." They sat facing each other. Silje had moved to the side, watching them like a tennis match.

"My niece told me you live here." *Oh, did she.* "You like it?"

"It suits me," said Falk carefully.

"But Italy is fucked. We have a far-right government now," Christian offered, and waited for a reaction. The chitchat was over, Falk surmised. The Interrogator was in the house. His next answer better land.

"The planet is fucked," he offered with a shrug. "It's the same thing everywhere. One might as well pick a place with the prettiest architecture."

"Amen," said Silje. The fake uncle shot her an annoyed glance.

"What did you think of the talk?" Christian made a head motion toward the reading room. The evening's crowd had dissipated; apart from the three of them and the bartender, the only people in the People's House were two teenagers languidly playing foosball, careful not to knock over the beers they'd set on the edge of the table.

Falk decided that until he understood the parameters of the test a little better, his best strategy was punkish insouciance. "Which one? You guys covered just about everything."

This, unexpectedly, made the Interrogator laugh, a full-body guffaw that shook the ice in the glasses. "That's true," he said. "But they're young, what do you expect? I'm not a part of any movement. I just want people to live their lives without fear, you know? Like you do."

"Sure." The sentiment was vague enough that it felt safe to agree.

The bartender cleared the table and brought three more bright red cocktails that, upon the first sip, turned out to be maximum-strength Negronis. Christian put down half of his in one gulp. "Why is that, by the way?"

"What do you mean?"

"Why aren't you afraid? Out and about like that. Why aren't they hunting you still?" He leaned forward, playing instantly drunk. Falk would bet good money that Christian's glass, unlike his, contained a soda with a splash of Campari for color. That's what he would do, if this were his op. "I'll tell you why, if you want."

Falk yawned. "Because I'm a triple agent. Everything is a false flag. Blah-blah-blah."

"No, *amico*. Because what you did was brave, but it didn't change a thing. How do you say? Jack squat. Sorry."

Falk glanced at Silje, who appeared to have powered down. Her scripted part in this was clearly over, but she didn't want to leave quite yet. It belatedly occurred to him that she might be a real fan and have signed up for the job because she wanted to meet him.

"No, hey, you're right," he said. "Nothing's different. No one's been punished. No one cares. That's why, I think, it may be time for all of us to shut up and do something else. Something real." *Too eager? Too eager. Fuck.*

"Alan Keegan cared. And the Nazis killed him for it." Christian fixed Falk with his stare again. A predatory stillness came over him, a tell. This was the crux of the test. But now Falk finally knew what to do.

"Alan Keegan," he said with a wince, picking the name up from the table like a dead cockroach in a napkin. "Alan Keegan *era un fottuto truffatore*. A hustler. He charged me fifty grand to publish the dossier. Bet you didn't see *that* in the obituaries."

Christian held his reaction in check, but out of the corner of his eye, Falk noticed Silje perk up. This slander seemingly squared with her worldview.

He doubled down. "Your speaker was only half wrong earlier. Flea-Collar was never an Agency front; we didn't run it. We didn't have to. Believe me, he'd take money from everyone. Us, the Kremlin, any British pol trying to tank a competitor." The audience was eating it up. "Most of OSINT is a black market for the kompromat the big boys are too big to touch. Fucking hell, whoever killed Keegan, it was probably just a deal gone wrong. He had no ideology to speak of. And by the way, I don't believe the Czech-nationalist thing for a second. They vet people at Radio Free Europe. No one who'd done jail time would ever get hired as a guard."

Falk stopped, fearing he'd gone too far. "Sorry," he added. "It just pisses me off." He took a swig of his drink. "Look, I'm not proud of my old job. But I'm not proud of the way I quit it, either. Leaking the dossier was a coward's move."

"*Va bene*," said Christian. "So what would a non-coward's move be? Shooting Harlow in the face? He did that himself."

Falk was still debating the right answer when he opened his mouth and said it.

"Not him. Asha Tamaskar."

"Who?"

"The bitch they got to replace him. Same thing but worse. She's the reason nothing stuck. It was her idea to sweep it all under the rug and leave me in this fucking . . . this *limbo*. Not a traitor, not a hero, not an American, not an exile. Nothing."

A pause fell, long enough for Falk to grow aware of the ambient sounds around him. The teens had moved to a space-themed pinball machine, and a stream of otherworldly bleeps and bloops mixed with the clatter. A melting ice cube shifted in a glass. He had finished the Negroni somewhere in the middle of the diatribe, and the taste of gin and bitter herbs was still coating his tongue. Mixing with it was a fair deal of stomach acid.

The hand he had just played was unplanned and reckless, but there was a logic behind it. If Tamaskar was right in her hunch, this meant that whatever information he fed Burnham right now, via whatever surrogates, would sooner or later get checked by Burnham's mole inside the Agency. Thanks to her virtuosity in arranging the Prague meet, they wouldn't find anything on Tamaskar herself, beyond a failed attempt to catch him last winter. Yet giving up her name, unprompted, could convince Burnham of the authenticity of Falk's grudge against the CIA faster than just about anything else. And knowing what he knew of the man, it might also help for the object of that grudge to be a nonwhite woman.

Or it could all blow up in his face right this second. That was always a possibility.

"Anyway." Falk got up, putting his palm on the table for balance as he did. "Sorry for the rant."

Silje stared up at him with an expression that made it difficult not to visualize other uses for this height differential. Christian texted with someone, keeping the phone away from view under the lip of the table.

"My niece and I," he said suddenly, with a lopsided grin that bespoke the sheer absurdity of the notion, "like to take trips. Do you travel? Or do your circumstances not allow it?"

"Within Europe, sure."

"We were thinking about Andorra for our next one. Have you been? You should."

"Andorra?" Falk swallowed hard. Suddenly his throat felt dry. "What's in Andorra?"

"Skiing, mostly," Silje volunteered. She really wanted to be a part of this. "Or shopping. They don't have a sales tax. Do you ski?"

"I especially recommend this spa they have," Christian continued over her. "It's right in the center of the city, enormous, all glass, you can't miss it."

"I see," said Falk. "And when, do you think, would be the best time to visit it?"

Christian texted a bit more, then put the phone away. "What's today, Tuesday? Honestly, I'd say before this weekend. Afternoons are best. It's less of a madhouse then."

He got up, too, sober as a judge, and threw a couple of bills on the counter. "*Allora*, I leave you two alone. Have another round." A hand, calloused to half hoof, squeezed Falk's. "An honor."

Falk sat back down, mostly to cover up vertigo. For a long moment, both he and Silje stared at the marble tabletop, sticky with a week's worth of spills. With the third person gone, sitting this close to each other was no longer a necessity but a choice.

A single sandal slipped to the floor with a quiet slap. Silje's bare foot found his shin and began a short trip upward. Outside, an Abarth 695 revved up and chirred away with one loud farewell parp of the turbocharger.

He turned to her, weighing the wisdom of the next step. Instead of doing the same, Silje coquettishly swiveled away. Then she leaned back, not ungracefully, and kept leaning until her laughing face was under his. Her breath was shallow and hot. One of the teens whooped in sarcastic appreciation.

By all operational standards, this was a blunder. By the standards of a rogue ex-officer about to cross over, it was exactly the kind of blunder demanded of him.

"I biked here," Falk finally said, looking down. "But you know where I live."

■ ■ ■

Tbilisi, Georgia
March 27, 2024

The Georgian Intelligence Service compound stood north of the city center, on the low shore of the Tbilisi Reservoir. The name of the street was Utsnob Gmirta, "Unknown Heroes." They were clearly almost there: For the last two or three minutes, the car had been driving along the same waffle-patterned ferroconcrete fence with curls of razor wire on top. Asha Tamaskar knew the fence's name—PO-2 wall slab, once the most ubiquitous surface of dour Soviet life. She even knew the name of its designer, Boris Lakhman. And that Puma once made a sneaker with a sole based on it. As an expert, she was fully in her element. The only thing she didn't know was what the hell waited on the other side of the wall.

Talking Spaleta into letting her go to Georgia, surprisingly, had not been the hardest part. Once again, the best cover story was the truth, with a couple of details tweezed out: Tamaskar told the acting director that Lisichenko had had contact with Falk and might know his whereabouts. Dave Patero's data dump only corroborated this.

"Look, I know it's a weird ask," she had added apologetically. "It may seem below my pay grade. But the situation is sensitive."

"How so?"

"Because Georgia is a fucking paradox, pardon my language. The world's most anti-Russian country—well, second most—with a pro-Russian government and a quarter million Russian refugees. Half the locals want NATO and the EU, the other half keep a portrait of Stalin at home."

"Yeah, well," Spaleta had said, "he's a local boy made good."

"My point stands. It's factions within factions. Did they let her in to mess with the Russians? Did they arrest her to do them a favor? Hell, she could be dead in her cell tomorrow and we'll never know. Georgian prisons are historically great for that. In a way, the arrest itself confirms that she's got *something*. You see why I can't give this to a midlevel officer, right?"

"I am beginning to."

"It calls for someone who can walk into that building, blind them with a smile, and walk Lisichenko out five minutes later."

If Spaleta had some reservations about the blinding powers of Tamaskar's smile, he had wisely kept them to himself. "All right, all right. I'm convinced. But take a team with you. And use the jet."

If you insist, she had thought. "Thank you, sir."

The driver of the S-Class Mercedes that had picked her up at the airport was a local U.S. embassy staffer and obvious GIS agent named Merab. The car, he had explained with a touch of pride, was his own, bulletproofed at great expense and formerly part of the presidential fleet. A black escort Jeep with a custom floodlight rack rolled close behind, carrying two Special Activities blue badgers and two embassy Marines.

Merab had a well-curated beard, deep pockmarks, and eyes like two oil-slicked kalamata olives that kept lingering on her via the rearview mirror. His clothes befit a club promoter more than a spy. As a rule, Tamaskar wasn't into the type of man who'd wear a black shirt under a black suit, but this one, she hated to admit, made it work.

For a moment, her thoughts turned to her sorry dating history of the last two years. Being what she was, Tamaskar couldn't use the apps, openly or furtively, and the real-life options were limited, to say the least.

In her analyst days, she could at least date laterally within the Agency. Her ascension to the seventh floor had put an end to that, too. Most of her peers in the building were now men on the far side of fifty, and every outside hookup had to be weighed against the risk of entrapment, doxxing, blackmail, or straight assassination. None of it was exactly a turn-on. At least not for her. For some, maybe.

"*Et voilà, madame,*" said Merab, steering toward a metal gate that rolled open on their approach.

"You speak French?"

"A little. Us Georgians and the French, we have a kinship. We're bon vivants, too. At least when life lets us be."

The GIS building rose in front of them. Thanks to satellite pictures, she knew it to be a perfect triangle encircled by a round road for a rather Masonic-looking effect doubtlessly inspired by Washington, but you wouldn't guess any of that from the ground. The escort vehicle peeled away. Merab stopped the car and gallantly jogged around to open the door.

"Thank you," Tamaskar said, getting out. "I'd like to see the prisoner first, if you don't mind."

"This is just a formality. The big boss wants a few minutes of your time."

"How few?"

"Ten. Maybe twenty. You don't have to stay for the dinner."

"Dinner?!" They were halfway up the front steps. Tamaskar stopped and turned, searching his pockmarks for clues that he might be joking. "You have my schedule. The handoff is prearranged. The jet's wheels-up in an hour."

Merab shrugged. "Look, you know how it is. We're a small country. The guy needs to feel important. Like he's doing you a favor, not obeying an order."

"Are you sure it's the *country's* size that's the issue?" Tamaskar muttered. This unexpectedly cracked her companion up. He was still giggling a little as he handed her over to the locals at the entrance.

"I'll wait by the car. Good luck." Merab gave a conspiratorial wink, which made her feel something interesting but ill-timed, and fell back.

She passed through the security gauntlet and took the stairs to the GIS director's top-floor suite. The front room of the office had indeed been set up for a serious meal; a long conference table, pushed to the back wall, held a spread of local wines and cold appetizers. Tamaskar recognized satsivi, ajapsandali, pkhali, and lobio, but there were at least as many more she didn't know. Above all this bounty hung a U.S. flag, pinned up with thumbtacks. Four staffers greeted her by standing up at their desks in unison.

"Hello," she said, uncomfortable with the pomp. *Blind them with a smile.* So far it was the Georgians doing the blinding. But what for? This wasn't a goddamned state visit.

The director emerged from the inner sanctum, a fifty-something man with the profile of a heraldic lion and a gray mane to match. He wore jeans and a tactical quarter-zip with elbow patches. Tamaskar was relieved to see this getup—at least someone here meant business.

"Levan Gogoberidze, head of Intelligence," he said, fully enfolding her slight hand in his right paw and patting the resulting sandwich with his left. "Pleased to meet you in person. We missed you here in December."

"Deputy Director Asha Tamaskar." She pulled free. "And, uh, my apologies for December. Our last pop-in was a little hectic."

"So I heard." Levan reached past her for a pkhali, a purple bun of beet and walnut paste with a single pomegranate aril on top, and popped it in his mouth whole. "Don't fill up, by the way. Real food's coming soon."

"About that. I'm so sorry, but I can't really stay this time, either. We're in a real hurry to get Lisichenko stateside."

For a few seconds, Levan silently chewed. "My English is no good, and you don't speak Georgian, do you? I'm afraid that leaves one option." The last sentence was already in Russian.

"*Nu davaite*," she said, steeling herself for bad news. His English had been fine. No one ever switched to Russian for extra levity.

"Here's the problem." *Thought so*. "Things between us, they are not as simple as they once were. It's not 2004. A sizable faction in our parliament sees your agency as part of the global war party."

"A global what?"

"Lockheed, Fidelity, Vanguard, the CIA. All working in concert. They make money on the Ukraine war, you push us to open a second front."

"I can't believe what I am hearing," Tamaskar said, temporarily shocked back into English. "Where's your intelligence coming from, Reddit?"

"I'm not saying *I* believe it," said Levan. "Look, it's no secret that our government is playing both sides. One hand waves the Ukrainian flag, the other jerks off the Kremlin, pardon me. I suppose it can all look a little confusing from the outside. But in any case, this is no longer a political environment in which you order the music." *Order the music* was a Russian idiom; like most older Georgians, Levan spoke the language of the oppressor at the native level, with the syncopated, singsongy accent that was one of his country's greatest exports. His casual outfit made more sense now. What Tamaskar had mistaken for a show of in-the-trenches camaraderie was meant as an insult.

"I don't know if that applies here," she calmly replied.

"Perhaps not. Regardless, here's our counterproposal. You *interview* Lisichenko. Get whatever you need out of her. We can give you a clean room right here in the building—feel free to sweep it for devices. If she clams up, we can even lend you our experts on, uh, persuasion techniques. I think you'd agree that this constitutes more than full cooperation on our part, yes?" He seemed to wait for an actual answer. She gave a quick nod, to make him continue. "But that's the extent of it. She stays here, you go home. Everyone happy."

Right. Especially Katya. "Mr. Gogoberidze," she said, furiously enunciating. "Levan. I am a deputy director at the U.S. Central Intelligence Agency. I do not conduct interrogations myself. And I sure as fuck don't stand by and whistle while your goons pull out someone's fingernails on my behalf. Make no mistake: Your only choice right now is between honoring our two agencies' long relationship or burning it to a crisp."

"See, but that's the problem." Levan sounded genuinely exasperated. "Look at it from my perspective. Some skirt—sorry—prances into our country on an expired passport. Okay, whatever. Then the Russians call and demand we send her back, which, by the way, we're still obliged to do by extradition law. *Then* I find out the CIA wants this lady bad enough to send in a deputy director and a goddamn jet. So what am I, Levan Gogoberidze, to do? I'm like all of Georgia. We're all kids of your divorce. Forced to pick sides when the parents fight."

Tamaskar felt a measure of relief. Beneath all the flowery language, this was a simple shakedown.

"Which Russians?" she asked.

"Huh?"

"Who called you, exactly?"

"Our own Justice Ministry. All very official. Don't ask me who called *them.*" Levan shrugged. "Try the satsivi, at least. It's the proper old recipe—guinea fowl, not chicken."

"I'm good. So. What is it you want from me right now? What would it take for you to tell them you don't have her?"

The Georgian shook his large head in mock grief and switched back to English. "All business, all the time. So American. And here I thought you came from a different culture, closer to ours. You know we have the same word for bread, right? *Puri.*"

"My culture," said Tamaskar, "is Bloomfield Hills, Michigan." She waited a beat and decided to lighten things up. "Our word for bread is *Panera.*" The joke went over Levan's silver mane.

"I don't need anything from you right now." He moved in closer, breathing walnuts. "But I might soon. And it would be very good, when that moment comes, if you and I could talk directly and safely."

"So, essentially, you want my phone number."

"Your phone number, yes, but that's easy. A phone number that you and only you will pick up? Now that's worth something."

"You got it." She hated the self-satisfied *Godfather* vibe on which Levan had landed, and just wanted the conversation to end. Tamaskar wanted most conversations in her life to end as soon as possible. Except last December's with Falk, which she desperately needed to continue.

"Is that a yes?"

"You have my word." She stabbed a piece of guinea fowl with a fork, held it aloft until it stopped dripping white satsivi sauce back into the dish, then ate it. More walnuts. "Delicious. May I see the prisoner now?"

The director heaved an ironic sigh. "What prisoner?"

"The— Right. Thank you." Tamaskar did not smile.

A silent staffer led her to the building's second or third subterranean level and handed her over to a uniformed guard for a respectful patdown. Another guard buzzed open a pair of reinforced metal doors, painted white over the rivets. A third one took her down the narrow hallway that lay beyond.

The room was lit by a single strip of cold LED light. Katya Lisichenko sat with her elbows on a steel table, studying her own dirty fingernails. She looked thinner than in her booking photo; her hair had grown back to shoulder length. The Georgians had let her keep her own clothes—matching cashmere hoodie and sweats—which gave her a look of a business-class passenger who survived an airplane crash. When the door opened, she didn't lift her eyes, just winced at the scrape of the chair as her guest sat down opposite.

"Hi," said Tamaskar. "My name is Asha." She turned to the guard at the door. "Sir? Please wait outside. Thank you." She then repeated the phrase in Russian.

The man complied, finally earning Tamaskar some eye contact from the prisoner. The scowl of quiet disdain hadn't changed. *Good for you,* she thought.

"I'm here to take you to the U.S." The woman slowly nodded. "Is this where they kept you? Were you treated humanely?"

"Here's how this plays out, legally speaking," said Katya, ignoring the questions. Her voice, after what must have been days of silence, was a hollow rasp. She cleared her throat. "I am hereby making an official asylum request. Your conversation with me is the equivalent of an Asylum Merits interview. This makes my case active by the moment we leave this room."

Having read her file, Tamaskar knew all about Lisichenko's impressive education and experience, but the businesslike tone still took her aback. She hadn't been expecting tears or a hug or anything, but jeez. Even in prison, the woman still sounded like she was laying out the terms of a corporate acquisition.

"We'll have more time to get into all of this on the plane," she said.

"I'm not stepping out of here until you agree."

What is it with everyone playing hardball today? Tamaskar wanted to yell into the void. "Sure." She looked at Katya, met her glare, and corrected herself. "I agree. And anyway, the credible-fear standard has been more than met. You'll have a rock-solid case once we're on U.S. soil. Shall we?"

"Yeah. I'm just preparing myself." Katya got up. She was a full head taller than Tamaskar and all sharp angles, skin stretched taut over jutting collarbones.

"For what?"

A smile finally came to the prisoner's face, and she wished it hadn't. It was a smile of pity and pain and the worst kind of wisdom. "For not making it to U.S. soil."

■ ■ ■

Bethesda, Maryland
March 27, 2024

Jim pulled up to the house, already feeling the familiar combo of nostalgia and dread. The drive from Langley had taken him less than twenty minutes. The neighborhood was thick with E-ZPass warriors for various intelligence agencies across the Potomac; one of Otterbeck Senior's patented quips on the subject claimed that the local Starbucks was a SCIF (sensitive compartmentalized information facility). Another was about the dogs at the Cabin John dog park all having TS clearance. When you were a spy with a spy for a father, these were the kinds of dad jokes you got.

The house itself was a perfectly symmetrical redbrick Georgian, with white quoins running like zippers down every corner and two dormers on the roof that had once looked to Jim like a pair of permanently surprised eyes. He and his four sisters had come up behind those eyes—the sisters chaotically trading rooms as they grew and feuded and formed new alliances, him off to the side, an obscure princeling. Now the parents, Charles and Liz Otterbeck, lived here alone. This left eight of the house's ten bedrooms vacant save for the summers and holidays, when Jim's nieces and nephews flooded in.

Right now it stood even emptier than usual, with Liz away on some sort of fifty-something girls' trip with friends from Ensign College. Jim found his father enthusiastically pruning the hydrangeas in the back.

"Hey, whoa. You're kinda killing them," Jim said in lieu of a greeting.

Otterbeck Senior shrugged. "Mom said it needed to be done."

"Yeah," said Jim, examining a cut branch with a few buds already on it. "Weeks ago."

"So, how's work?" Charles asked once they were inside, bottles of Orangina in hand.

"Good. How's yours?"

"Good." Both smiled the same smile. It was a little ritual.

In truth, Jim always assumed that his father knew much more about his day-to-day than he of his father's. Having come up through Special Activities, Charles had shuffled through several executive stints near the top of the IC—if not at the icy peak itself, then somewhere above the tree line—before ending up back at the Agency, in Procurement. Experience had given him myriad formal and informal connections. With his leisurely drawl and the physique of a quarterback gone to seed, the elder Otterbeck was an easy man to like. Or so Jim had been told by others.

Whether these connections had propelled his own rise, especially his posting at Moscow Station with full diplomatic cover at twenty-eight, Jim would rather not know. Today, however, they were the reason he found himself at the family house on a Tuesday afternoon, drinking fizzy orange juice. He knew Charles knew, too. The unspoken question between them was how far into the chitchat he'd find the guts to ask for the favor he was there to ask.

They sat down in the den, in matching armchairs facing the fireplace. A little velvet-lined reliquary on the mantel contained Charles's declassified Hostile Action Service Medal from Bosnia: eagle, shield, compass rose.

"You see the Yale game?"

"Of course." A day or two ago, Charles's alma mater had exited March Madness in round two, at the hands of San Diego. "Hey, they did their best."

"When's Mom back?"

"Monday. You *know*."

Jim didn't, until he did. Sunday March 31 was Easter, recognized by the LDS but not treated as much of a holiday—unlike in Liz Otterbeck's current social circle, where it was bigger than Christmas. She often found it easier to quietly split for the week than to let the Bethesda ladies dwell on the difference.

"I hear they moved you to Covert," said Charles, wheeling closer to real talk. "How's working for the Indian gal?"

"*Dad.*"

"Hey. As long as she's not in your way."

Jim glanced around the room for new conversation topics. Twelve or so years earlier, his parents had had the whole ground floor expensively renovated, turning it into a suite where Grandpa Otterbeck could "age in place," but the patriarch spoiled the plan by dying instead. The den became a den again, though, in Jim's eyes, not quite; the spirit of an old man's bedroom was still there somehow, lying in wait for Charles and Liz to grow sufficiently decrepit.

"All right, son." Charles set the coffee aside. "I can't help you if you don't talk." It was far too easy to imagine his father saying the same thing in Serbian while holding up a car-battery clamp. Jim shook the image off.

"Right," he said, a British tic he had picked up in London that refused to go away. "I, uh, okay, this is stupid."

"Spit it out."

Jim sighed. "Dad, I need advice. I was part of an important op. Can't say any more, obviously, but, like, really important." He hated how childish this sounded; *everyone regresses when they talk to their fathers*, he thought.

Just keep going. "And, false modesty aside, I did a fantastic job. But now Spaleta's given it to someone else, and I'm supposed to go back to busywork. Do I try to make my case before him, or do I let it go?"

"Yeah, well," said Charles, "chain of command is chain of command." He dropped into a stage whisper, putting his palm cartoonishly to one side of his mouth. "Even if it's a drip like Burt."

Jim took a nervous swig of his Orangina. "But what if, and this is a hypothetical, of course, what if—"

"Son. Breathe."

"What if there was a component to the op that was not necessarily on the books?" he blurted out and froze in immediate violent regret.

Charles leaned forward in his chair. "Aha. So what you're saying is, you might have some leverage here, and you're asking me whether to cash it in or bank it. See, that's a whole different dilemma. And now I understand all the stammering. I thought you were just being you."

He stoically ignored the dig. "So?"

"So. My first advice is not to clutch your pearls too hard. Every other mission has a little stink on it. We're not wedding planners. Things go wrong in the field. If every mess we make ended up in a congressional hearing, we might as well close up shop. You see someone cut a corner and fall all over yourself to report it, you might end up looking naive. Not to mention, a rat."

"That's a good point. So you're saying, forget it."

"Not necessarily. The thing about all leverage is, someone's getting lifted up and someone's getting knocked down. Who should be the one lifted up?"

"Me?" Jim offered, shrugging.

"*Bzzt.* Wrong. It should be whoever will be most impressed by you. Which isn't the same as the biggest boss. Sometimes it's the guy you could have ruined but didn't. Are you getting me?"

"Barely. It sounds like you're advocating for blackmail."

"What I'm advocating for is your career." Charles appeared to relish his ability to help, as if Jim were nine and needed his bicycle seat adjusted. "Did your op have a name?"

Jim cleared his throat. "Birdbath."

"Jesus Christ. You know Churchill personally banned the Brits from using silly codes, right? *Do not make me inform a widow,*" he huffed, uncorking a decent Churchill imitation, "*that her husband perished in Operation Bunnyhug.*"

Both laughed. Weirdly, Jim thought, this was shaping up as one of their better interactions in recent memory. He was almost disappointed when his phone buzzed.

He glanced at the screen. A notification from Instagram. There was only one account there that he hadn't muted.

"Crap. I need to go. Work."

"Go get 'em," drawled Charles from his armchair, saluting with the Orangina. "You know the drill: Man up and do the work. Read the people. Read the room. You'll get there."

"Thanks, Dad. Say hi to Mom." In the time it took to utter these six syllables, Jim was out of the house, the slam of the front door bisecting *hi* and *Mom.*

The Otterbot hadn't seen action in months; he had almost forgotten it existed. The new picture in the "hidden requests" folder, surrounded by porn spam, was a red Alfa Romeo. A fake license plate had been crudely photoshopped atop the real one, reading *A E80W.* The description, as usual, was a meaningless pile of emoji, hiding the five-character string that identified it as a genuine communication from Falk.

Alfa Romeo, according to the code they had set up back in Prague, meant Felix Burnham. *It worked. They've contacted him. He is going to the meet.*

Red meant *now.*

The rest required some googling, which Jim did, recklessly, from behind the wheel while gunning his decidedly not Alfa Romeo toward the river. "E80" was a real highway, but that hardly narrowed things down: an international designation, it stretched, under dozens of local names, from Tehran to Lisbon. Even if Jim took just the part west of Pisa (W), it still covered over 1,300 miles.

Finally, and far too late by his own admission, he noticed the fake license plate's foreshortened format. Most European countries would have more than five characters; this suggested a dwarf state. The only one along the E80 route was Andorra. Hence the A.

I still hate you, Ari Falk.

Just as Jim wanted to floor the gas in triumph, the traffic ahead slowed to a crawl: DC drones, on the way to their Virginia hives. Steering with one hand, he popped the glove box, shook a clean phone out of its Faraday sleeve, and called Tamaskar's. No answer. He switched phones and called into work the regular way, rattling off his ID and department code to the switchboard.

"Deputy Director Tamaskar's office." The assistant, Valerie, a piece of work.

"Is she in? It's urgent."

"Oh, hey, Jim," said the assistant. "Sorry, she's out of pocket. Left last night."

"And went where?"

Valerie let her silence speak to the inanity of the question, then deigned to throw him a bone. "Took an Agency jet."

Fan-tastic, he thought. Then he said it out loud, the same way it had sounded in his head. "Fan-tastic."

"She should be back on the comms in a few hours."

"Right. I see." This was a lie. He felt as blind as he had in that Prague hallway, a part of something but unsure of what, expected to perform without the luxury of knowing the script, the venue, or his own character. "Okay, Valerie, look, I need to get on the first flight to Andorra. Or whatever's closest to Andorra. I don't actually know if they have an airport."

"I'm not your assistant, though." That Gen Z *though* felt deliberate.

"I am aware of that. But it's for DD/AC."

"Good. Then she'll confirm once she's back on the comms," said Valerie sadistically.

Jim hung up and punched the headliner. The westbound American Legion Memorial Bridge was bumper to bumper. The one on a burly Yukon in front of him had a sticker reading *My Kid Beat Up Your Honor Student.*

He opened the app once again and pressed a little heart, confirming receipt.

Man up and do the work. He'd have to figure out the next part himself.

■ ■ ■

The night outside smelled like almond bloom and creosote. Their rides idled by the foot of the stairs: Merab smoking by his limo, the two U.S. Marines leaning against the escort Jeep. They saw the women and trotted up the front steps to escort them down. The initial plan had been to put Katya into the Jeep with them. "Absolutely not," Katya said, freezing in place. "I go with her or I don't go." The Marines looked at Tamaskar, who shrugged her assent.

The two of them got into the back seat of the Benz, Katya on the right as the taller one. She immediately buckled up, making Merab turn with a cartoonish frown. "What, you don't trust me?"

"Not one bit," said Katya.

"Damn," said Merab. "Nice to meet you, too." He then repeated his story about the limo having once been part of the presidential fleet. The cars took off, the Jeep first this time.

Tamaskar could understand some of Lisichenko's unease: Each time the woman had tried to leave Russia ended in disaster. But it also implied something else, something yet unsaid. She carried herself like a bearer of secrets, careful not to trip and spill. Tamaskar had seen this type of apprehension in assets before. It usually meant the real deal. It was always the ones with nothing to tell who wouldn't stop talking. Katya knew her worth—and it appeared to terrify her.

In any case, the almost certainly bugged GIS vehicle wasn't the place to ask. Perhaps she'd be up for a debrief on the plane.

The caravan took a ramp onto the Kakheti Highway and headed toward the airport. Katya stared out of the passenger-side window, each passing lamp reflecting in her wet hair; she had demanded a shower before they left and was now looking a little closer to her pre-prison self from the file photos. Tamaskar suddenly remembered that she had a travel cosmetics kit in her bag and offered it. After some hesitation, Katya silently mouthed thanks and began to riffle through its contents. "Oh, cool, I love that one," she said, pulling out a Korean vitamin C serum.

In retrospect, Asha should have recognized the drone earlier. Both the thing and the sound. The latter came first—that eerie buzz of tiny propellers straining in four-part harmony, the theme song of modern warfare. Then the drone itself, a simple Chinese-made Mavic, swam into view over the almond trees. It wheeled toward the road in a high, smooth arc, stopping three hundred feet or so above the divider, and hung there for a second like a giant hummingbird before banking right and disappearing. From the ease of its movements, Tamaskar could tell that it had no payload attached to it. Despite knowing what this likely meant, she felt herself relaxing.

The feeling lasted several seconds at most. When the whine came back, it sounded harder and lower. A second drone, moving at twice the speed—thanks to its spotter cousin, it now knew exactly where it was heading—slashed across the dark sky and dropped like a hawk onto the Jeep in front of them.

At the last possible moment, the driver must have noticed it, too. The Jeep attempted an evasive maneuver, barreling across the divider and into the empty oncoming lane. The drone corrected in mid-fall, tumbling left over itself as it made contact.

She expected a crash, a fireball. What she saw was worse. The drone's payload must have been an armor-piercing HEAT warhead, which sent a jet of hot copper streaming through the target at 5,000 feet per second. One half of the Jeep had ceased to exist before the other half had time to explode.

The hit reversed the car's momentum entirely, pushing its disintegrating body backward into the Benz's windshield. Katya screamed. Merab, silent and precise in a way his previous manner hadn't portended, swung right onto the shoulder. The Jeep's remains flew past Tamaskar's window, close enough that the flames licked the glass. A wave of infernal heat rolled through the car. An oncoming semi hit the brakes and jackknifed into a ditch with a metallic groan.

Merab climbed back onto the roadway, turned off the headlights, accelerated to ninety and drove in hard zigzags, anticipating a double tap. Tamaskar and Katya found themselves grabbing onto each other as they sank into the back seat. Staying below the window line made little defensive sense in this type of attack, but at least it prevented them from being thrown from side to side at every turn.

"It's okay," said Tamaskar, breathing hard in order to breathe at all. "It's going to be okay." She fit a nervous titter between two exhalations. "But, boy, someone *really* doesn't want you free."

"Yup." In the passing slashes of sodium light, Katya's face toggled between gray and lemon yellow. Her lower lip trembled a bit; otherwise, she held herself together about as well as anyone Tamaskar had ever met.

"Two klicks to the airport," said Merab, overtaking an oblivious late-night Lada.

"Good. Get us there." Behind them, the Lada's driver laid into the horn. Merab responded with an automatic Georgian curse.

Now or never. Tamaskar locked eyes with Katya's, inches away, and spoke in short half sentences to the rhythm of their combined breath. "Look, if you have anything on Felix Burnham. If you're holding on to something, hoping to sell it later. Which is smart—I would do the same. But, Katya, I think it's time. Whatever you got, you can tell me."

Katya said nothing, but her grip on Tamaskar's upper arm tightened for a moment. She seemed to be on the verge of a decision.

"*Ibiolamat,*" repeated Merab through clenched teeth. The telltale quadraphonic buzz had returned.

"It's the spotter again," said Katya, looking up.

Tamaskar's mind raced. The Agency jet had a mobile electromagnetic-warfare system on board, built specifically for jamming enemy comms; it created a 200-yard safety dome around itself. The last time, the bomber had taken about thirty seconds to arrive once the spotter relayed the coordinates. They still had a chance.

"How close are we?" she shouted.

"Close. One klick max."

A small one, but a chance nonetheless. "Keep driving. Not to the terminal. Straight to the plane."

Merab glanced back at her. "What do you mean, straight—"

"What it sounds like."

Merab shrugged, downshifted, and threw the wheel to the left. The car skidded onto a rough service road, barely making the turn; a full G of lateral acceleration made the seat belt feel like it was going to cut her in half. The buzz grew weaker as the spotter drone fell away.

Tamaskar lifted her head and hazarded a look. The lights of the airfield shone in front of them. A tall wire fence separated the apron from the track. One more bend and she saw the jet. It was parked in an underlit area at the far end of the tarmac, ready to go, lights on. The EW system, too, hopefully.

"Hang on!" Merab yelped, flooring the gas. The Benz bounded up a small man-made bank, smashed through the fence, and, briefly airborne, bucked onto the field. For a moment that seemed to stretch beyond real time, its windshield held nothing but the night sky.

And in that sky, the bomber drone, homing in.

The limo crashed onto the tarmac grille-first. The metal skid plate threw up a shower of sparks; a piece of the bumper swung loose. A length of fence wire had caught on an axle and trailed behind them, popping off pole after pole with a repeating whiplike swish. Merab lost control of the steering wheel for a second, regained it, braked, put the car in reverse to dislodge the wire, then locked the front wheels and swung it into a wide, tire-burning J-turn toward the plane.

The engine stalled out. Every warning light came on at once. Merab mashed the start button, then punched the dash and sagged in his seat, spent. The drone had cleared the fence and was rocketing toward them, its insectoid body pregnant with payload.

The jet glowed several hundred feet away, an unattainable vision of safety. Tamaskar thought about getting out and running toward the plane, but the idea itself used up the last second she might have had to execute it. A strange silence overtook the car and everyone inside. The only sound to remain was the dull buzz of approaching death.

Then it, too, stopped.

She opened her eyes, which she didn't know she had closed. The drone's propellers had frozen in midair; inertia sent it tumbling forward a few more yards before it met the tarmac. With no electronic sensors telling it to detonate, the nerfed warhead gonged against concrete like an empty milk canister. Cheap plastic parts scattered in all directions.

"We're in the dome," she said, trying to will away nausea. "We made it."

A single sob escaped Katya's chest, mutating halfway into a hysterical snicker. In the front, Merab sat slumped over the steering wheel. The Marines were already running from the plane toward the car, weapons out and at the ready.

"Okay, listen," Katya suddenly said through her teeth. "This is the thing that's not on the video. They told Burnham to hire some people. Specific people. Killers. For a specific operation."

"Yes?"

"They used a code name. Grendel. That's it."

"Thank you," said Tamaskar. She reached over to touch Merab's forearm. "And thank *you*. You saved our lives."

The Georgian didn't answer, turn around, or acknowledge her in any way. She saw, with some surprise, that he was staring at his phone; the screen threw a blue tint over his expressionless face.

Everyone deals with shock differently, Tamaskar thought. It wasn't like she knew the man well. Still, something about his hunched stillness bothered her. The Marines were about thirty paces out now, their barking voices music to her ears.

"Merab? You okay there, bud?"

Merab sharply exhaled, straightened his back, and shoved the phone in his pocket. She caught a glimpse of a photo: a girl, black hair, no older than ten.

When he turned around, his kalamata-olive eyes were full of tears. "I'm so sorry," he said, taking out a handgun.

Katya understood first. She lunged at him diagonally from her seat, trying to get an arm around his throat. Merab pistol-whipped her right to left, slamming her head against the center pillar. Then he pointed the gun at Tamaskar and restarted the engine.

"Out. Now."

"Merab, what—"

The agent leaned over, still holding her at gunpoint, opened the door with his free hand, and pushed her harder than she'd ever been pushed.

Tamaskar's body remembered some of the basic training even when her mind didn't: She rounded her shoulders and rolled a full turn before coming to a stop. The instant she hit the apron, the Mercedes tore away, acceleration flinging the door shut an inch above her head. An acrid cloud of tire and diesel smoke—red in the car's taillights, then black—enveloped her.

"Ma'am? Are you okay?" One of the Marines slid into a crouch next to Tamaskar. The other two raised their M27s and took aim at the Benz through the dissipating haze.

"I'm fine," Tamaskar said, getting up. Shredded fabric caked against her freshly skinned knees. The jet revved its engines, preparing for an emergency takeoff.

Inside the limo, Katya had come to. Tamaskar could hear her screaming in the back seat. A Marine let loose a tentative volley, aiming for the back wheels and missing; another followed suit, two or three bullets pocking the armored trunk. The car swerved, almost flipping over in the process.

"Hold your fire!" Tamaskar barked. "Hold your fucking fire! They crash, she dies."

The chain of command was murky at best. The men shared a hard glance before grudgingly lowering their rifles. She realized, in a flash of empathy, that they already knew or suspected the fate of their comrades in the Jeep. She, a civilian, was asking a lot.

The Benz steadied itself. It weaved around the dead drone, giving the unexploded ordinance as wide a berth as possible, and headed toward the same breach in the fence it had made just a few seconds ago. Inside, Katya kept screaming, a single, short, repeating phrase; the roar of the jet kept drowning her out.

Four or five syllables, over and over. This wasn't just a wail of pain or despair. It was a message. It was *information.*

Before Tamaskar knew what she was doing, she found herself sprinting after the car, into what had just been a line of fire. Finally she got herself downwind and clear enough of the turbine roar to hear something.

"Find me in the West!" Katya managed to lower the passenger-side window and yelled into the opening. "Find me in the West!"

At first she thought she misheard. The window slid back up; Merab had taken over the controls. Katya hit the glass with her fists, chanting the inscrutable phrase at the top of her lungs with each strike.

"Find me in the West!"

Her voice grew hoarser and fainter. The battered limousine roared up the bank, onto the road, and was gone.

"Ma'am." A Marine touched Tamaskar's shoulder and pointed to the plane. Another knelt by the remnants of the drone, taking pictures.

She nodded, turned back, then turned around, searching for words. "I'm very sorry about your friends. We won't let this go." This kind of talk had never been her forte, but she could think of nothing else to say. "I *promise* you someone will burn for this."

"Yes, ma'am." They just wanted her on the plane and out of there. Fair enough. Tamaskar stepped on the stairs, gripping the handrail. Along the horizon and across the tarmac, blue and red police lights were beginning to bloom, same as everywhere else in the world.

CHAPTER SIX

Andorra
March 28, 2024

Falk got off the bus and saw it from a mile away. Silje's fake uncle may have lied about many things, starting with his name, but he wasn't kidding about Caldea Spa. You couldn't miss it. A glass pyramid designed to mimic either an alien spaceship or a quartz crystal cluster, it was the tallest building in the country. Granted, the country was eighteen miles wide.

He stretched and looked around. Beyond the rooftops of Andorra la Vella, yellowish brushland reared up like a theater backdrop. The microstate sat at the bottom of a deep valley; Andorrans had kept their statehood intact by staying invisible even to their immediate neighbors. Banks, hotels, duty-free malls, and chintzy casinos accumulated like silt on the banks of the river snaking along the valley floor. A Eurotrash Wakanda.

Three dozen tourists or so, most of them French, had disembarked with Falk. He loitered for a few minutes, taking in the skyless skyline, to let the group dissolve into the shopping district. Then he found the embankment and joined the general flow of foot traffic, heading east. The spa's gleaming spire removed any need for a map.

Ironically, he could really use a shower. The trek from Pisa had taken twenty-eight hours. The FlixBus that had deposited Falk on the spot was his third in a row; the first took him to Milan, the second from Milan to Toulouse. Despite having technically left the EU, he hadn't had to reach for his crisp new passport once. That must have been part of Andorra's appeal to his suitors. No taxes and an incurious border service: a gray zone in the middle of Europe, shot through with gray money.

Falk wasn't really sure what, or whom, to expect at the loosely scheduled rendezvous. The chances that he'd walk into the building and see Felix Burnham holding court in a terry-cloth robe seemed remote. Considering the total secrecy around his whereabouts, Christian wouldn't have been able to mention Andorra in the presence of a day player like Silje. So it would be prudent to prepare for yet another entrance exam.

Still, he couldn't shake the intoxicating sense of closing in on the target. He felt it in his limbs, his lungs, the way his brain sped through new data. This wasn't a good thing. It was that stage of an op when even the best got impatient and restless—which meant sloppy, which meant exposed, which meant dead.

Falk forced himself to slow down his steps and his breath. *Be a tourist. Gawk.* On the opposite bank stood an ugly bronze sculpture of a melted clock sprouting tree limbs; he crossed a footbridge to get a better look. What he had assumed was a local Dalí rip-off turned out to be an actual late-career Dalí, though hardly better for it. He sauntered thoughtfully around the sculpture, at a fraction of the speed his body was screaming at him to do, and saw Jim Otterbeck.

The young officer loitered across the plaza, photographing the sculpture (and Falk) on his phone. He had dressed for a rather romantic idea of a Eurotrip, with Jude Law in *The Talented Mr. Ripley* his apparent inspiration: a linen suit from J.Crew, boat shoes, and a straw hat. Falk was dying to inform him that it made him look more like a Nazi hiding out in postwar Argentina. Sadly, they had to play strangers.

Falk had sent up a flare the same night he got the invitation, firing off coded messages from his own bed while Silje snored next to him. The op being as bare-bones as it was, poor Jim would have to combine the duties of a watcher and a courier. His first task was to tail Falk from the bus station and make sure that no one else did. The second was to hand-deliver the only piece of hardware the mission required: an inconspicuous beacon that Falk could smuggle with him into Burnham's lair.

He was happy to see Jim, straw hat or not. It felt good to be in the presence of someone who knew him, even if they couldn't talk or acknowledge each other. Falk was not exactly starved for human company, yet every single interaction in his life since 2021—even sex with Silje, unexpectedly and rather needlessly acrobatic—had a layer of playacting to it. The only exception, the only time he was fully himself and not performing a part, must have been last December's chat with Asha Tamaskar. Falk flashed back to it often, if only to remember what his own unmodulated voice sounded like.

Otterbeck took a few more photos of the square, shoved the phone in his pocket, and headed in Falk's direction. Despite the weight of the moment, Falk found himself wondering if Jim had bothered to install a local SIM card: Andorra's roaming charges were the highest in the world. If the young agent's photos auto-uploaded to the cloud, he had just lost about a hundred euro in one minute.

He turned sideways and looked at the river, positioning his body just so. Otterbeck squeezed between Falk and the sculpture, touched the rim of his straw hat in a deniable greeting, and padded toward an eyewear shop at the far end of the plaza.

Falk resumed his walk, both hands in his hoodie's kangaroo pocket. A furtive grin waxed and waned on his face. If he'd had a direct line to Tamaskar, he would have texted her, like one proud parent to the other: *Our boy's getting better at brush passes.*

The new object in his pocket was a key fob to an old Fiat—exactly the kind of car Falk could plausibly own back in Pisa. A push of the unlock button sent out a signal at 434 MHz, like any regular key; piggybacking on it was an ultra-wideband ping, traceable from anywhere in the world and broadcasting every other nanosecond until the battery ran out. For the op's purposes, he wouldn't need anything fancier than that.

Inside, the spa looked large enough to give Andorra's entire population a simultaneous bath if needed. The lobby, all milky glass and would-be calming blue tones, smelled reassuringly of chlorine—like a bad hotel or a good hospital. In the absence of any clear instructions, Falk went up to the reception desk and bought a pair of black swimming trunks and a day pass under the name Richard Daniels, hoping this would trigger some kind of response. A clerk in a crisp uniform mechanically handed him a towel, a folded robe, and a magnetic bracelet with a locker number. Falk was about to wander away when her monitor showed something that made her check twice.

"Orange bath?" she called after him, with a soft Catalan accent.

"Excuse me?"

"Richard Daniels. You left a message last night to ask if you could reserve our orange bath, right?" *Sure.* "I'm sorry, sir, but it is first come, first serve."

"I'll live," Falk said. "Thank you."

There it was again, the feverish thrill of invisible crosshairs locking onto the target. Except he was a target, too. Someone else, somewhere close, at this very moment, was equally tickled that everything was going to plan.

The men's locker room, the size of a basketball court and designed to process guests by the busful, stood nearly empty. Falk changed in a narrow two-way booth that made him feel like a horse in a racetrack starting stall, shoving his things into a small locker on the other side. Stripping off the clothes in which he had spent two days on a bus felt great. Parting with the phone and the fob did not.

The orange bath, in a semiprivate nook above the main pool area, turned out to be just that: a large hot tub with dozens of fresh oranges floating on the surface as an Instagram-friendly gimmick. The tang of citrus rind hung in the wet air. In the tub's far end, submerged to the chest, sat a man with the physique of a Laughing Buddha, though none of the good cheer. Mid-forties, bald but for a horseshoe of thin brown hair, rough-hewn features. Not Burnham. Not Uncle Christian. Not Stan Vlasic the ex-Sac.

Falk waded in, worrying the oranges. A pair of small colorless eyes openly followed him. Last he checked, Caldea wasn't a place for same-sex assignations. For a minute, they sat in silence among the bobbing fruit, like two capybaras. New Age music wafted up from the main pool.

The last moment of plausible deniability. The elation was gone. It may have been something as simple as being nearly naked in front of a stranger or the man's heavy stare, but all of a sudden, Falk felt out of place and out of his depth.

"Hey," he said.

"Armband." The voice was a lazy rasp.

"Armband?"

The man sighed and stood up. Water cascaded off his bluish-white belly; a single tattoo, reading *XXV,* covered a distended smallpox-vaccine scar on his left forearm. He had on the same type of magnetic bracelet as Falk and everyone else in the spa. He tapped it with his right hand. "*Genau. Wir müssen zuerst die Armbänder tauschen.*"

"I don't speak German," said Falk automatically, but then again, he didn't have to. *Clever bastards.* He slipped off his bracelet and sent it skimming across the water. The man caught it, took his off, and left it on the edge of the pool.

"Thank you." His English was both hard and chewy. "We are done. See you outside." He climbed out, causing a little tsunami, and left with an orange for the road.

Falk picked up the bracelet and walked back, dripping, his mind in overdrive. *First of all, no reason to panic.* In fact, this was good news. Being checked for bugs meant he was about to be taken into some kind of inner sanctum. The strip-and-swap was just a more elegant version of the body search he had been expecting on arrival.

There was nothing incriminating in his locker. The clothes were clean—well, metaphorically clean; Burnham's men were welcome to sniff along every seam. The phone was a burner, befitting a man on the run. The one he had used to contact Otterbeck lay on the bottom of the Arno back in Pisa. And the key fob was indistinguishable from the real thing to anyone without an advanced engineering degree. Even if the German had one, he wouldn't have the time to take it apart and study every little circuit. In the worst-case scenario, he'd just throw it away as a precaution.

"See you outside" was promising, too. In planning the day over the Otterbot, Falk and Jim had decided against the junior agent following him into the Caldea building. For all they knew, this was Burnham territory already, with a CCTV system tapped to identify everyone going in and out. Instead, Otterbeck was to hang across the street and watch the entrance to the spa's underground garage. Falk had no means of alerting him now, but with a little luck, he might see them drive off and get the car's plates.

He found the new locker—it was in some elite crevice of the building that required buzzing in—and opened it, with some caution. Inside sat a neat stack of new clothes and a shoebox. Underwear, jeans, socks, a pair of basic Adidas, and a heather gray T-shirt: all with the tags still on, all in Falk's exact sizes, and all the kind of stuff he would actually wear. He unfolded the shirt and was not particularly surprised to see the winged-*P* Pixies logo on the front.

Falk threw on the clothes and walked out, wincing in the Andorran daylight. The German had somehow pulled up the car already. It was an old Opel Mokka, psoriatic from sun damage, with a pair of non-EU plates Falk had never seen before: Set against a background of red, white, and black was the unfamiliar country code DR. Puzzled, he almost forgot to scan the street for Otterbeck. The field liaison and his stupid straw hat were nowhere to be found. He must have staked out the wrong entrance. Unable to dawdle any longer, Falk got in.

"Don't worry," said the driver, misinterpreting his sideways glances as they peeled off. "You don't have a tail on you."

"I know."

"You did before." The German expertly muscled into the traffic. His driving manner suggested a former pro—a cabbie or a trucker.

"Comes with the territory." Falk smiled, stifling a twitch of terror. Otterbeck being blown in his capacity as a watcher was survivable. A rogue ex-CIA officer *should* have ticks on him. If Burnham's men had noticed the brush pass, however, it was game over.

"Let me guess," he added. "The weirdo by the clock." Same strategy as earlier: Give up what you know they already know, and nothing more.

"Correct. That's why we have to do all this. But it's over now. You'll be safe where we're going."

"Good to hear."

"Also." The driver leaned over and opened the glove box. Despite having just emerged from a bath, he already reeked of fresh sweat, which didn't bode well for the rest of the journey. Inside was something Falk hadn't seen in at least a decade and a half: a book of CD-Rs in soft plastic sleeves. "Felix says you're a music fan. He told me to take some music for the trip and let you pick."

Felix says. Just like that. Either he finally had the organization's confidence, or discretion no longer mattered because you can say anything to a dead man.

"That's thoughtful of him. And, uh, how long a trip are we talking here?" Falk asked thumbing through the disks.

The man cracked a grin that looked like his first in a year. "Let me say it like so. You will have time to play them all."

■ ■ ■

McLean, Virginia
March 28, 2024

She had wanted to come to the office straight from the airport debrief, but Spaleta wouldn't hear of it. So instead Asha Tamaskar had spent all Wednesday in bed, trying to watch a show about fancy Realtors—or were they interior decorators?—and wishing she was at work. Having to deal with whatever horrors had piled up on the hated maple desk would be vastly preferable to being stuck at home with a cat named Blixa and her own brain for company. Neither was helpful in a crisis.

Every time Tamaskar let her focus wander away from the screen, memories of the Tbilisi attack flooded in—maddening snippets running on four or five simultaneous loops. The whine of the bomber drone, the obliterated Jeep, Merab's face a frozen mask as he pushed her out of the car, Katya's repeating scream, all at the same time.

Finally she put herself to half sleep with the help of the strongest melatonin pills and CBD gummies that wouldn't show up on an Agency drug screen, but she still woke up in the middle of the night. The phone clock read 3:12. Tamaskar cupped Blixa's head with both hands, peered into his yellow eyes, said, "Fuck this, right?" and made him nod a little in agreement, took a very cold shower to lift the pill haze, and drove to Langley.

"Asha. Where to even begin." Tamaskar lifted her eyes. It was five hours later now, though she could barely tell where the elapsed time had gone. Burt Spaleta stood in the doorway, still in his track shorts; he ran before work and kept a suit in his office. "How you holdin' up?"

"Fine," she said. "Do the families know?"

"Yes. I just got off the phone with the DoD. Worst part of the job."

"Are we at war with Georgia yet?"

The attempt at humor was feeble enough that he answered seriously. "They're swearing up and down it was Russian nonstate actors."

"Russia doesn't have a 'nonstate' anything."

"That's what I told them. May I?" The acting director sat down on the visitor sofa, indicating the beginning of a serious talk. She walked over and perched on the opposite end.

"Look, Asha. The Georgians' loyalties are a mess right now. We can't be absolutely sure this wasn't their hit and that you weren't the target." Tamaskar shook her head no, which only made Spaleta speak louder. "So, I came to say two things. One, how profoundly sorry I am for letting you go with so little protection. If you need anything, anything at all, I'm here for you and so is the Agency."

She decided to hurry him along before he offered her a hug or a paid leave. "And the second thing?"

"The White House wants us to play it down. *Way* down. Getting publicly mad at Tbilisi would make the Kremlin happy, which may have been the goal all along. Privately, though, I've been told our hands are untied, within reason. There will be retribution, but it would have to be smart. If you feel up to it, I want you on that team."

She shook her head again. "Thank you, but I . . . Well, sir, I disagree with your whole premise. The only target was Lisichenko."

Spaleta chewed his lips. "What makes you so sure?"

"She was supposed to be in the Jeep, with the Marines. It got hit first.

Everything after that was improvisation. Hell, they blackmailed the driver in real time by sending him a photo of someone—his daughter, I assume. Tactically brilliant, sure, but still a desperation move. To me, it suggests that whoever did this got ahold of our initial exfil plan, but they weren't getting updates on it."

Tamaskar noticed that having to reason through the whole ordeal out loud was making her feel markedly better. As long as she stayed in analyst mode, everything that had happened hadn't happened to *her*.

"Then there's the fact that even under duress, the driver let me go," she added, and blinked away another flash of Merab's face.

"Maybe he liked you," said Spaleta.

"Not to mention that the Georgians had every chance to kill me in the comfort of their own prison basement. They could have fed me a polonium pkhali if they wanted to."

The acting director nodded glumly, conceding the point. "So who wants Lisichenko dead this badly?"

"That's easy. The real owners of Orlan Finans. Military intelligence. The GRU." Another thought occurred to her. "Ironically, they couldn't get to her while she was in Georgian custody. Until we gave them a lucky break. The airport transfer was their window of opportunity."

Spaleta looked genuinely appalled. "My god."

"Think of it this way," Tamaskar said. "This proves we were right on the money. Whatever Lisichenko knows is so high-value that five U.S. citizens were acceptable collateral."

The boss glanced at the door, making sure it was shut. The hallway outside was quiet; at 8:20 a.m., the seventh floor still stood half-empty.

"I don't love some of your implications here," he said after a pause.

"Such as?"

"Well, for starters, that the Russians are insane enough to try this. I realize that Ukraine has changed everyone's risk calculus, but what you're describing is an act of war."

"They think we *are* at war. And they still think of Georgia as their backyard."

"Then there's your leak theory. Thing is, Asha, that exfil plan went from my own desk straight to the embassy."

For a second, Tamaskar entertained a crazy idea that she should come clean to him about the real op. The urge abated as soon as it appeared. What form would that confession even take? *On a possibly related note, sir, I am in the process of smoking out a mole on this very floor. Just something I've been tinkering with in my spare time. Can't tell you much more at the moment, since you yourself are not absolved yet, but do stay tuned.*

"It wouldn't be the world's first bugged embassy," she offered instead.

"Think there's a chance Lisichenko is still alive?" Spaleta suddenly asked, sounding almost plaintive. "Your debrief mentions she shouted something—what was it? 'Find me?'"

Tamaskar nodded. "Something like that. But seeing how their opening move was to drop a HEAT charge on a car they thought she was in . . . I'm not hopeful."

"Yeah. All right. Had to ask." Spaleta stood up with a grunt. "What a mess. Once again, so sorry that you had to go through all this. I'm not ready to buy your version of the events yet—too many leaps. Horses, not zebras, remember. But your conduct was nothing short of heroic. I'm putting you up for a Medal of Merit."

For what? Not dying? she wanted to snap. "Thank you, sir."

"Thank *you*." The acting director headed toward the exit, Tamaskar back to the desk. Outside, she heard Valerie settling in at her station, five minutes early as usual. Like most of the Agency, her assistant would know nothing about what had happened in Tbilisi and thus wouldn't be compelled to pantomime concern or empathy. She was beginning to prefer it this way.

For the next few minutes, or maybe hours, Tamaskar forced herself to catch up on the department reports and intel briefs. She had missed a lot, and nothing at all. Half the world was on fire as usual. Waves of refugees lapping at the marble plinth of Europe, far-right scum ascendant in the wake. Same two or three stories everywhere. The System, whirring along.

The desktop vibrated. She unlocked the top drawer. Inside, the clean phone she had used on occasion to contact Otterbeck was skating merrily across the papers, propelled by its own buzz.

"Asha. May I call you Asha?" said a familiar voice. "This is Levan." The Georgian-accented rasp jolted her right back into the screeching Mercedes.

"Are you insane?!" She clamped her free hand around the phone's mouthpiece. "I know I gave you this number, but now is *not* the time—"

"Which is why I'm not calling you with empty apologies," the GIS director cut in. "I am calling with information. I figured that's what you need most right now."

"And why should I believe anything you tell me?"

"Why?!" The voice cracked a bit, or perhaps it was the connection. "If nothing else, because I just gave an order to execute a man who served me *veroi i pravdoi*"—faithfully and truthfully—"for twenty years. Maybe that's why."

"Merab?" The name felt hollow on her lips, a sound with all substance ripped out. Levan fell silent. Perhaps he didn't want to say it, either.

"Look, here's all I know," he continued after a pause. "You can take it as proof that we're on the same side. Or you can throw it away and treat us as enemies. I'll understand. But just know that I am keeping nothing to myself."

"Fine," she said. "Talk."

"The drones hopped frequencies to avoid interference at the airport. At some point they even used the Wi-Fi band. This suggests that the controller was very close. Our best guess is that they were operated out of a Russian cargo plane on the tarmac. The same aircraft took off three minutes later, despite all planes being grounded after the firefight. I'll send you the tail number."

"Was Lisichenko on it?"

"It's very likely. She was not in the car."

"Any blood in the vehicle?"

"None of hers," said Levan harshly.

Tamaskar didn't ask him to elaborate. "Anything else?"

"Yes. A small thing. I looked into her file. Did you know it wasn't the first time she left Russia illegally? Two years ago, she tried the same in Estonia."

"So?"

"So I called them. Estonians and us, we have a good working relationship. It helps having a common problem, you know."

"And?" She felt the last of her patience drain away.

"It was a strange case. They say she crossed the border on March 1, 2022." He gave the time and the place; Tamaskar hastily wrote them down. "Then, two days later, she showed up *again.*"

"What do you mean?"

"That there seem to be two Lisichenkos. One real, and one who's got her old passport."

"Thank you, Levan," she said. "This is helpful."

"I know this means nothing to you or the families of these soldiers," Gogoberidze added, "but I am truly sorry. Sorry this happened in my house, on my watch. Please know I am in your debt. If you ever need anything else, call anytime." He hung up first, freeing her of the need to say anything in return.

Find me in the West.

The scream echoed in Tamaskar's head anew, flooding her senses all at once: the red and black smoke, the smell of oil and burned rubber, the tarmac lights and the muzzle flashes.

Find me in the West, find me in the West, find me in the West.

An hour later, she had.

She called Spaleta on the direct line, complained about headaches and inability to focus, and asked for a three-day stress leave, which he was only too happy to grant. Even as she talked, Tamaskar was buying an airline ticket to Miami and arranging a cat sitter for Blixa.

"Very glad you're doing this," the acting director said. "Oh. Almost forgot. Last thing I'm going to bother you with, sorry. That Ottenberg character, he's back on the Russia task force, right? Like I asked?"

She pretended to rack her mental Rolodex. "Otterbeck? I'm sure he is. He is nothing if not a trouper."

"So, uh, why is he in Andorra right now?"

"He's *where*?"

But Spaleta had already hung up.

■ ■ ■

Baden-Württemberg, Germany
March 29, 2024

The Opel puttered through postcard countryside. As far as Falk could tell without his phone or a map, they had been going northeast the whole time, tracing the Rhine from the left. By sunset, the land around them was still France, but the last few towns they'd passed had names like Altkirch and Wittenheim. In a more relaxed state of mind, he might have mused about the ways countries shaded and bled into each other: A true political map of the world would be a watercolor. Around midnight, they entered Germany via some minor bridge crossing north of Strasbourg.

The driver—his name, he had reluctantly volunteered, was Rudi—clearly knew these parts well. He drove from memory even in the dark, barely glancing at road signs. When they ran out of gas the first time, Rudi refilled the tank from a canister in the trunk; the second time, he parked in the fallow fields half a mile from the gas station and walked there and back with said canister. Falk found these precautions a little naive, considering the national borders they'd crossed along the way. Surely they'd gotten on a camera or two. Perhaps that's what the strange license plates were for.

He'd been wanting to ask about those, but the mood in the car did not seem conducive to a chat. Apart from the music, they rode in a somewhat saturnine silence. Rudi's CD-Rs turned out to contain mostly smooth jazz, so after a couple of blind tries, Falk gave up on DJing. The driver responded by finding a smooth-jazz station on the radio and stuck with it even after it changed its format to Mostly Static.

The tense vibe had several possible explanations, including a very unpleasant one: This was a one-way trip. Falk had spent the first hour coolly guessing who or what might have done him in—Otterbeck, Silje, the key fob to the nonexistent Fiat, Burnham's mole inside the CIA, or some unknown unknown he hadn't yet thought of. As time stretched on, however, this scenario seemed less and less plausible. *Let's say I'm blown. Interrogating me is useless. I don't know anything they don't. The logical move would be simply to call off the meet and have me show up to an empty tub. The second logical move would be to kill me right away and toss the body into some Andorran ravine. Neither has happened.*

Another reason for Rudi's discomfort would have something to do with the forearm tattoo Falk had noticed in the spa. *XXV* was a neo-Nazi marker, though a marginally subtler one than the usual eagles and runes.

It stood for *25,* which stood for *BE* (second and fifth letters of the alphabet), which in turn stood for *Blut und Ehre,* "blood and honor," a onetime Hitler Youth slogan.

To his retroactive embarrassment, at no point during a three-month audition to join Burnham's crew of bigots had it occurred to Falk that he might be putting himself in danger as a Jew. Orphaned at five, he had grown up bouncing around the heavily Christian foster-care system and partly retained the childhood impression that being Jewish meant curly hair and an unusual name. While antisemitism puzzled and irked him, so did the idea that shared genes meant instant kinship with strangers across the globe. And for someone in his line of work, an ability to lean both into and out of American whiteness frankly felt like an asset.

A car ride next to a guy with a *25* tattoo, however, made quick work of all that nuance. That was the only upside of dealing with Nazis: Things got real simple real fast.

Or maybe Rudi is just a big fan of Adele's third album. Falk yawned, stole a glance at the driver's porcine profile, then looked out into the moonless night for some hint as to their whereabouts. They might as well be driving through a tunnel.

He was weighing the pros and cons of taking an actual nap when Rudi's phone buzzed, startling both of them. The German groped for it in his many pockets for four full rings. When he finally fished it out, he pressed it hard to his left ear, to make sure Falk wouldn't hear the other side of the conversation. "*Servus. Bin fast da.*" He paused to listen. "*Genau hier? Bist du sicher? Na klar. Wie du meinst.*"

Falk's German vocabulary consisted of about twenty words he had picked up from Klaus Staubermann, his late colleague at the Riga Station. One of them was the Berliner's omnipresent *genau*, which, combined with *hier*, must have meant "right here." The driver had sounded slightly surprised when he said it, then compliant. A change of plan, then. A new set of instructions agreed to.

He felt sleep evaporate from his body, every cell on alert. Rudi flipped on the high beams and squinted, searching for some sign in the darkness ahead. Falk followed his gaze and saw nothing but the even pulse of the dotted divider in the pool of light.

"Hey," he said, now feigning the drowsiness that had been real moments ago, "want me to take over for a while? You've been at it for what, eleven hours?"

"Not now," said Rudi through his teeth.

"At least tell me if we're getting there tonight or tomorrow. If it's tomorrow, I'll get some sleep."

"Not *now*," the driver repeated. A moment later, he had seen whatever he needed to see: a tree, a roadside bench, a kilometer marker. Falk could read it in his subtly slackening posture.

He was already bracing for Rudi to hit the brakes, but the force with which the German did it still caught Falk by surprise. The Opel screeched to an ugly, wiggling stop on the shoulder. Dust swirled up in the lights.

The driver looked him up and down, now openly measuring the opponent. Falk, for his part, had done the same calculations at the very start of the trip. There were no weapons in the car. They had both had some combat training—Rudi's more extensive, if Falk had to guess, his own a little fresher. Rudi also had at least fifty pounds on him, but seated side by side with seat belts on, that didn't really matter. It all came down to the speed and force of the opening blow. After that, things would get ugly for both of them, with an unclear outcome.

Behind the German's head, a black hilltop lit up along the edge like a paper cutout; a pair of headlights dawned over it and dipped, coming down an invisible side path toward the road. The best time to strike would be if and when they got Rudi's attention.

"I think we have company," Falk said, hoping to speed things along.

To his credit, the driver didn't move a muscle. The lights drew closer; he could hear the engine now, too, a grumbling V8 in a low gear.

"Good." Rudi nodded, without taking his eyes off Falk. "Now get out of the car, please."

"Why?"

The German sighed. The headlights beat into the cabin, forming a halo around his bald head. "Because we're here."

The strange vehicle accelerated, as if preparing to T-bone the Opel. Falk looked directly into the advancing beams until his eyes began to water. Four full feet off the ground, oddly close together: a vintage Land Rover. But bright, too bright, so refurbished.

"Been a pleasure." He unbuckled and got out. The moment he did, the Opel rattled off, taking away Rudi, his body odor, his smooth jazz, and his tattoo.

The Rover barreled onto the road, turned, and came to a stop facing Falk. The doors opened. Two silhouettes. He stood wincing in the light, ready for whatever came his way next.

The last thing he expected, and the first thing he got, was a hug.

"Finally!" A familiar voice—British, or nearly British, with a Germanic edge—boomed in his ear.

Up close and backlit, Alan Keegan's murderer looked thinner, less substantial, than the patrician persona in his videos. Some people—mostly actors, but a few politicians, too—were born for the camera to such an extent that there was something unsettling about them in real life, without the mediating presence of a lens. Felix Burnham was one of those. He wore a freshly oiled Barbour Bedale with the collar up, which, combined with the car, added up to a rather ridiculous country-squire cosplay.

"I trust the trip wasn't too dull." Burnham gave Falk's back a resonant slap and disengaged, though not before giving his right bicep a squeeze with his left hand. "Rudolf may be my favorite reindeer, but he's not exactly a sparkling personality." Falk noticed that he kept moving his shoulders as he spoke, a constant half shrug, half shimmy of impatient excitement. An apt single word to describe his demeanor would be *squirmy*. But there was an undeniable charm to it, too.

Falk smiled in the face of the enemy. "It was fine."

"Brilliant." Burnham spun toward the other man, who'd hung back politely on what Falk had thought was the passenger's side but was, of course, the driver's. "Speaking of sparkling. *Stanley*."

A bottle of Dom Pérignon moved into the spotlight, followed by Stan Vlasic, all six-ten of him. An octopus-sized palm covered the neck from the top to the label. In his other hand, fanned out between the fingers, were three champagne flutes. Unlike Burnham, the disgraced former Sac was *more* intimidating in person. Falk glanced at his pug nose and swiftly refocused on the bottle, careful not to betray even a hint of recognition.

"Welcome, brother." Vlasic twisted out the cork using only his thumb and forefinger, a strongman's party trick. The pop echoed off the hills like a silenced gunshot. "Good to have you here. Big fan of your work in '21."

"Agency man?" Falk turned to Burnham. "Shit, now I don't feel special." Smirks all around.

Vlasic distributed the foaming flutes; Burnham glanced into his, glowered, and mumbled, "Good god, man, tilt when you pour." For a second, he held it aloft over Falk's forehead, as if to bless him rather than toast him; they clinked glasses, Vlasic too forcefully.

"Great year, 2008," Burnham said, meaning the champagne. Falk had taken his glug without bothering to register the taste. He did make a mental note that it was ice cold. This suggested that the welcome wagon hadn't traveled very far to pick him up.

He tried imagining what they'd look like to an outside observer right now: three madmen in the middle of nowhere, huddled in front of an idling antique, drinking from cut-crystal stemware at two a.m. *Just take me to the goddamned hideout*, Falk thought, suddenly so tired he could barely stay on his feet.

"Hell of a welcome," he said, to say something. The weight of the last three months was hitting him all at once. As a case officer, he had run assets but had never been one. At the end of the day, he always got to go home and be more or less himself. Even as a man on the run, he still retained the general mental shape of Ari Falk, a luxury he hadn't appreciated until now; his cover had never required him to transform into someone whose views he'd find reprehensible. This, however? This was harder than basic training, harder than Moscow. The constant, draining pretense, every breath a lie; and all of it just to get here, all of it leading up to this absurd roadside tableau. *Take me to the hideout, give me the fob back, let me press that button, and I'm done. I'm done. You can kill me right after. I can't keep this up.*

"All right," Burnham said, his tone shifting to businesslike, and threw the rest of the drink away with a flick of the wrist. About $50 worth of brut arced into roadside bushes. "Look. You're smart, so I expect you'll have a lot of questions. All of them will get answered, though possibly not at the pace you're used to. Some of our security procedures will look to you like lack of trust. That's normal, and I won't begrudge you a little impatience. But there is one answer I feel I owe you right away, officer Ari Falk of the United States' Central Intelligence Agency. You must be dying to know what it is I actually *do* here."

Falk nodded, feeling the taste of the champagne turn metallic in his mouth. "It has crossed my mind."

"What I do," said Burnham, "is the Harrowing of Hell."

"What's that?"

Burnham adopted a look of professorial disappointment. "Did they teach you nothing at Yale? The liberation of the dead. A medieval apocryphon. In the three days between His death and resurrection, Jesus stormed the underworld and released the unbaptized righteous to Heaven. Well, Ari, *I'm* dead. This is *my* three days. So I'm down here freeing some souls, too. Yours. His." He glanced at Vlasic, who took this as a cue, chugged the rest of his Dom like a beer, and got behind the wheel. "Congratulations, my Old Testament friend. You are out of Asha Tamaskar's limbo." With that, he hopped into the back of the Rover, took up one side bench, and patted the other in invitation.

Even in his exhausted state, Falk recognized the wording. It was his own. He had used the limbo analogy with Silje and Christian at the Casa del Popolo. Behind the self-admiring prattle, Burnham was letting him know two things: that the vetting process had been more thorough than he could imagine, and that it was now over.

He'd been checked and approved. He was past the looking glass.

"Well, halle-fucking-lujah," he said, climbing in.

CHAPTER SEVEN

Dulles International Airport, DC
March 29, 2024

Jim Otterbeck looked a mess. Two transatlantic flights in one day had left their mark. His normally smooth cheeks had sprouted untidy blond fuzz, as if he'd fallen face-first into sawdust; the beige linen suit he, for some reason, had on seemed to consist of nothing but creases. To cap it off, he had burst blood vessels in both of his eyes, giving him the appearance of a stressed-out rabbit.

"Take your time. Start whenever." Tamaskar smiled at him across the plastic tablecloth. She had picked the airport's least appealing deli for the meet—a no-name nook between a Hudson News and an Auntie Anne's, serving prepackaged salads and overpriced water.

"Right." Jim rubbed his eyes. "Sorry, ma'am. I'm still kind of gathering my thoughts."

"No worries." Magnanimity came easy, fueled as it was by secret pride. After a single day's weakness, her glossy facade was back up: full makeup, new Moscot frames, not a hair out of place. What swirling terror it held back was nobody's business, least of all Otterbeck's.

"Mind if I just show you?" He took out his phone. "Here. Scroll from this one."

Tamaskar was prepared to see almost anything, but not, it turned out, a casual close-up of Ari Falk. The facade held, barely.

The agent stood in a city square, looking slightly past the camera. An amorphous bronze sculpture dirtied the foreground. Falk's hair had grown back since the first and last time she saw him, nearing its normal messy state but coming in with a stronger salt-to-pepper ratio than before; the dark bags under his eyes were more pronounced. Otherwise, he looked his usual rail-thin, tightly wound, somehow avian self.

Was it possible to miss someone you'd met only once for just a few minutes and hadn't spoken to since? Or was it just trauma manifesting itself in a novel way? She tabled the thought for later.

"Did you do the pass?"

"I did."

"Anyone see you?"

Jim shook his head. "I don't think so."

"Good." The next picture, a smudged snap at the far end of the phone's zoom capacity, showed Falk exiting some architecturally ambitious structure. The raw-cement canopy above the doorway, inlaid with glass triangles, doubled as a footbridge across the street.

"What is this place?"

"A spa. It's where they told him to go. He was in and out in half an hour."

"Why the costume change?" Instead of the black hoodie Falk had worn in the previous photo, he had on a gray T-shirt.

Otterbeck shrugged. "It's pretty warm there."

"Nope." She tapped the image, zooming in. "These jeans are a shade darker. The shoes are different. They gave him new clothes inside. This means they probably have the beacon, too. Expect him to go dark until he figures out a way to send a message."

"Not necessarily," said Otterbeck with an undertone of mischief, and swiped to the next photo for her. This one was shot *from* the footbridge—a top-down view of Falk getting into an ugly little sedan. The driver's face was obscured by the car's A-pillar.

She let him bask in this achievement for exactly two seconds. "Please tell me you got the plates."

Otterbeck sighed and went back to rubbing his eyes. "Yes and no."

"What the fuck does that mean? Also, don't do that. Get some eye drops. There's a pharmacy a few gates down."

"Sorry." He swiped to the last photo, which showed the car driving off. "It's a fake plate. There's no such thing as a DR country code."

Tamaskar felt her lips break out in a smile, as if someone else was stretching them out. "Jim, this is *great.* I mean, yes, it's fake, but in a way that helps us. There's a ninety-nine percent chance this car is going to Germany."

DR: Deutsches Reich. She had heard of the so-called Reichsbürger before: half right-wing movement, half cult, they were the Euro equivalent of the Three Percenters. Their unifying belief held that the current German state was an illegitimate occupying power. Just as with every other anti-government group in the world, the lockdowns of 2020 had turbocharged their madness; the most delusional banded into militias, stockpiled arms, and printed their own passports. And, apparently, license plates.

There was no way Felix Burnham would buy into this bullshit, but as a tactical alliance, it made sense. The "citizens of the Reich" were mad sticklers for privacy. They owned vast tracts of private land. Conflict-averse local authorities were under orders to humor them as much as possible. To be among the Reichsbürger was to be relatively invisible.

Of course Burnham's own roots helped, too. Born Philipp Brenner in the East, he must have still held a so-called yellow certificate in his old name, confirming his historic citizenship. The Reichsbürger, who for some reason revered these certificates as the only legitimate form of ID, would often try to use them in daily life; some even had success crossing EU borders with them. This immediately explained the ease of Burnham's vanishing act. A German but not really German, hiding *inside* Germany but not truly *in* Germany: It all fit.

And then there was Grendel. The name of Burnham's operation, according to Lisichenko. The monster from *Beowulf.*

"How do you know this?" Otterbeck asked.

"Google it," she said. "It's a fun rabbit hole, I promise. Now, before I go, we need to explain your trip. Not much Russia business in Andorra."

"I was actually thinking we'd lean into it," said Otterbeck. "If Spaleta has the Sacs searching for Falk, just tell him I went off the reservation and flew to look for him there. Let them stomp around that spa for the next week." He scrolled back to the first photo: Falk by the bronze sculpture. "I took the liberty of sending it to myself as an anonymous tip the moment I took it. The timing is hinky, but you can finesse it in the report."

"James Otterbeck. You do surprise me."

"Yeah, well," he said. "I mean, I know you all think of me as a careerist little weasel anyway. Might as well weaponize it."

"It's still insubordination." Tamaskar grinned. "Someone's been around Ari Falk too much. I think he's beginning to influence you."

"Gross," said Otterbeck. He got up and left, buying an eight-dollar peach Snapple on the way out.

Tamaskar checked her phone. The flight to Miami was not boarding for two more hours. An astute watcher might notice that she was going on a supposed beach vacation without any luggage; to mitigate that risk, she bought a suitcase in the nearest store and spent the remaining free time filling it up with the cheapest crap she could find.

The gun stayed in her purse, alongside an official letter to the TSA allowing her to carry it on board. She had told Spaleta she'd feel unsafe without it, which happened to be true.

■ ■ ■

Schwarzwald, Germany
March 29, 2024

In picturing Burnham's lair, Falk hadn't been expecting a castle—though on some level, perhaps he had. The building in front of them was a four-story slab of Swabian Baroque, uplit in stripes by dozens of in-ground floodlights. Onion-domed turrets marked each corner; Roman statues crowded the roof of the portico. The Rover came to a stop between the entrance and a perfectly centered fountain. More lights, fitted with red and blue gels, illuminated the lone angel figure on top.

"You like? I don't," said Burnham, watching Falk watch the surroundings. "There's a level of eighteenth-century ornamentation that crosses into body horror. Just absolutely *slithering* with detail."

"Sorry to be rude," Falk replied, "but what the fuck is this place?"

"Ah." Burnham waved his hand dismissively. "A certain prince has been receptive to our ideas. Wants to help the movement." Vlasic killed the engine. They waited while he padded around the car to open the back gate for his master. "Thinks we'll make him the new kaiser. I'm in no hurry to disabuse him of that delusion."

The trio walked toward the portico, gravel crunching underfoot. Two armed guards in tactical gear snapped off a quick salute, ignored by Burnham. Vlasic nodded in response. They were his men, Falk surmised—it made sense that he'd be running the organization's paramilitary side.

"It's too late for a celebratory dinner, alas," said Burnham. They were walking down the endless main corridor, marble with a soft runner rug in the middle. All lights were off; an army of someone's ancestors stared from the walls, though all Falk could really see was moonlight glare on the paint. "It will have to be a celebratory brunch instead. Meanwhile, pick a room. There's about three hundred to choose from."

"How many people do you have in here?"

Burnham shrugged. "Maybe forty at any given point. The locals come and go. For them, it's more of an event space. You seem disappointed. Did you expect something else?"

"I don't know," Falk said. "A gladiator school, I guess. Men running drills in the yard. That sort of thing."

"Right. Alpha Academy made flesh. Imagine the smell." Burnham burst out laughing. "Would it shock you to learn that there are women here, too? And not a harem of depraved Eastern European models you're picturing right now—sorry, old boy. Proper *Hausfrauen*. Families. A couple of kids here and there. Anyway." He opened the nearest door, looked inside, and came back out. "This should do. I trust you won't mind if our Stanley stays close by. You're still in the delousing stage, so to speak." Vlasic grinned, gave Falk a mock salute, and went into the next room over.

"I understand," Falk said. "Thanks for picking me up."

"Night-night."

He walked in. The room looked like a premium suite at a slightly musty hotel: a rolltop desk, a bed under a fringed velvet canopy, a gilded mirror where a TV would normally be hung. The cleaning costs on this place alone must be quite a drain on the GRU budget, Falk thought. A key turned twice in the lock, caging him in for the night.

Falk was staring at the gaunt, half-familiar man in the mirror, wondering if he'd be able to sleep at all, when exhaustion hit him like a truck.

He hadn't had a moment's rest since Pisa, two days ago. He climbed into the creaking bed in his—technically Burnham's—clothes, shut his eyes, and plunged into a deep sleep that felt more like a fainting spell. The last thing he heard was the whir of the ceiling camera, adjusting itself slightly for a better angle.

■ ■ ■

Sea Ranch, California
March 29, 2024

The old man closed his laptop and looked out the window at the Monterey pines standing sentry around the house. Squint past the trunks and you could almost, but never quite, see the ocean. The view was much better from the second floor, but his favorite armchair stood here, in the conversation pit whose walls doubled as bookshelves. He could, he supposed, have it moved to the upstairs study. The man even considered it for a second before deciding that that would be madness. Comfort was a hard-won thing, decades in the making: the silver Moroccan tea tray at arm's reach, his favorite books nearby, the foyer in the line of sight, the leather ottoman scuffed and deflated to the right degree and positioned close enough to the fireplace to warm one's toes without toasting them. A delicate ecosystem.

This must be age, the man thought. Infants and the elderly alike hate to see a routine disrupted, the former because they had just acquired one, the latter because it's about to be taken away. *Then again,* he quickly corrected himself, *when wasn't I like this?* For as long as he remembered himself, everything around him had to be just right. At school. At home. At work. In society at large.

Over the last forty years or so, the world outside these timber walls had benefited as much from his pathological yen for harmony as the world within. Borders redrawn, regimes changed, lives saved and ended: The old man had been instrumental in moving some very heavy furniture indeed. And for a while the general state of things almost satisfied him. Almost.

And now it was all slipping away again.

"There you are," said Jane, as if he'd be anywhere else. He smiled at his wife as she walked up to him, still wreathed in the chill of her afternoon beach walk, and swapped the empty cup on the tray for a stack of newspapers. "Shall I brew a fresh pot?"

"A tisane. I've had enough excitement for the day."

"Aw," she said in mock compassion, which he knew happened to mask real sympathy. "Then perhaps I better take this." She reached for the copy of the *Times*.

"Just the crossword," the man said, snatching the paper back. He was already up on most of the day's developments. Tucked deep into the org chart at one of his European companies was a twelve-person department tasked solely with assembling his morning briefings. The result of their work was a daily collage of mainstream news in every political hue, cut with (and often refuted by) original reporting, OSINT, and illegal intercepts of illegal intercepts by three of the world's top intelligence agencies. If it had been an actual publication, it would have been the most accurate news source on Earth—which is why even the people putting it together weren't allowed to see the whole document.

"Any calls?" he asked. The house had no phone, and neither did its two inhabitants. Instead, Jane's daily walks took her to the Sea Ranch Lodge, where the nice receptionist let her use the hotel's line to check a certain voicemail.

"Yes." Jane emerged from the kitchen. "That abominable would-be despot."

"I'm afraid you'll have to be more specific, dear."

"The not-quite-Brit." She knit her brow, then snapped her fingers. "Felix Burnham."

"What did he say?"

"He wanted to let you know that someone has arrived and that it's all *going to plan,*" Jane said, affecting the late queen's coo for the last three words. To his ear, it sounded more like Julia Child. "We have chamomile and ginger."

"Ginger, please and thank you." The old man shook the Arts & Leisure section out of the *Times* and let the rest fall to the floor. A certain calm spread through him, a warm sense that things still might, just might, work out. That the world, so hopelessly off-axis as of late, could be course-corrected after all.

He groaned as he reached for his favorite pen on the bookshelf, then sighed as he made himself comfortable again. *And to think I almost ruined this setup for the view. There's always another way.* He glanced outside one more time and immediately identified which three pine trees he would need to cut down in order to see the ocean from his chair.

■ ■ ■

Falk woke up to the sun streaming through the curtains. The dream had involved Asha Tamaskar, but in what context—threatening, erotic, absurd—he couldn't remember. The gap between deep sleep and full consciousness was a hairline fissure, half a second at most, but nothing had traveled across it. That half a second before his spy brain came back online, however, was filled with the purest panic he had ever experienced.

On the tufted footboard bench lay his clothes from the Andorran spa, all freshly laundered, folded, and laid out as if for a photo shoot. Ten percent courtesy, ninety percent domination: message received. His phone and watch, also collected by Rudi, naturally weren't there. Nor, more important, was the key fob with the built-in beacon.

Falk had showered and almost dressed when someone knocked on the door. From the weight of the fist involved, he guessed his neighbor Vlasic.

"Let's not pretend you have to do that," he yelled. The ex-Sac unlocked the door and walked in, mid-smirk.

"'Sup?"

"Hey. They're waiting downstairs."

Falk zipped up the newly clean hoodie and followed him out. "What time is it, by the way?"

Vlasic turned his head. "Dinnertime, dude. You were out for fifteen hours. Tough week, huh?" At least for the moment, he seemed to genuinely enjoy having another American male of his age around. The assembled internationale must have grated on his soldier nerves at least a little.

"You could say that."

Burnham hadn't been kidding about a celebratory meal. A long table, set across what must have once been a formal reception hall, held enough food and wine for a midsize wedding. A couple of guards walked the room's perimeter, casually toting Heckler & Koch assault rifles. The guests, twelve or so men and a couple of older women, appeared to be a mix of full-time Burnhamites and the local Reichsbürger elite. Falk recognized the two Orlok mercs from the photos Asha had shown him; they sat off to the side, conversing quietly over beers in gutter Russian.

The man himself presided at the head of the table, wearing his idea of a casual weekend outfit: white dress shirt, cream linen jacket, and pink slacks. Upon seeing the new arrivals, he got up and gestured to an empty seat beside him. All conversations stopped. Gilded frippery aside, there was a definite whiff of the barrack in the room.

"*Meine Damen und Herren,*" Burnham said, "*Der Falke ist gelandet.* Please meet a new addition to our aviary, a reformed raptor, Mr. Ari Falk."

Smiles and nods all around. Falk took his place, discreetly scanning the faces for reactions to the name Ari. A server in a modified black-and-white dirndl emerged from the wings and silently poured him a glass of Spätburgunder. The last thing in the world he wanted ten minutes after waking up was red wine, but he took a sip out of politeness.

"Too sharp, right?" Burnham said, evidently attuned to Falk's every microexpression. He gestured for the woman to pour him some, too, tried it, and grimaced. "Watch this. Old Oxford trick." He raised the wine in his right hand, covered the rim with his left, and violently swung the glass down and back up, almost smashing it against the table. "Instant aeration. A risky move, but the difference is palpable."

An *insane* move for a man in a white shirt, Falk thought. Revealing, too: One would have to be extremely confident in his control over his actions. He made a mental note. Burnham wiped his red-slicked fingers with a cloth napkin, tossed it aside, and took a swig.

"Well, that opened up nicely," he said. "Try it yourself." Falk gingerly repeated the trick, feeling like he was being tested. He spilled only a few drops.

"*Nebo i zemlya,*" he said in Russian, an idiom for a vast difference. It was his turn to do some testing. In his videos, Burnham always preened about having read Tolstoy in the original.

"Heaven and earth indeed," Burnham said. "Beautiful language."

With this, he seemed to have lost interest in Falk for the next hour. Wisps of hushed German conversation hung over the table. Demure all-female staff, floating in and out of the hall's hidden recesses, cleared the plates and served dessert. Most of the guests said their goodbyes, shook the host's hand, and took off, leaving behind the core group of hard-looking men.

"There he is!" Burnham exclaimed in English and clapped. Falk followed the line of his eyes and saw Rudi. The fat gofer loitered in the doors, seemingly cowed by the honor—he must have seldom, if ever, made it inside the castle before. It took the boss's explicit hand signal for him to unglue himself from the doorjamb, walk up to Burnham, and hand him a little plastic bag. Falk overheard a terse "*Alles in Ordnung.*"

Burnham glanced inside the bag, nodded, and upended it on the table in front of Falk. Inside were his wallet, watch, keys to the Pisan Airbnb, and the Fiat fob. It took all Falk's self-control not to go for the fob first.

"Thank you for your patience, Ari," Burnham said. "As promised, the delousing is almost complete. We took the liberty of disposing of your phone. Sorry about that, but as you may have noticed, we have a 'no phones, no computers' policy out here."

"It would be strange if you didn't," Falk replied, leisurely putting on the watch.

"Hang on a sec, Chief." On the opposite end of the table, Stan Vlasic got up, all the dudebro geniality gone from his face. He loped over, bent down next to Burnham, and whispered in his ear at length. He then reached across the entire tabletop, which presented no challenge to him, grabbed the fob from under Falk's nose, and began to consider it from every angle. The process made him look like an ape studying a walnut.

"Say the same thing aloud," Burnham suggested. "Let him explain."

"Let me explain what?" Falk adopted a look of bored dismay, as if to say *This is unpleasant, but I don't really care how it shakes out.*

"Chief, you've read the reports," said Vlasic. "Same as I did. He *biked* to Casa del Popolo. She didn't see him drive *once* over a full week of observation. And there were no car keys or documents found at the house. So what is this thing?"

Even in a moment of such precarity, a part of Falk was a little hurt to learn that Silje had gone home with him as an integral part of her assignment. *Oh well. Right back atcha.*

"I see." He chuckled. "This, gentlemen, is what happens when Special Activities tries to do analysis."

This got Vlasic's goat pretty good. The ex-Sac glared at him from Burnham's side, jowls moving like pistons under the pink skin. The Russian mercenaries laughed, after one translated the quip to the other. Everyone in the room was now tuned in, including the guys with the assault rifles.

"First of all, *obviously*, I bought the car for cash under a different name," Falk continued. "I am not a moron. The point of a getaway vehicle is to get away, no? Who drives in the center of Pisa? And I paid the old owner extra to keep it in his garage. Tradecraft 101. Honestly, bro, you're welcome to that piece of shit. Zero to sixty in sixty seconds." This made Burnham crack a smile. "I can give you the address right now."

"It's a start," said Vlasic. "Rudi, go contact Christian." *Goddamn it.* The offer was, of course, a bluff.

"But look, there's an even easier way," Falk quickly said, monitoring Burnham's face out of a corner of his eye. The goal was to convince Burnham—not Vlasic, not Rudi, not the Russians. "You have the thing in your hand. Click it. Take it apart. Hit it with a hammer. What do you think it will do, blow up?"

He swiveled toward the mercs, remembering Tamaskar's words. *There's a demolition expert here, fuck's sake.* "Hey, lads," he yelled in Russian, knowing Burnham would understand, but Vlasic wouldn't. "Anyone know anything about explosives? Come take a look. This dude thinks I came here straight from the Q Branch."

"All right, all right. Enough." Burnham cleared his throat. "Stanley, do settle down. I appreciate the fervor, but your social skills need work. Ever heard of 'Trust but verify'? Or course you have. Reagan's favorite saying. Well, by the very properties of the coordinating conjunction at its center, it also means 'Verify but trust.' Our friend here *has* been verified. And not just by you or Rudi or Christian or Silje."

He took the fob from Vlasic's hand and tossed it to Falk across the wine-stained table. Falk caught it, almost clicking it right there and then. His finger froze over the unlock button.

One click, and the hideout's precise location would hit Jim Otterbeck's phone. One click, and his months-long job would be done.

Yet something about Burnham's very last sentence, though clearly intended as comfort, put Falk more on edge than anything that had come before.

"Everyone out of the room," said Burnham calmly. "Yes, you, too, gentlemen," he called out to the guards. "Not you, Ari. You stay for a minute."

Rudi, the Russians, and a pissed-off Vlasic shuffled toward the exit. The rifle contingent reluctantly followed. Burnham and Falk sat in the empty reception hall, under a ludicrous chandelier, studying each other.

"Now, if you are at all concerned about your status," said Burnham finally, "here is what I have been authorized to say to you. Your old friend—your *very* old friend—says hi. I don't know what name you know him by, but his message to you is simple. All is conditionally forgiven. Bygones are bygones. Prove yourself in action, and you will be safe."

"Thank you," said Falk, through a screen of fine red mist filling up his field of vision.

"You'll receive your marching orders tomorrow. For now, relax. Our lovely servers are off-limits, I must warn you, but if you have any needs in that department, tell Stanley and he'll arrange a visitation."

"I'm fine." The mist darkened.

"Good man."

It took several minutes for Falk to make his way upstairs and find his room, or maybe another one just like it. Once inside, he dashed straight to the toilet and puked out the dinner and the wine, until the only thing left for his body to eject was foaming bile.

Then he lifted the foot of the ancient bed, put the fob under it, and smashed it a dozen or so times until the pieces were small enough to go into the toilet bowl, too.

His first and wildest instincts had been right. Deniable Russian money. A high-level CIA cover. No fingerprints on either. Felix Burnham was a Cormorant op.

Cormorant was real, alive, active, an invisible third party in the new East-West standoff, just as he had been in the old one. A ghost in the machine of modern history.

It was Cormorant who'd had Petra and Keegan followed and killed, to contain the mystery of Burnham's financing.

Any attempt to stop Burnham on Asha Tamaskar's part would mean her end.

Any attempt on Falk's part to contact her or Otterbeck would mean putting them in mortal danger.

At least he was in. He didn't yet know in *what*—that would come tomorrow—but he was in, and would stay in, because the only way out was through. Unlike in the hackneyed quote, however, he'd have to go this way alone.

■ ■ ■

Miami Beach, Florida
March 30, 2024

Kate Liss was furious. If she had been going to her usual morning yoga, it would have ruined her concentration. Luckily, this time the text from work caught her on the way to a spin class, so she was able to channel her ire into pure pedal-pushing aggression instead.

Just who the hell did Ilya think he was? She had taken the job with one explicit stipulation: *work from home only*. LQuid Labs had a physical office—a penthouse suite in an aparthotel on Collins, in Surfside—but it skeeved her out. The type of people who came in and out of there were not Kate's crowd. (Take security: What's the point of a shiny, all-American crypto start-up if you keep hiring the same type of ugly bruiser who'd be lucky to guard a shopping mall back in Russia?) Yet Ilya, the founder, kept calling her in. First it was monthly, for big-picture strategy sessions. Fine. Then weekly briefings, each of which could have been an email. And now an emergency in-person meeting on a Saturday? At ten a.m.? Fucking hell. It's like Covid was all for nothing.

Maybe he was under pressure to justify the office costs. Fair enough, since she knew he kept billing Moscow for twice the actual rent. But so what? She'd seen the numbers. They had all the money in the world. Even doubled, the rent on a penthouse in some shitty building, on a dumb sandbank that would be underwater in ten years anyway, was less than a rounding error. Her salary alone was five times that.

Or hey, maybe Ilya was just into her. Plausible, in fact probable, not even altogether unwelcome, but what the fuck. In Kate's experience with amorous bosses, this normally entailed late nights, not weekend mornings.

The class came to an end with an instructor-led round of self-applause. Kate dismounted, still vaguely annoyed but mostly pacified: The endorphins did their job. On the way to the showers, she even paused by the hallway mirror and found the light good enough, and her skin glowing enough in it, to take a few photos. At least three or four classmates stood around doing the same; no one with her bone structure, though, Kate noted, and felt her mood improve a little more. By the time she got to the building, she was almost okay.

The LQuid Labs office was a repurposed five-bedroom apartment, with elevator doors opening directly onto a round foyer with the guard's desk. Today it stood empty, which was frankly a relief. Kate badged in and marched straight to the bay-facing conference room, where staff meetings tended to take place. The clack of her Ferragamos echoed through the suite, announcing her loudly enough that anyone present would normally pop out and say hi. No one did.

"Ilya?" A heap of documents lay strewn across the conference table, a highly atypical sight. There had to have been an all-hands-on-deck situation. She came in to check it out. Up close, the paper selection made no sense: banking statements, customs forms, packing slips, even a takeout menu.

"Ilya? Hello?" No response. Instead, a set of automated shades came to life, unspooling over every floor-to-ceiling window.

"Ilya, *nu ne smeshno, blyad.* This isn't fucking funny." Kate spun around, anxious to leave the rapidly darkening room, and shrieked.

Behind the luxury facade, she was still a girl from a mining town. She'd had guns pointed at her before. Just never by a woman in tortoiseshell glasses.

■ ■ ■

She really did look a little like Lisichenko, this one. Same cheekbones. But where the real article was all hostile, defiant energy, the fugazi version, despite every cosmetic treatment known to modern womanhood, just looked tired and mad. Years of a double life would do that to a gal.

"Sit down," Tamaskar said. Liss half fell into the nearest chair, which, in an accidental bit of slapstick, rolled backward until she grabbed the table to stop it.

"Stay there. Slide your phone over." She did.

"All right. I'm not going to keep pointing this thing at you. But try anything and I'll shoot way before you're up on your feet. Especially in those." She used the gun to indicate the woman's thousand-dollar heels, then set it down on the table. In truth, she did it because her hand was beginning to shake, which would put the lie to the coldly competent vibe she was trying to project.

"My boss is going to be here any minute," said Liss.

"No he's not," Tamaskar scoffed. "Ilya Chapurin is in Key West with his Cuban boyfriend. None of your security guys are coming in, either. Screaming won't help, the floor below you is unoccupied. The cameras are off. Have we covered every possible bluff? Good." Ironically, she was the one bluffing. Having arrived the previous afternoon, Tamaskar had only been able to scope out the building once.

Liss bit her lip. "There's no money in here."

"You don't seriously think I'm here to rob you. Can we please move it along? The faster we start, the faster we finish."

"Well, what do you want, lady? Information? I don't know anything. We're a fintech start-up. We build products that make it easier to convert crypto to fiat and back, that's it. And I don't even do *that*. I'm on the sales side."

"What you do in your spare time does not concern me," said Tamaskar. "I'm interested in your main line of work: sitting on a giant bag of Kremlin money."

"I have no idea what you're talking about."

"Okay, let's start with the easy stuff then. What's your real name?"

"Kate . . . Fine, you got me. Katya Lisichenko. I shortened it for the Americans."

"Keep her name out of your fucking mouth," Tamaskar barked, surprising herself. She thought she had been largely performing this persona for the other woman's benefit, but apparently it was there all along. "I said your *real* one."

Liss stared at her in confusion that, for the first time, read as genuine. It occurred to Tamaskar that she might be simply unaware of her cover's origin.

"All right, long version it is," she said. "It's two years ago. Your country has just invaded Ukraine for some goddamn reason and is about to be cut off from the world's financial systems as a result. So your bosses at Orlan Finans hand you a drive with hundreds of millions in crypto, a passport in a new name, and a ticket. This part you obviously know. Here's one you might not: They had to act so fast, they just took your new identity from the nearest colleague who looked kind of like you. It was a clever choice, too. The real Katya Lisichenko was up to her ears in GRU associations from her last place of work. No one would let her out of Russia, certainly not during a war. What would she need a passport for?"

"The *real* Katya Lisichenko?"

"Yes. Kate Liss is a copy of a copy."

The woman fell silent for a while. When she spoke up again, her voice was different, quiet and dull. She sounded like an actress who just finished her big scene and was now telling the PA her lunch order. "I was wondering why they gave me a Ukrainian last name. Seemed like a strange joke to make at the moment."

"Good," said Tamaskar. "We're talking. Let's keep talking. Now, obviously, you couldn't just waltz into the United States and cash out. That would create a—what is it you douchebags call it? A *taxable event*. No, you needed a whole new infrastructure around it. That's why they sent *you*, not just the money itself. So you dressed it up. Hired a few tech guys, called it a dumb name. Best job in the world. Bet they even let you skim off the top a little. All you have to do is not ask any questions and occasionally move some of it to whatever crypto wallet they tell you. Right?" The false Katya blankly stared at the glass tabletop.

"Do you even know who's on the other side of these transactions?" Tamaskar pressed. "Do you know you've been financing some of the worst people in the world? Including those who, if they come to power, will make sure an ambitious woman like you stays home barefoot and pregnant."

"Oh my god, stop." It was Liss's turn to sneer now. "Not this sanctimonious bullshit. What are you, CIA? NSA? ATF? Yeah, all great guys, I'm sure. You're happy they let you into their club? A little Brown lady with a big career? So important, you're going to die in a one-bedroom apartment with a cat. Maybe a medal on the wall, for catching the scary Russian. All while your bosses make billion-dollar deals with Saudi Arabia. Talk about the worst people in the world, Jesus. It's all a scam. Either you scam the scammers or you're too dumb to."

Tamaskar decided to let her rant until she tired herself out. She visualized a protective field, a carapace, an energy shield for Liss's words to bounce against; even so, a few poisoned pellets got through. The one about the cat hurt.

"Why are you even here?" the woman continued to yell. "If you know everything, what do you need me for? Let me guess—nothing better to do. You don't love anyone. You don't *have* anyone. All you have is this. You do this or you're no one. Me, I'm myself whoever I work for, whatever my name is. Because I am a person. You're just your job."

All right, enough of this. "What is Grendel?"

"What's what?" Judging by the speed with which the word knocked Liss off her high horse, she had heard it before. Tamaskar put her palm on the gun for emphasis. "Grendel. What is it?"

"An account."

"Whose?"

"I don't know. It's a string of numbers. They all are."

"Show me."

She recognized the new look on Liss's face. The woman was doing every turncoat's mental math: the short-term risks of staying mum versus the potentially terrible cost of talking.

"I'll need protection," she finally said.

"You're already stateside with three names to choose from. Doesn't get safer than that."

Liss thought a little more, then indicated she was about to get up. Tamaskar grabbed the gun and followed her out to the warren of cubicles set up in what, in an apartment, would have been the living room.

"I show this to you and we're good," said Liss, logging into a laptop via a thumb scanner. "Right?"

"Never better." *What a waste of an asset*, Tamaskar thought. Flipping someone like Kate Liss would have given Covert Activities access to a massive trove of first-grade intel. But CA was compromised, and there was no way to bring her in through proper channels without exposing the rest of the operation. Cut out the cancer first.

Liss signed into a proprietary interface and pulled up what looked like a long ledger. "Whoa, okay, correction," she said. "Grendel is a whole bunch of accounts."

Tamaskar looked over her shoulder. The list of payments went on for screen after screen, each with a new recipient. Most were in bitcoin and ether. Unusually, a few of the numbers had a plus sign next to them.

"Looks like some of it is funds coming *to* you."

"Yeah, I don't know what to tell you," said Liss. "This is Ilya's shit."

"Do you mind?" Tamaskar squeezed in front of the computer and pushed her aside. "Go sit over there." She pointed at a spot within her peripheral vision. Liss reluctantly changed chairs. Tamaskar showed her the gun once more, this time eliciting a teenager-style eye roll, and kept scrolling.

Looking for patterns in massive amounts of data was not just her forte, the thing that made her name and reputation as an analyst, but one of her favorite things to do. Despite the intensity of the moment, she found herself getting sucked in by the work.

A dozen or so screens in, she felt that familiar, ineffable brain itch that was the first sign of success. She didn't see the pattern itself yet, but already knew there was one. Tamaskar scrolled backward, then forward again. *There*: A few of the amounts repeated, down to the smallest fraction, as credit and debit. There was always enough time between transactions so it didn't jump out at first, but the more she looked, the more these coincidences kept piling up. Moreover, each time it happened, the back-and-forth was followed by a large outgoing payment.

By the time she rewound the list back three months, she was sure she wasn't reading order into chaos: The same bits of crypto kept coming in and out, regardless of the rate fluctuations in between. It made no sense.

Except it did. You just had to look at it as a different system.

"Hey," Tamaskar called out, "can you embed nonfinancial data within cryptocurrency?"

"Yes, of course. Dates, times, pictures. Tokens. Porn links. You name it."

"Encoded?"

"If you want."

"In that case, I have news for you. Grendel is not a ledger, it's a switchboard. Someone's using it to send messages back and forth. You're buying information from one party and passing it on to another, except the payment and the information are the same thing."

"May I remind you that I don't care?" Liss responded, having apparently adjusted to the situation enough to be catty.

Tamaskar sighed. "And may *I* remind you that I'm five foot three and have no upper-body strength, so shooting you is the only move I got?" She opened one of the double transactions. A block of letters and numbers filled half the screen. "Now, can you extract and decode what it says?"

"Ilya can."

"Then get over here and be Ilya."

"Christ." Liss came back, sat in Tamaskar's place, and logged out and back in, pulling up the command-line interface to override the biometric reader. *Credit where credit is due*, Tamaskar thought; *girl knows what she's doing*. The process took her several minutes. "There. It's some crap in German."

"Let me see." The ASCII text on the screen read *Terminkalender*, followed by times and places. "It's a hack of someone's appointment schedule. Let's try one more."

Wrapped in the next in-and-out transaction was an architectural blueprint of a building. Tamaskar didn't need to wonder which one; the file name, *Hardthöhe*, spoke for itself. It was a very, very famous address in Bonn.

"*Next.*"

Line by line, the code on the screen transfigured into a low-res photo scan: a fifty-something in a suit, getting out of a black sedan. Someone had drawn a circle around the car's license plate and added a string of data over it. Tamaskar recognized it as a VIN number.

She also recognized the man. She had *met* the man, at a Ukraine Defense Contact Group summit at Ramstein. He hadn't taken his post yet, but was already floating the proposal that would deliver him into it: long-range U.S. missiles on German soil. Dark Eagles, SM-6s, Tomahawks, all pointed east.

"Hey," said Liss, whipping around. She now seemed more alarmed by what she was seeing than by the gun at her back. "Hey, lady, I have nothing to do with this. You have to believe me. It's the first time I'm seeing any of it."

"I believe you. I also believed you when you said you didn't care," Tamaskar said.

"Yes, but this is too much," Liss stammered. "This is not me. Okay?"

"Get ahold of yourself. Ilya's not back until Monday."

"So?"

"So you have forty-eight hours to disappear." Tamaskar slammed the laptop shut, grabbed it, and headed out to the foyer. The elevator was still there; the building was, indeed, all but empty.

"Don't leave me like this," Liss called out in desperation from the depths of the office. "They'll find me. Please. Look, my name is Yulia, okay?! Do you hear me? Yulia Baranova!"

"Not for long," Tamaskar muttered into the closing doors.

The elevator began to move. She leaned back against its wall, breathing fast and shallow, her mind in roaring overdrive but doing donuts around a single thought. She almost walked out into the street with the gun still in her hand, shoving it into her purse, next to the laptop, at the last moment.

Collins Avenue, in this stretch, was mostly low-rise condos that seemed to come in two states: under construction and in decay. Tamaskar sped-walked south for a few blocks, toward the part recently renamed the Jimmy Buffett Memorial Highway, then took out her clean phone.

"Is he online yet?"

"No, still dark," said Otterbeck. "I keep staring at the map, waiting for the dot to pop up."

"Jim, there's new developments. You need to pull him."

"How can I pull him when he's dark?"

Tamaskar's head spun; she slowed her steps and sat down on the nearest bus bench. Humid Florida air felt like Saran wrap around her whole body. Her heart beat so fast she thought she might pass out. Part of it was the adrenaline comedown, part something else.

"He'll figure it out," Otterbeck offered, trying to be helpful. "He'll steal a phone or something. You know him."

"Yeah. You're right. Yeah." Tamaskar hung up.

A bus came, disgorged a couple of elderly locals, and left, and still she sat on the bench, poring over her own feelings like an intel brief, because they didn't line up with her sense of self at all.

She had just won the battle. She uncovered Burnham's mission: a GRU-funded assassination plot against Florian Reschke, Germany's new minister of defense. A plot someone at her beloved Agency either abetted or tolerated.

And yet she was more worried about Ari Falk than anything else.

"Oh, *fuck*," she said out loud. The false Lisichenko had been wrong—the one time, and in the one aspect, where Tamaskar would have preferred her to be right.

She was not her job. And she did love someone.

CHAPTER EIGHT

Schwarzwald, Germany
March 30, 2024

On the second night, owing perhaps to his new status, the intrusion was more subtle: Someone slipped a piece of paper under the door. Falk woke, this time from a nightmare where he fought a shapeless mass that was and wasn't Cormorant, and found the note on the rug. Written in a slanted doctor's scrawl on the Alpha Academy letterhead (fist, sword, etc.), it was a personal invitation to lunch from Professor Felix Burnham. It requested Mr. Falk's presence by the fountain at noon sharp.

Burnham surprised him by pulling up in a mid-sixties Pagoda roadster. He was driving himself this time, and had dressed for the occasion like even more of a P. G. Wodehouse character than usual.

"Are we, uh, going somewhere?" Falk asked, climbing in.

"Sadly, not too far." Burnham gunned the engine. "Indulge me. I've been pupating here for years. I like to give myself an illusion of freedom every once in a while."

The ride took four minutes at the reckless average of 80-odd mph over gravel and cobblestone. Short but still insane for private property, Falk thought: The estate must have been at least five miles in diameter.

The car screeched to a stop by a pseudo-fortress of mossy brick, surrounded by old oaks and elms. Somehow, even without the vats in the back and the pervasive smell of yeast in the air, it was immediately recognizable as a brewery.

"Changing minds and making beers," Falk said.

"Ha. Well, the prince may not believe in taxes, but the government still does. Nothing like a failing little enterprise to keep it at bay." Burnham walked to the barn doors in the back of the building and rolled them open with the gusto of a man who gets to do physical work only as a treat. Inside was a damp, vaulted dining hall, with all the tables pushed to the walls but one, preset with a lacy cloth and Meissen porcelain. The sight struck Falk as something out of a Kubrick movie or simply a continuation of a bad dream. A silent server—male this time—brought fizzy water and ladled some Flädlesuppe onto the plates.

They began to eat, Falk stealthily checking the corners for cameras. A part of him fixated on the rolled-up crepe strips that unfolded like tentacles in the broth. Another part calculated the speed and strength needed to break Burnham's neck, grab the keys to the Pagoda, and drive away.

But what would that accomplish? Whatever plan Cormorant had already put in motion might still proceed. Proving that Keegan's murder hadn't been stochastic would be impossible without the real culprit alive. And any retaliation would target Asha first. The only play was to wait.

Burnham misread his darting looks. "Part of Germany's sick fascination with American Blackness," he said. It took Falk several seconds to understand what he meant: The top of the wooden bar in the back of the room held a row of "jazzmen" figurines. "Must be the Jesse Owens effect still."

"I can see why you like the place," Falk quipped. Since his cover persona was not racist but merely misogynistic, he figured he could afford a light jab. Staying too obsequious might trip some alarms.

To his surprise, Burnham took offense. "Come on. I expect better of you. Just because I detest identity politics doesn't make me a caveman like Rudi."

"Sorry. I— Look, I . . ." It was weirdly hard to figure out how much or how little he could say while staying in character. "Isn't the whole thing a deflection, ultimately? Five billionaires control the global flow of data, so let's all argue about the skin tone of a mermaid instead."

Burnham laughed. "But can't you see that that's the only way to make them do something about the billionaires? You have to harness whatever makes people angriest, and right now it's the fear of becoming a minority. You say deflection, I say disruption."

"So you're what, a leftist at heart?"

"I am a Bakunin-style anarchist if I'm anything at all," said Burnham, finishing his soup. "I want a vast tapestry of self-rule. I want people deciding their own fate, not nation-states and corporations. But you can't say that out loud without consigning yourself to the loony bin." He gestured for a change of plates. "God, it's nice to talk to someone who's not an idiot for a change."

The next course was a pale stack of weisswurst with a cowpat of mash. "Speaking of idiots," Falk said once the server was out of earshot, "the Reichsbürger? Come on. This has to be a ploy."

"Whatever do you mean? I find them delightful," Burnham said with a crooked smirk. "By the way, did you know that a big part of their dream is to negotiate a proper World War Two surrender as their first act in power? A nation so thoroughly cucked, it boggles the mind."

"You talk about it from such a remove," said Falk. "Aren't you German?"

"Mmm. Complicated, my boy. Complicated." Burnham winced,

paused, took a bread roll, and ate the whole thing before continuing. "Yes, I grew up in Dresden. My family moved to America as refugees just before the Wall fell. I was stateless for most of my formative years, thirteen to twenty. The weird kid in the corner with a book of Rilke poems. Did I mention we were living in Cleveland at the time?" He chuckled, and so, despite himself, did Falk.

"By the age of eighteen," Burnham went on, "I had made some money doing odd jobs, and was dying to see old friends because I'd made no new ones. So I blew it all on a plane ticket home. You can imagine how those boors at passport control looked at me, with my brown Refugee Travel Document. But to the kids back in Dresden, I was already an American, see? So I had a pretty good time. Fucked every girl from my school I ever had a childhood crush on. Barely forced myself to get back."

"Nice," Falk said, cringing inside. *Is he really opening up to me, or does he talk to everyone like that?*

"I promise you there's a point to this," said Burnham. "A couple of years later, we got *naturalized.* What a word. I still remember that idiotic pledge: 'I renounce every foreign prince and potentate!' Such flowery language, such banality. All those poor Mexicans around me, barely forming the same sentences. Each as valuable a citizen as I. And my parents—oh, they were so delighted. I couldn't tell them I *missed* being stateless. Turns out, my normal state, my base condition, Ari, is that of not belonging anywhere at all. I liked being an American fine, but I liked being *nothing* so much more." He pushed the plate away. "I'm sure you get this, as a Jew."

"To an extent."

"Ugh," said Burnham. "Now I'm sentimental. Never get sentimental at lunch."

"Last night, you mentioned my marching orders," Falk said. He'd had enough of the man's musings.

"Right. To the business at hand, then," said Burnham. "Though I do enjoy just chatting with you, in case that wasn't clear yet."

"Thank you. Same."

"The job is exceedingly simple. On Tuesday, I want you to take Oleg and Kostya and go to Bonn."

"What's in Bonn?" Falk asked. The perspective of a day trip with two Orlok mercenaries in tow didn't thrill him, but the idea of going outside did: Even stripped of all devices, he'd finally be able to learn the hideout's location. All it required was to count the turns and guess at distances until they passed by anything that looked or sounded memorable. This was a basic skill from Falk's Camp Peary days; he could do it with a hood over his head, and had, in fact.

"A person from whom I've been buying vital intel," said Burnham. "I just got word from the U.S. that our current comms channel has been rumbled. A new one, in these circumstances, means in-person courier service. Luckily, it's a nice drive, even with those two animals stinking up the auto."

"So what do I need them for?" Falk asked, already dreading the answer.

"Let's put it this way." Burnham paused. "Sometimes a new channel means deleting the old one."

That was that, then. He was being sent out on a hit. "Don't you, uh, already have a guy with proper training for this kind of stuff?"

"Who, Stanley?" Burnham laughed. "Stanley is my *Glücksschwein*, my lucky pig. I need someone with an actual brain overseeing things. No, no, you, Ari, are a crucial piece of this puzzle. I'm sorry I can't reveal the whole picture to you quite yet, but trust me, you are. We couldn't have set it in motion without you."

"Well, in that case," said Falk, "I do have to ask. You 'got word' from the U.S.? How?"

Burnham smiled, reached into his breast pocket, and produced a new iPhone. After several days of involuntary digital detox, the very sight of it felt oddly thrilling. "I know, I know, unfair. Rex facit legem."

"Quod licet Jovi, non licet bovi," Falk responded. *That's right, I went to a good school, too, fucker.* "A little unsafe, though, no?"

"Well, obviously, it's just a box now," said Burnham. "There's no SIM card. And there's no signal anywhere on the property. Since I've, um, educated the prince about the perils of 5G, he's spent about a million putting in jammers." He laughed a wheezing laugh. "Oh, amazing, Trempel's! Otto, *du hast dich selbst übertroffen.*"

The server brought in a round turquoise pastry box, held together by a silk bow he ceremoniously proceeded to untie. Inside was a chocolate torte with lacy red piping. Bits of gold leaf fluttered on top.

"I'm not much of a dessert guy," Falk said, his mind elsewhere. If Burnham had a working phone with no SIM and no cellular signal, this had to mean an internet hot spot somewhere on the premises. It would most likely be in whatever room Burnham used to record his videos, and would turn on and off at his command.

"Some men find a sweet tooth feminine. A terrible mistake." Burnham was already devouring his slice. "Oh well, more for me. Otto, put Mr. Falk's portion back in the box. See, Ari," he continued through a mouthful of chocolate, "small-scale is the only true luxury left. A product like Trempel's is achievable only by a true family business. A dynasty outlasting any regime. The moment they open a second location is the moment greed wins and quality dies." He was quoting his own lecture now; Falk was getting a private show, The Felix Burnham Experience.

Thousands of men go into debt to hear this stuff, Falk fleetingly thought. He wasn't listening. Jittery excitement coursed through him, a sugar rush without any need for cake. He had just received his marching orders—just not the kind Burnham meant.

■ ■ ■

McLean, Virginia
April 1, 2024

Miami seemed to have done to Deputy Director Tamaskar the exact opposite of what Miami was supposed to do to people: She had come back wired, impatient, spinning at twice her usual rpm. Whenever someone spoke to her, she either barely listened, saying "uh-huh" with a glassy stare, or spooled invisible yarn around her index finger in the international get-to-the-point gesture. The first thing she had done after coming in on Monday, inexplicably, was get rid of Harlow's desk and order a new one, letting Valerie pick one at random from the office catalogue. From her panicked call over the weekend, Jim knew it all must have had something to do with Falk's vanishing, but little else.

He, in the meantime, had taken his lumps for the unsanctioned trip to Andorra, and was now firmly chained to his desk on the Russia floor. His foreseeable future looked bleaker than Russia's: Regional Impoverishment Trends all the way to the horizon and beyond. Frankly, Jim had been expecting that his selfless offer to fall on his sword for the boss would merit at least some loyalty in return. Instead, Tamaskar seemed to have forgotten about his existence at all.

So, when she finally texted him on Monday afternoon and told him to pick up a file from a guy named Dave Patero at the Operations Support Branch, Jim met the news with half relief and half chagrin. If this had been any other kind of relationship, he'd feel used.

Having to schlep to the OSB in person was classic Langley kabuki. Secret files moved through the system at a snail's pace; it was often easier to literally walk something across town than to get the permission to email it. (In 2021, when FleaCollar published the Harlow Dossier, employees without top-level clearance could theoretically be fined or fired for laying eyes on it, despite the fact it was available to everyone in the world.) As Jim passed the branch's own extra-stringent security perimeter, the guards made him give up his devices, as if the whole building was a SCIF. He walked in already pre-annoyed.

The sensation deepened once he made it to the ninth floor. The rumors had been true: The unofficial OSB uniform was shorts, sweats, and band tees. A building full of Falks. Jim, in his rep tie, felt sarcastic glances from cubicle after cubicle as he strode past. He tried to hold his head high. *Feast your eyes, nerds, here's what a real Agency man looks like.*

Patero, a walking goatee in an aloha shirt, met him by the coffee machine, handed him a manila envelope, said "peace," and was about to leave when Jim noticed something. "Wait," he called out, "this has no SCI stamp on it."

Patero turned around. "That's right, because I'm not SCI. Despite what your ladyboss explicitly promised."

"Yeah," said Jim, "she does that. So why didn't you just email it? You know I had to drag my butt here all the way from the Campus, right?"

"Well, if you care to hear *my* theory," Patero said with a smirk, "it's that none of this is on the books, and she's picking out the most expendable minions she can find."

Jim had not heard it phrased quite like this yet, and didn't like how close to the bone it cut. "Don't—don't say that. Jesus."

"Yeah, whatever, Book of Mormon," said Patero and walked away carrying a full cup of coffee with no lid. Jim stifled an urge to clap behind his ears so he'd spill it.

"That's a letter to HR right there," he mumbled instead.

Tamaskar sat in her office, drumming her fingers on the new glass desk. She waved Jim in, grabbed the envelope without saying a word, and shook its contents onto the desktop. It was a stack of blown-up, time-stamped screenshots from European highway cameras, all featuring the familiar Opel Mokka with the Deutsches Reich plates.

"Should I go?" Jim asked.

"What? No, of course not. Stay. Help me make sense of this." Tamaskar began to arrange the photos in chronological order. The first camera had the Opel at the Andorran–French checkpoint, the second caught it speeding through a tunnel near Lyon. Jim went in from the other end and found the most recent image, from 11:52 p.m. on March 29. It showed the car—barely; the picture was mostly dark—on a bridge across a wide placid river. "Crossing the Rhine," he said.

"Yes, so, south of Germany. But we knew that. I was hoping for more. Fuck!" Tamaskar shoved the papers to the floor and stared at her own knees through the desk. Jim had never seen her like this.

"It's only been a couple of days," he said, not knowing what else to offer.

"Jim." Tamaskar lifted her head. "Jim." And then, shockingly, she took his hand in hers. It was hot and dry. "You found him for me once. I need you to do it again. Go there."

"It's—" he stammered. "I— I'll be out of a job. If I tell them it was your order, you might be, too. And if I don't, I'll probably go to prison."

She squeezed harder, then let his hand go. "Not if we win."

"But I don't even know what the win looks like!" Jim's exasperation broke through. He considered reining it in and didn't. "To be honest, I don't think you've ever read me in fully."

"No shit," Tamaskar said, sounding a little more like herself. "For your own protection. But I'll say this much. The thing we're staring down, it's big enough that none, *none*, of this will matter if we manage to stop it. And all I need to stop it is the ability to get in touch with Falk. That's it."

"I don't know, ma'am."

"I'll let you take the jet," she said with a touch of mischief.

"I'm not a child," Jim muttered, hating the fact that this was working. "Okay, fine, I'll go. *Not* because of the jet, mind you, but because it's actually doable. If he's with the hardcore Reichsbürger, they have only so many bases. And the local police must keep tabs on all of them."

"Act fast," Tamaskar said, handing him the bridge photo.

Jim had swung by his apartment to grab some basics and was on his way to the FBO when his father called. As usual, he took a moment to find the right tone before picking up.

"Hey, Dad," he said, having landed on "suspiciously breezy."

"Got a sec? I need to talk to you."

"Sure, go ahead. I'm not doing anything."

Charles laughed. "That's good to hear. Last week you asked me for some advice."

"Yeah," said Jim, "sorry about that. It was a moment of weakness."

"It was, but still. You know I would never tell you to disrespect the chain of command. However, in some cases, especially when it comes to conflicting orders, one does have to make a decision. Don't make the stupid one."

"What are you talking about?"

Charles sighed. "Just turn the goddamn car around."

The shock almost made Jim crash instead; he had to pull to the shoulder of the Dulles Greenway to process what he had heard. Not least of all, his father swearing.

"You okay there?" Over the hands-free connection, it sounded like the car itself was talking.

"I'm fine. How do you know?"

"It's my job to know. And your op name wasn't much of a riddle, either. Birdbath—bird—falcon—Falk. Should have listened to Churchill."

"Dad, I can't discuss any of this."

"Of course you can. Because it's not a real op. It's cowboy bullshit.

Cowgirl, in this case. Or wait, is this offensive, too? They've got a whole thing with cows, don't they?"

"Enough!" Jim yelled, or rather yelped. "Stop it. You sound like Burnham."

"Who?"

"Never mind."

"Your grandfather was head of division at thirty-seven," Charles said, "and I know you're dying to beat that. Well, Lucky Jim, through no effort of your own, you have been dealt some good cards. Find the best way to play them." He hung up.

Jim sat on the side of the road, hands on the wheel, teeth clenched. The FBO was ten or so minutes out; the plane was wheels-up in twenty. Nineteen. Eighteen. Every time another car whipped by, the blast of air hitting the driver's side felt like a slap.

■ ■ ■

Schwarzwald, Germany
April 1, 2024

Falk lay in bed, staring up at the canopy and silently repeating the number of Asha Tamaskar's clean phone. Step one was to get his hands on any device capable of dialing it. Step two was to find a signal, which meant either sneaking past the jammers and off the property—an hourlong hike—or somehow hopping on Burnham's Wi-Fi.

He had spent the entire day quietly researching ways to do this and was close to despair. The rules of castle life appeared rigid enough to make any subterfuge impossible. When people like Rudi visited the compound, they gave up their phones and computers. The staff used cheap plastic walkie-talkies. It was quite possible that Burnham's iPhone, and whatever router he used to get online, were the only game in town.

From a few context clues, like the armed guards' tendency to crowd a certain landing on a certain staircase, Falk had figured out that Burnham's private quarters were on the second floor in the main building's east wing. Going there would be the world's dumbest suicide mission. Besides, unless the man's password was BurnhamRules4Ever, Falk was not tech-savvy enough to get on the network anyway.

He had briefly considered buttonholing a waiter or a gardener and simply asking about the castle's location or bribing one to smuggle a note outside. That idea died at lunch, the moment Falk saw a guard take a young kitchen staffer out to the hallway and nearly brain him with the butt of his rifle.

"Whoa. What's that about?" he asked Oleg the demolition expert, who was watching the beatdown with a huge grin on his face. They had been eating together in preparation for the Bonn trip. Falk spoke to him and Kostya in Russian, hoping it would loosen their tongues a little.

"The usual. Snuck a phone in. You wanna know the funny part? It wasn't the guard who saw him." Snitching, Kostya sidled in to explain, was so pervasive at the castle that people stuck working together would rat each other out for the tiniest infraction so the other person wouldn't do it to them first. As everywhere, systems of suppression created systems of betrayal.

But every system had a flaw, and that flaw almost always had to do with human nature. *Think.*

Around midnight, a solution presented itself. It was desperate, risky, and ethically repugnant. The need to warn Tamaskar, however, outweighed all other concerns. Falk jumped off the bed, put his shoes on, thought about it, took them back off, and slipped outside.

He began by visiting the kitchen, just off the ground-floor reception hall. The cutlery had been dutifully locked up—God forbid someone would get their hands on a butter knife in a place bristling with automatic weapons—but just as he had hoped, the cooks had left their walkie-talkies to charge overnight. He stole two, threw away their charging stands (this way, the loss would be less evident in the morning), then opened the fridge and ate a cold duck leg as his cover. Upon returning to the room, he hid the radios under the mattress and banged on the wall.

"What?" Vlasic yelled through two feet of Swabian masonry.

"Can you come in?"

The ex-Sac showed up a minute later, looking a little sleepy. "What's up?" he said, gruff but without malice. "Hey, you're not still pissy about the other night, are you? I was just doing due diligence. You'd have done the same."

"No worries at all," Falk said. "So, tomorrow's a big day for me. Heading to Bonn with the Russians."

"Yeah, I heard."

"I don't mind telling you, bro, I'm a little on edge. First mission and all."

Vlasic gave him an ironic squint. "You fishing for weed? Drug-free zone, I'm afraid. The chief is pretty fucking strict on that front. Haven't had a puff in a year myself."

"No. But he did mention the option of, uh, female company." Falk cleared his throat. "Would be nice to take my mind off things."

"My *man*!" The giant guffawed. "Ha ha, no problem. I'll make a call. Tell you what, I'll even move rooms for the night. Give you a little privacy."

"Appreciate that. So these women," said Falk, "who are they?"

Vlasic stared at him, puzzled. "What do you mean?"

"Are they . . . vetted? Discreet? Are they, like, friends of the cause or something?"

"Nah, they're just local talent. Well, 'local.' Mostly the Balkans,

Moldova, you know the drill. But we've had no issues so far." He seemed to have interpreted Falk's concern his own way. "Believe me, whatever you've got in mind is nothing compared to what goes down here when the prince is in town. I've seen some *Caligula*-grade shit. You're not a pervert, are you? Not going to choke her to death or anything?"

"No," Falk said slowly, "I am not going to choke her to death or anything."

"Good." Vlasic headed to the door.

It was now or never. "You said you'd make a call. How? I thought phones didn't work here."

"They don't. I'll have to drive out to the road. So yeah, your dick just cost me thirty minutes of sleep, thanks for asking. Next time, get horned up earlier."

"Oh shit," Falk said, "I'm sorry."

"All part of the job, believe it or not. Have fun." Vlasic stepped out, still cackling.

For the next hour, Falk paced the room, muttering abuse at himself as he made his preparations. He estimated the chances of the plan working out at about five percent. He was also uncomfortable with it in other ways he didn't have the time or mental capacity to analyze.

On the one hand, there was enough of a professional kinship between a spy and a sex worker to treat whoever was on her way as a colleague: the cover persona, the manipulation skills, the rehearsed lines and faked reactions, the need to keep a piece of one's soul locked up and inaccessible. On the other, his old job as a case officer made him more of a pimp. After all, running native assets mostly involved taking advantage of other people's misfortunes, addictions, and vulnerabilities. Sometimes recruitment was a long seduction. Sometimes it was just money on the dresser.

When the knock came, he took a moment to collect himself. The woman at the door was about thirty, dressed in a shapeless overcoat designed for a dramatic later reveal; she wore her red-dyed hair in a bun pierced by a decorative chopstick. Her face was frozen in a professional smile. The road to the castle must have been like going to visit Dracula. Perhaps she'd heard all about the prince's proclivities or even experienced them firsthand. Falk allowed himself to feel bad for one more second, then decisively turned that part off—just like she was probably doing at the same time. Two people, steeling themselves for something neither wanted.

"*Grüß Gott*," she said earnestly. "*Ich heiße* Krista."

"Hi, Krista. Do you speak English, by any chance?"

"Better than German." Falk placed her accent as Albanian.

"Okay." He lowered his voice. "First things first. I don't need anything from you. You can just sit here for, I don't know, twenty minutes. I can stay in the bathroom if you want."

"Oh god," said Krista. "Is this going to be weird?"

"No, I swear. I just have a couple of questions. Did you drive here alone?"

"Yes. Why?! You're already creeping me out."

"I know. I'm sorry. Did they take your phone and search you?"

"Yes. Very annoying. But it pays extra, so whatever."

"Is this your first time here? Don't spare my feelings or anything."

She smirked. "It is not."

"Last question. They ever search you on your way out?"

"No. What am I going to do, steal a candelabra?"

"Good. Okay. In this case, I will need you to do me a very simple favor." Falk reached under the mattress and got one of the walkie-talkies; he had scratched Tamaskar's number into its side. "Take this with you. The range on this thing is about eight kilometers. When you're out on the road but not too far, dial this number on your cell and put the radio next to it. Don't stop the car. When the call's over, toss it out the window."

"Huh?"

"I know it sounds insane. But it's the only way I can talk to someone I really need to talk to."

Krista thought for a bit. "Five hundred extra."

Falk looked around for his watch, a vintage Longines he had bought ten years ago to celebrate getting the Riga job. "I don't have any cash, but here, take this. It's not a fake and it costs four times that."

"I know it's not a fake because it's old as fuck." Krista regarded it with some skepticism. "This is all still very weird, by the way. Just so you know."

"I do. And thank you."

They sat on the bed for a few minutes. "God, it's so boring without a phone," she said. "Can I go already, or do you have a reputation to protect?"

Falk chuckled and nodded. Krista shoved the walkie-talkie in her coat and put on the Longines. "Best I ever had. *Tschüss.*"

The moment she left, he locked himself in the bath with the second radio and began to count. Three to five minutes to get out of the building and into the car; five to seven more to get her phone back and clear the perimeter. The next eight to twelve minutes of Falk's life would be torture.

As, if the plan went south, would be the rest of it.

In the end, he didn't know exactly how much time had passed, because his watch was gone, but it felt like half an hour at least. The walkie-talkie came to life with a loud click, followed by the rustle of static.

"All right, psycho, I'm dialing now," said Krista. Falk listened to the unsure beeps; this seemed to take another whole minute.

Finally, Tamaskar's voice. Wan, faraway, filtered through three separate membranes. As slight as his chances of making it home. And as missed as home itself, wherever it might be.

"Hello? Hello?!"

"Hey, Asha," he said. "It's Ari."

"My god. Listen, I—"

"No, me first. Burnham is a Cormorant op. Stand down. Don't make a move. Forget the whole thing. Tell Jim to forget it, too. I'll try to take care of it on my end."

"What?!"

He realized he had never uttered that odd nickname in front of her. "Cormorant. From the dossier. He's real. He's financing Burnham through the Russians."

Tamaskar either took this information in stride or was too overwhelmed to process it. "Now you listen to *me.* I'm not standing down. Burnham's planning a hit against—"

The void swallowed her next words. Krista's car had to be reaching the end of the walkie-talkie range.

"What?"

Hiss, crackle. The voice returned, crumbling into syllables. "—schke. Florian Reschke. It's too big, Ari. We have to act—" More hiss. "Just tell me where you are, and run!"

"I don't—" Falk realized something. "But someone does. Krista! Hey! Are you listening to all this? Can you tell us the address you just went to? The name of the castle?"

"Wait, is someone *else* on this fucking call?!" Even through the interference, Tamaskar's outrage was audible across half the world.

"Krista!" he whisper-yelled, crouching on the tiled floor. "Your location! Where are you?!"

A tsunami of static met him, followed by dead silence. Falk pressed the talk button several more times, turned off the radio, resisted a strong desire to smash it, and walked out of the bathroom.

Stan Vlasic stood on the other side of the unmussed bed, a Glock in his outstretched arm at shoulder level. To aim at Falk's head, he had to point it slightly down.

"Should have choked her, bro," he said. "You'd be in way less trouble."

■ ■ ■

Tamaskar stared at the phone in her hand, breathing hard. The call had caught her on the roof of the three-story parking lot behind the New Headquarters Building. It was twilight, and the treetops surrounding the lot were just beginning to sprout leaves; the combined effect was that of a strange, foglike diffusion all around, as if the world were going soft-focus.

She was struggling to grasp what Falk's words "Burnham is a Cormorant op" meant. The Harlow Dossier, as she remembered it, had made Cormorant sound like a civilian who once financed Harlow's off-the-books adventures as chief of Moscow Station. He was thus just as likely to be an oligarch as a politician. (He would also have to be in his late eighties; there wasn't anyone that age at the Agency itself, but plenty of options across the Potomac.) His métier appeared to be finding and funding ops that united rival forces across seemingly impossible divides—like the joint GRU/CIA attempt to install a third-party Russian president. And now, apparently, a plot to take out an overambitious German defense minister.

None of this changed her priorities: Prevent the attack and save her agent, not necessarily in that order.

Tamaskar briefly considered contacting the Germans. She had

enough proof. Kate Liss's laptop lay locked inside her office safe. On it was clear evidence of Russian operatives buying intel on Reschke's movements around Bonn and forwarding it to Burnham. This alone should be enough to spur the BND to action. But it would also mean either exposing Falk as a CIA agent operating under their noses or sacrificing him along with the rest of Burnham's gang.

She thought about running to Spaleta's office. Until the extent of Cormorant's sway over the Agency was clear, however, this was not an option.

The last thing Tamaskar had heard through the storm of glitches were the words "the name of the castle." At least that's what she thought Falk had said. Well, this was *something* to go on. She got into the car and dialed Otterbeck, who should have landed in Munich already.

The call didn't go through. She sent a message. An automated text bubble informed her that the recipient didn't exist.

So Jim didn't just ditch the clean phone, he had taken care to erase the number. She had no time to analyze this new wrinkle. There was only one demonstrably uncorrupted party left to whom she could turn. Fully aware of the irony, she opened the phone's browser and typed in FleaCollar.

The OSINT portal had only grown stronger since its founder's death; thousands of Keegan's fans and friends around the world had poured their grief into donations. Tamaskar scrolled to the bottom, past investigations of secret Nazi music festivals, black-market grain trade routes, and the deepfake porn industry, until she found the site's anonymized tip line. After one last twitch of hesitation, she typed in a short message.

Re: right-wing influencer Felix Burnham. Look at CASTLES in Southern Germany.

■ ■ ■

It had admittedly been a while since Falk got hit in the face, but he didn't remember it feeling as if his whole head disintegrated in a single flash of white light. He had to give props to Vlasic. The man was a natural.

The second blow, to the abdomen, folded him in half and sent him clutching the bedpost for support. The third one crashed down on the top of his head like a cartoon anvil. Falk slid onto the floor and pulled his knees to his stomach. He hadn't gotten a single swing in.

Oleg and Kostya were the first to arrive. Listening to their quick, alarmed conversation was painful in more ways than one—their English was close to nonexistent and Vlasic, in classic blue-badger fashion, spoke nothing but.

"You break face?" Oleg asked. "Bad, will mess up story."

"Nyet," the ex-Sac replied, mocking him, "I no break face. Plus, come on," he added in his normal voice, "it doesn't even matter." The last phrase, tragically, made Kostya think of a song by the band Linkin Park, which he kept humming for the next several minutes as the duo dragged half-conscious Falk to the top floor. Vlasic walked in front, hands in pockets.

The next thing Falk heard was Burnham's voice, though it wasn't addressed to him or anyone around him. It filtered through a set of pillar-flanked double doors, too loud and mellifluous to be a part of any real conversation. He must have been taping something. Vlasic knocked as quietly as he could; an aide in all black opened the door just wide enough to pop his head out.

"Shh," he said. "We're live."

Vlasic pointed at Falk's bloodied face. "This is pretty fucking urgent, too. I can't have random people seeing this. And I need instructions from the chief."

The aide looked up and down the empty hallway, then at Falk. "Ugh, fine," he said. "We'll be done in a minute. Bring him in. Is he going to make any noise, though?"

"No he is not." Vlasic easily tore off a large piece of Falk's T-shirt, pressed the sides of his face with his thumb and index finger to unclench his jaw, and stuck the fabric in. "You guys have gaffer tape in there, right?"

They taped up his mouth and carried him in. On the other side of the door was a small, jewel-like ballroom with mirrored walls and a trompe l'oeil ceiling. It was the type of space where an aristocrat's children would put on a puppet performance for Papá. Burnham had commandeered the far end of the room; he sat in a Rococo chair in front of a ring light, orating into an iPhone set on a tripod. Arranged in a C-shape around him were several gray fabric gobos, like those in a recording studio, not so much to dampen the sound but to block off the room's identifying details. A few more aides stood by, listening in awe.

Falk's captors sat him down on the floor by the doors and stood by. "I'll take a few more questions now," Burnham said, checking his phone. "Ooh, that's a nice one. 'Do you believe in absolute good and evil?' writes Roman Calvary from Detroit. First of all, cool handle, Roman. Unless, of course, you misspelled *cavalry*."

Falk noticed that Burnham sounded more American now. During their lunch, he had been leaning heavily into his Oxford side, "sorry old boy" and all.

"What *I* believe is that good and evil are subject to depreciation at scale. Let me explain. See, Roman, these concepts are at their strongest on the human level. Kindness, fidelity—good. Deceit, cruelty—evil. It's the very fabric of humanity. But scale up and they cease to exist altogether. It is ridiculous to apply the concept of, say, kindness to a nation-state. Do you really think any countries or forms of government or corporations are inherently better than others? Of course not. On the macro level, the world is composed of gray actors looking out for their self-interest. Sometimes that self-interest aligns with, say, giving everyone a car and free education, to goose up some indicator or another. And sometimes it aligns with, say, an urgent need to annex the neighboring state, or having five percent of the population over sixty die of preventable disease."

Christ, Falk thought. *Thanks for the backstage pass.* He wondered why Burnham was doing a livecast at two a.m., then realized it was prime time in the United States, where most of Burnham's target audience was. He looked around for the source of the internet signal, as per his earlier hunch, until he espied a wireless router blinking away under the catering table. On the table itself was the usual array of water and snacks, plus a familiar turquoise box: the cake he had declined during his first, and now last, lunch as Burnham's golden boy.

He focused on the router. Plugged into it was a second device, smaller and flatter, with four short antennas that made it look like a robotic insect playing dead. Falk guessed it provided some kind of beefed-up VPN functionality, scrambling the livecast's origin and diverting unwanted visitors. The aide who let them in waved to get Burnham's attention, then pointed to Falk. "All right, men and boys, time to wrap it up," said Burnham, glancing to the side.

Falk looked at the device again and saw a thin, treacherous, improbably winding path forward.

Oleg stood closest to him. Still seated, Falk slowly pulled in his feet and shifted his weight to his back. He rehearsed the move several times in his mind, accounting and correcting for the bad tendon.

Then he pressed his palms into the wall and kicked out his right leg, instantly breaking Oleg's kneecap.

The next part was crucial—he had to get up *as he did this*, otherwise he'd lose the one second of advantage he had. Amazingly, his precalculation turned out correct. The kick with the right leg, combined with a push off the wall, created the momentum he needed to stand on his left one. By the time Oleg screamed and hit the ground, Falk was already past him and mid-dive toward the catering table.

Vlasic and Kostya ran at him from one side, Burnham's men from another. Food flew as the flimsy table came crashing down on top of him. "Stop! Cut the stream!" an aide yelled.

Falk's hand was two inches away from the box when Vlasic's steel-cap boot stomped it into the parquet.

At least three people helped flip him on his back and held him down while he gagged on a piece of his own T-shirt. The next shoe that hit him, a few seconds later, smashed his nose. Falk didn't have to wonder to whom it belonged. It was a wine-colored oxford.

■ ■ ■

He lost track of time surprisingly quickly. No sunlight reached the basement, and the ceiling lamp in its metal cage was weak but always on, so once Falk had fallen asleep and woken up two or three times, the concept of a "day" became very abstract.

They had stuck him under the brewery, that much he knew. The stench of yeast, strong enough to seep in even through a broken nose, was a dead giveaway. The cell itself was a damp square cut out of a larger space; the floor sloped toward a trench drain by the back wall, which made his filthy mattress—the room's only amenity—lie slightly aslant as well. It might have once been part of a cellar, where lager beer fermented at close-to-freezing temperatures for months before bottling.

Ignorance of time turned into hyperawareness of space. It wasn't long before Falk knew every scratch on every brick in the cell. He knew when to duck when pacing, to avoid hitting his forehead on a low beam, and was soon doing it with eyes closed, as a sport. He knew which three floor tiles were loose. There was nothing exciting underneath, however, just a layer of older and shittier tile.

Food came at irregular intervals, sometimes when he was asleep. Gone were the days of freshly pressed clothes and elegantly worded notes; now he woke up to a cold plate of chicken and rice on the floor. At least they weren't feeding him the kind of horror-movie slop Falk had expected from his surroundings. He was pretty sure it was microwave dinners from Lidl.

The roughest part was hygiene, as it always is. Once a day, though also at random intervals, an armed guard in a KN95 mask took Falk to a disgusting bathroom at the end of the hallway and waited in full sight for five minutes. The rest of the time, he used the drain.

From what Falk could tell, he had no neighbors. After a while, he decided to turn this to his advantage. He talked to himself. He sang a cappella renditions of songs by Pavement, Spoon, and, once he was really sure no one was listening, Lana Del Rey. He composed a poem in bad Russian and recited it a dozen times in various voices, but sadly had forgotten it the next "morning."

Time flowed in and out of itself like wax in a lava lamp, elastic and nonlinear, free of goals, ambitions, analysis, or after a while, even fear. No one came down to interrogate, intimidate, or torture him. The only real mystery was why Burnham had bothered to keep him alive to begin with, and Falk didn't feel like solving it. Perhaps he was being held as exchange or blackmail fodder. Or undergoing his own lagering process—getting his mind softened up before its contents could be tapped and the container discarded.

On what felt like the seventh or eighth day, he got his answer regardless. The locks clanged, but instead of the masked guard, in stepped Stan

Vlasic. He checked the corners, made Falk get up and hug the wall, lifted the mattress and set it on its side, and finally waved someone in. The someone was Burnham himself, dressed for an English gardening session in wellies and a Woolly Pully jumper.

"Thank you, Stanley. Give us a minute," he said to Vlasic.

"You sure, Chief? He might get feisty again."

"Yes. It'll be fine."

"All right. I'll be outside." Vlasic gave Falk a warning look before walking out. Falk sat back down on the floor. Even after days without human contact, he had zero interest in a conversation.

"You dumb fuck," Burnham said unexpectedly. "You really think you did something with that call, don't you. When all you've achieved was a slight hiccup in a plan that has more redundancies than you can possibly imagine."

"And I'm sure you're going to tell me all about it," Falk said and yawned. The yawn was performative, and a terrible idea: His jaw still ached from the previous week's drubbing.

"Nothing changes. That's all I want you to take away from this. You sacrificed Asha Tamaskar, and *nothing changes.* You will still die. Florian Reschke will still die. They're still going to find your body in an abandoned car in Bonn, next to the Russian mercenary responsible for the hit. Terrible what kind of brutality these so-called Eco-Socialists are capable of, isn't it."

Falk must have flinched despite himself, because Burnham enthusiastically began to elaborate. *The man's need for validation is just bottomless,* Falk thought. If he weren't about to be murdered, this would have been very funny.

"That's right. Sorry to disappoint, old boy. You *are* a crucial piece of the puzzle, that part is true. But having the CIA on your tail was always the sum total of your value to me. Once the deed is done, tracing your movements over the last months will lead them straight to those hard-left lunatics."

"So that's why you had them handle my intake so publicly," said Falk. "Clever."

"Why thank you."

"And that's why I'm still alive. So my corpse is still fresh by the time you're done with Reschke, which I'm guessing is tonight. Hey, just out of curiosity, did you hire Kostya to kill Oleg or vice versa?"

Burnham mimed applause. "Bravo. I'd say you catch on fast, but clearly not fast enough."

"Actually, I still don't get it," said Falk. "I mean, I get the *how*. It's even somewhat elegant. My compliments to Cor—to our old friend. But *why*? Other than carrying water for Russia, what does killing a German minister accomplish? Where are *you* in all this?"

"First of all," said Burnham, "it's my plan. As you lot like to say, 'Don't deny me my agency.' As for the why . . . How shall I explain it to such a blinkered warhorse? Okay. Consider the pandemic."

"Oh boy. I take it back, I don't care. Shoot me now."

"Did people really believe that the vaccine was poison?" Burnham went on, unruffled. "Of course not, even if they *believe* they believed it. But as a metaphor for another, more insidious poison, the poison of the nanny state, it gave them a way to focus their grievances. Likewise, I don't literally believe the German state is worse than any other. But one must keep the pressure on. Will the Bundestag fold overnight? No. But will the next kanzler think twice about letting in the next million refugees? Will simple animal fear guide a few lawmakers away from the globalist agenda and toward their own people's interests? Yes and yes." He looked at Falk, pleased with his own eloquence.

"You know," said Falk, "I keep thinking about that last response you gave on your livecast before I, uh, crashed the party. It sounded a lot like what someone said to me once. 'Institutions can't be moral, only people can.'"

"Smart man."

"Except he meant a completely different thing. He was trying to remind me that institutions are *composed* of people."

"Ah, that." Burnham wrinkled his nose. "Bit of a middlebrow fallacy, that. It's like saying, 'Cats are atoms.' They are, technically, but it's irrelevant to what a cat is. Still, at least your fellow was on the right track."

"Yes," said Falk. "Yes, he was. Until you had him killed. His name was Alan Keegan."

For several seconds, Burnham stood there not saying anything. "All right," he finally muttered, more to himself than to Falk. "This was fun." He turned on his heel, about to call in Vlasic. Falk belatedly understood the utility of the floor drain and why the mattress was on its side.

"Hang on," he said very fast, getting up. "Do you have a recording of that livecast? I'd love to rewatch it with you. Just that final answer. Consider it my last wish."

Burnham looked genuinely taken aback. There was no way he could say no to a request like this, a fact so obvious it made the situation a bit of a trap. And yet vanity still won out.

"There's no signal here, remember?"

"I'm sure you can get someone to turn it on."

"All right." Burnham chuckled. "You're an odd bird, Falk. Hope you don't mind if Stanley joins us, in case you decide to try anything again." He took his walkie-talkie, gave a terse command in German, and called in Vlasic, who came in holstering his gun.

For thirty seconds or so, the three of them stood there looking at Burnham's iPhone and waiting for the bars. The video began to play; Burnham dragged the red dot to the last minute of its two-and-a-half-hour running time. "Hope it's worth it," he said to Falk.

"So do I," Falk replied.

The screen Burnham, framed wide to show off his suit, talked about good and evil again. He kept his legs crossed European style; the shoe that would, in less than a minute, break Falk's nose swung gently back and forth like a pendulum at the bottom of the shot.

". . . preventable disease. All right, men and boys, time to wrap it up."

"Satisfied?" asked the real Burnham.

"Almost. To the very end, please. There's like five seconds left."

"This little shit is trying to see if he messed up the 'cast," said Vlasic. "Don't worry, Chief. I stopped him. It was just a little—"

A muffled din issued from the phone's speaker. The screen Burnham frowned and turned his head.

"Stop! Cut the stream!"

The shot was tight enough that none of the behind-the-scenes commotion had made it into the frame.

Yet wide enough so that, a second before the stream cut off, a few out-of-focus objects did tumble into the far background.

Including a pastry box of a uniquely piercing turquoise color.

"Trempel's," said Falk. "Small-scale is the only true luxury left."

The screen went black. Burnham and Vlasic stared up at him with two comically distinct expressions—Vlasic grasping nothing at all, Burnham everything at once.

"You scheming Jew filth," said Burnham, pushing every sound through clenched teeth. A fast, insistent vibration had taken over his entire body, making his shoulders twist and twitch and his silver hair flop over his eyebrows.

"Gentlemen. You can go ahead and kill me, Stan." Falk exhaled and closed his eyes, resigning himself to the dark.

"Chief?"

"Give me the gun. I'll do it myself."

"*Chief.*" Vlasic sounded like he was trying to call Burnham's attention to something happening beyond the cell. The grinding whine of a barn door opening. A stampede of boots one floor up, beating dust out of the ceiling and into the caged lamp's light.

The voices, when they became audible, were all German except one, a familiar, out-of-breath Yankee yelp.

"He's down there! No, like, a floor down! Uh, *unter*!"

Falk's eyes flew open. Whatever else his fate held, he was not going to let the last words he ever heard be Jim Otterbeck's.

CHAPTER NINE

McLean, Virginia
April 8, 2024

"Again," Spaleta said. "Again, slower, and like I'm five." Despite the pseudo-gruff tone, the director was clearly in an excellent mood. Fresh from the Senate confirmation, he had finally lost the *acting* qualifier; congratulatory notes lay in heaps on the desk.

Tamaskar smiled. "Sir, I believe that Officer Falk's decision, of his own accord, to investigate, infiltrate, and subvert this terrorist ring is commendable enough for him to be reinstated. At least in some minor capacity."

"His own accord," Spaleta repeated, not mocking her but not exactly buying it, either. "And you found out when?"

"Seven days ago, when he tried to contact me. He wasn't able to give the compound's location. Luckily, OSINT researchers at FleaCollar pinpointed it later the same night, from a background detail in one of Burnham's videos."

Spaleta shook his head and got up. "Well, I guess it's not the craziest thing to happen last week. What bugs me, Asha, is that you didn't feel the need to inform me right there and then."

This was the tricky part. She made a show of choosing her words carefully, as if they hadn't been pre-chosen and rehearsed hours ago.

"I know, sir, and I'm sorry. It just didn't seem believable or actionable at the time. And once it was, the Germans took it over and ran with it. Officer Otterbeck was only there to extract Falk. It's all in the debrief, but I'll file a detailed report as well, of course."

"Still. Would've been nice to share in some of the glory." Spaleta aimed a remote at the TV in the corner and put on CNN with the volume down. Above the chyron *Crisis in Germany*, Florian Reschke was speaking into a stack of branded microphones. He stood outdoors, with the Hardthöhe defense ministry complex in the background; spring wind kept whipping his hair back.

"Good optics. Meet the next kanzler, huh."

"I have, actually," Tamaskar said.

"Same. Nice guy. All in all, a net positive."

Someone here doesn't think so, she almost blurted out. Instead, she took it for the gracious conversation ender it was.

Falk sat in a lounge area by the elevators, sporting fresh bandages and the tense mien of someone waiting for a test result. The Germans had given him camo pants and a khaki jacket with a flag patch, which made him look less like a soldier than a punk who shops at army surplus. Two Security Protective Service officers loitered unobtrusively nearby. She slowed her steps on approach, hoping her heartbeat would take the cue and slow down as well.

"How did it go?" he asked.

"I mean, you're in the building, and not in cuffs," she said, shrugging. "That's progress."

"Fair enough." Falk stood up.

"I have something for you." Tamaskar riffled in her bag and handed him an envelope from State. She already knew what was inside: Falk's brand-new passport, his first in his own name in three years. She couldn't help opening it earlier, to sneak a glance at the photo for a quick dopamine hit.

"Wow." Falk seemed briefly overwhelmed. He strained for a jokey response until he found one. "Hey, that's two out of two times we met. Now I'll be expecting you to keep handing me passports."

"One small difference. This one's real." It was a rush job by the personal request of the director, which boded well for her reinstatement request.

"Thank you so much." He gave her a brief, intensely awkward hug. "All right, I better find a hotel and get out of all this stolen valor."

"*Stollen* valor," Tamaskar said, a German pun so bad she had to squeeze her own eyes shut in embarrassment. She also belatedly realized that, after seven years in the field and two more on the run, Falk must have nowhere to go. "Come on. We have accommodations for returning officers."

"Is that what I am?" He looked directly in her eyes.

She met his gaze. "Is that what you want to be?"

"I don't know," he said. "If you're my superior, it means we can't go get a drink."

She froze for long enough that the SPS officers began to pay attention. Of all the day's possible scenarios, this was the one she wanted the most and had subsequently prepared for the least.

"As it happens, not yet," she finally replied. "Spaleta is thinking on it. You a beer guy or a wine guy?"

"Would it be obnoxious to say a cocktail guy?"

"Yes," Tamaskar said. "Absolutely. But I do know a place that makes a great Sidecar."

■ ■ ■

They had tumbled into bed almost as soon as she managed to unlock her front door, but it wasn't the kind of adrenaline ardor that sometimes follows shared trauma. It wasn't drunk fumbling, either. It was something else, much stranger and more profound: They made love like a couple who had known each other for years, got torn apart, and finally reunited. Considering that their time together up to that point had consisted of one conversation, one glitching phone call, and three cocktails each, the intensity of it even scared Falk a bit. Every touch made him realize that, in some way, he had been thinking about Asha every day since Prague.

By early morning, this weird and immediate adhesion of two souls had become so self-evident it was hard to talk around and harder to fathom where to go from there. So they lay in bed muttering insane things to each other, strewn with words like *always* and *never*, which hadn't been a part of Falk's lexicon since his first overseas posting wrung the life out of his first and only serious relationship.

Unless, of course, one counted a certain young woman back in 2021, whose name he had promised to forget because she did, too.

Predawn light crept around the curtains. A black cat jumped on the bed and began to rub against Falk's foot. "That's Blixa," Tamaskar said. "He's not really affectionate, he's just hungry."

"Blixa, like Blixa Bargeld? From the Bad Seeds and so on?"

"Who?" She laughed and got up, grabbing a robe. The cat immediately forgot Falk and trotted past her into the kitchen. "If you want coffee, speak now."

"I do but I can't," Falk said, getting up, too. "I have an exciting day of getting my nose rebroken and fixed ahead of me."

Tamaskar came back and stood by the door. "Wait, do you even have FEP still?"

"Nope. Looks like my reintegration into American life will start with about fifty grand of medical debt. Which seems appropriate." Falk found and put on his T-shirt. "Unless, of course, you want to marry me real quick." He cringed the moment the joke escaped his mouth, because some of the things they had said in full seriousness hours ago hadn't been that far removed from it.

"I don't know about that," she replied, thankfully taking it in stride. "You're kind of a slut."

"What! Silje? That was part of the cover."

"Yeah, yeah. That's what they all say." Tamaskar cracked up. "Then you call me, like, four days later and there's someone on the line named Krista. Imagine my reaction." That made Falk laugh, too.

She drank her coffee in a few gulps. "All right. A shower and I'm off. You can stay here if you want, but do check in at the quarters at some point today. Otherwise there will be questions."

"Are you safe?" Falk asked. "At work, I mean? Considering you just pissed off someone very powerful, and we still don't know who he is."

Tamaskar shrugged. "We know he isn't one of us, that's good enough for now. Spaleta's been on the level throughout." She headed into the shower, with no flirtatious subtext to her movements: The topic of Cormorant had taken all romance out of the room. Falk sat in the spotless kitchen—Tamaskar seemed to view it mostly as the room where her coffee machine stood—and tried to wrestle his mind back into its normal analytical mode.

The ultimate goal of targeting Florian Reschke had been consistent enough with the little that Falk knew about Cormorant: that for decades his main interest lay in reshaping the U.S.-Russia relationship from the ground up. Reschke's plan to place American long-range missiles on German soil, exacerbating the standoff over Ukraine, must have been a massive thorn in his side.

But why would he choose to do this through Felix Burnham, of all people? Why not just use the GRU or Orlok or someone like Vlasic directly?

Tamaskar came back in full makeup, and he lost his train of thought. She had her DD/CA armor back on: black chinos, a white silk shirt, and a slightly oversize jacket with shoulder pads. As it tends to happen when two people can't decide how earnest to make their first goodbye, an awkward pause ensued. "All right, hero," she finally said, swerving hard in the other direction. "Break a nose."

"Ain't no heroes in this mess," Falk said. "Except maybe you."

"Well," said Tamaskar, "there is one. Katya Lisichenko."

He remembered the name but little else. "What does she have to do with this?"

"Oh, god, right." She looked at her watch. "I guess I have five more minutes."

Fifteen minutes later, Falk still sat there slack-jawed, struggling under the onslaught of new information. A junior bank executive he had briefly—and, he thought, unsuccessfully—attempted to recruit sight unseen in 2021 turned out to possess the pluck and courage of his very best assets. Trying to escape Russia, getting turned away at the border, and figuring out it had been foul play was one thing; her next actions were quite another. Going back to work as if nothing happened. Rising through the ranks of a vile system, lying in wait the whole time. Looking for just the right moment to strike out against her masters. Laying a professional-grade trap at the Angleterre. And then risking it all to get the evidence to him.

The only way out is through.

Except she hadn't gotten through, had she. "If she's still alive," Falk said, "we must get her free."

"Agreed. Though not optimistic." Tamaskar looked at her watch again. "Oh fuck, now I'm really late."

She gave him an almost automatic peck on the cheek, which turned into a deep kiss, which almost turned into more before they disengaged. "Please behave. I'll see you tonight." She grabbed her purse—more of a dumpling-shaped black leather satchel—and headed to the door.

"You know what's still bothering me about all this?" Falk called out to her back. "The fact that they ended up at the same border crossing."

Tamaskar sighed and turned. "I'll give you thirty more seconds. Go."

He spoke faster. "Look, she could have left the country a million different ways. Even in the *very* specific case of fleeing to Estonia by car, she was much likelier to end up at the big Narva crossing, not that weird truck corridor. It's a hell of a coincidence. I hate coincidences."

"All right, I'll play. Orlan Finans couldn't let her leave, because then there would be two Lisichenkos in the West. But they also couldn't just kill or jail her, because she was GRU-adjacent. So they *steered* her toward the same crossing their bagman—bagwoman?—had used two days prior. This way, the Estonians did their job for them. It's actually kind of genius."

"And how do you steer someone?"

Tamaskar made an exasperated noise, took a black Moleskine out of her purse, and handed it to Falk. "Can you read my longhand?" He looked and nodded. "It's from a Georgian source who filled me in on the whole situation. This is like the tenth worst breach I've committed this week, so fuck it, you can sit here and go over the notes. Maybe you'll see something. I really gotta run." She gave him another kiss, quick but real, and was off.

The nose-job appointment was not for two more hours. Falk spent a few minutes aimlessly walking around Asha's house, lost and besotted, marveling at the degree of trust she had in him. Or was it pity? He wasn't a charity case for her, was he? He shook the paranoia away, sat down on the sofa in the tidy living room, and opened the notebook to the last filled-in page.

The words stampeded across the paper at a 45-degree slant, an instant transcript of a hurried phone call. A few question marks and parentheticals, in the same but cooler hand, must have been added later.

Exited R at APP Shamilkina (sp.?) 3/3/22
Entered Est. at Luhamaa (sp.?)
On foot w/2 ppl + dog (1 taxi?)
KL stopped, others let in
Iosif + Viktoria Dobrovolsky
Prev. xing: approx. 3/1/22???
KL escorted back to NML

The hasty abbreviations were more or less self-evident, at least to Falk. KL was Katya Lisichenko, APP was Russian for "automotive checkpoint," NML was no-man's-land. Iosif and Viktoria Dobrovolsky must have been the couple with the dog that got into *Est.* while Katya got sent back to *R*. Since they all arrived together, it stood to reason they had traveled from Moscow together as well, hence the *1 taxi* guess.

"And that, Blixa," said Falk to the cat, who had perched on the chair across the room to watch him work, "is how you steer someone." He took his new phone—Tamaskar's former burner—and typed the couple's names in the search bar.

Dignified, unsmiling middle-aged faces. Hundreds of bylines and appearances in old-school opposition media: interviews on Echo of Moscow, columns in *Novaya Gazeta*, blog posts on Lenta.ru. Almost every outlet they had written for was long dead, decimated, declared an "undesirable organization," or taken over by the state; reading their Google histories was like visiting a virtual cemetery of free speech in Russia. Viktoria seemed to specialize in book reviews, Iosif in satirical op-eds about current events. In short, these two were the last people you would expect to do dirty work for a GRU slush fund.

Despairing to find anything of use, he limited his search to the last two years. Apart from their Facebook posts and the like, the engine returned a single result, in English.

> Dr. and Prof. Dobrovolsky have been Free Pen Foundation Fellows since 2019. In early 2022, after both were designated "foreign agents" by the Kremlin, FPF sponsored and assisted their relocation to Oslo. They are currently at work on *Many Voices, Many Russias*, a comprehensive history of Soviet and post-Soviet cultural imperialism as seen through the lens of the literature of Native and colonized peoples. It is scheduled to be published by FPF Press in 2027.

A typical path for well-meaning exiles with no audience left at home, Falk thought. He felt as bad for the Dobrovolskys as he did for all new Russia's rejects, clinging to fragile sinecures abroad while waiting in vain for their mad motherland to come to its senses. His real sympathy, however, was for the ones without a fancy Western foundation to pull them out.

Falk tapped the FPF logo at the top, to see whom else it supported, and flinched. Looking at him from the site's front page, in black and white, was a familiar bespectacled face.

IN MEMORIAM

Free Pen Foundation's 2023 Aletheia Award Laureate

ALAN KEEGAN

The photographer had caught him in a half turn away from the camera, as if between two poses. It was a great shot. The awkward, apologetic smile was very Alan.

So: The nonprofit that gave Katya a ride to the fateful border crossing was the same nonprofit that got Keegan to abandon his usual caution and come to Prague. For a humanitarian organization, Free Pen sure did a lot of shoving people toward their doom.

Namely, the people who, knowingly or not, stood in the way of a plan to finance Felix Burnham with GRU cash.

Sometimes online research meant secret overlay networks, ZeroFox, Everbridge, and Cybersixgill; other times, it meant a ten-second visit to Wikipedia. Falk opened the entry for Free Pen, saw the line *created in 2003 via onetime anonymous donation*, and closed it.

Falk got up, spooking the cat, who hissed and parkoured off the hallway wall into the bedroom. "Sorry, Blixa," he yelled, "I gotta go." He downloaded Uber, ruining the phone's clean bill of health, and set Daniel Watts's somehow still functional e-bank account as the payment method.

The first destination Falk put in was 1000 Colonial Farm Road, because typing "CIA" felt stupid. After a few seconds' thought, he changed it to Dulles Airport.

■ ■ ■

She arrived at the office in a pleasant daze, her mind a kaleidoscope of last night's highlights. Valerie complimented her "aura," a word she had never used before, which could have been a subtle warning to tone down the grin. Tamaskar shook her head and forced herself to dive into work. Somehow the state of the world today felt like a little less of a wildfire atop a chemical spill than usual.

Among the avalanche of new items calling for her attention, two caught it first. One was a calendar invite, festooned with every kind of urgency icon available: an all-hands, in-person senior leadership meeting in fifteen minutes. The other was a long, heartfelt, somewhat indulgently worded resignation notice from Jim Otterbeck.

The conclave took place in the building's largest SCIF, which, save a heavier door and a guarded honeycomb cubby for electronic devices by the entrance, looked like a regular conference room. Tamaskar locked her phone and badged in; a dozen division and staff heads were already milling around the table. She saw the Agency's general counsel, so things had to be serious.

A few minutes passed in tense, expectant small talk while more men and women arrived. Tamaskar exchanged nods with the Operations Support Branch supervisor who had half-jokingly asked her to take away Patero. Charles Otterbeck, Jim's father from Procurement, came in, sat straight down, and stared daggers at her across the table. He had to know about his son's decision and appeared to have concluded it was somehow her fault.

Spaleta walked in accompanied by a slight, sharp-shouldered woman Tamaskar recognized. "All right," he said, gesturing for everyone to sit down, "without further ado, Kim Lawton, liaison to the National Security Council." He grabbed a chair, content to be a listener. Lawton chose to stay on her feet. Before beginning, she glanced around the room, making one millisecond of eye contact with each participant.

"Thank you, sir." She spoke in the crisp, regionless dialect government types often affect as a stand-in for competence. "Some overnight updates on the Felix Burnham matter. As you may have guessed, the White House is primarily concerned with the awkward issue of his double citizenship. The thinking is as follows. He is a German subject, caught by Germans on German soil, has resided there for years, and is currently being held at a supermax facility in Stuttgart. Burnham's U.S. passport is, and I am quoting directly here, 'an accident of history.'"

A few people nodded. Someone murmured, "Makes sense."

"In support of this point of view," Lawton continued, "we are not to treat it as our operation or, frankly, our business. This means no victory lap of any kind. In return, the BND are willing to overlook the presence of one or two Agency men on the premises." As she delivered this line, she looked first at Otterbeck Senior, then at Tamaskar. "As for Stanley Vlasic—"

The head of Special Activities chimed in: "At our rendition facility and cooperating fully."

"Thank you, Kim," said Spaleta from his chair. "Now, the bad news. With Burnham's group about to be reclassified as a terrorist organization, we are taking a hard look at his followers at the Agency. It brings me no pleasure to say that even the most cursory, single-day sweep found over two dozen officers, analysts, and support staff—all male, big shock, I know—with premium-tier subscriptions to Alpha Academy." He picked up a folded sheet of paper and shot a quick look at the general counsel, who nodded her approval. "Worse yet, now that the Germans have access to Burnham's accounting, there is evidence of money moving the *other* way, too. Three names stand out in particular: Scott Boyle in Science and Tech, Edward Minkin in Procurement, and David Patero at the Operations Support Branch. I urge the heads of the affected units to coordinate. My advice is to make a real, tough, and public example of these assholes."

Acquiescent mutterings all around. The OSB supervisor looked almost happy. So there it was, Tamaskar thought: the world's most anticlimactic mole reveal. Any one, or two, or all of these men, or someone else entirely, could have spied on her for Burnham, and the only twist was that it no longer mattered. They could shoot all three and dump the bodies by the Nathan Hale statue, and it would only convince a new set of hurt boys that their pain should be someone else's. One of them would become the next Burnham, and this one's fans would be better at hiding their affiliation. Until, that is, they didn't have to hide it at all.

"What about the subscribers?" someone asked.

Spaleta shrugged. "Look, what can you do. Burnham makes lonely guys feel smart and powerful. So, to an extent, do we. There's always going to be a small overlap. It's like cops and race. *Some of those who work forces*, you know?" It sounded like a song lyric, so, of course, Tamaskar did not.

"Finally, and to end on a nicer note," the director added, "a big hand for Deputy Director Tamaskar of CovAc, who has shown exceptional courage under literal fire, and whose Medal of Merit paperwork I had the pleasure of starting earlier today."

She stood up, less basking in applause than swimming against it. Her head throbbed. All she wanted was to get into bed with Falk. Not even to fuck. Just literally get into bed, pull the covers over her head, and lie there until the day was a distant memory.

The people around her were saying nice things and leaving. (Or, in the case of Charles Otterbeck, simply leaving.) "Thanks, everyone," Spaleta said. "Asha, stay for a sec?"

"Of course."

A small bottleneck formed outside the doors while everyone picked up their electronics. Spaleta patiently waited for the room to clear, but once it had, his demeanor didn't change. Deep State Nice was still the order of the day.

"Congrats again," he said. "So, hey, I'm pretty sure you know what this is about. You've had some contact with Patero over the last weeks. What's the exposure?"

"His TS/SCI has been revoked earlier, so not huge. I just had him do some grunt work. But yeah. Now I understand how Burnham used to stay one move ahead of us. It's so funny," she said, not even close to smiling. "I was convinced it was a much bigger thing than it was. Ari—uh, Falk—still is. He thinks Burnham is just a contractor, and the mastermind is some ancient civilian stateside."

To her surprise, Spaleta's face darkened in a way she hadn't seen before. "You shouldn't say things like that, Asha."

"Why?"

"You know why." He seemed to will himself back into his normal spirit. "I mean, you heard what Kim said. Not our man, not our op. No ties to the United States."

"Right." Tamaskar nodded, suddenly very anxious to leave the reinforced room.

When she got to her office, her phone was ringing. The buzz came from her own burner, which made her smile again.

"Ugh, clingy," she said into the receiver. She meant it as a lighthearted gag and was immediately terrified that the intent wouldn't come across over the phone. "Shouldn't you be in surgery right now?"

Falk sounded too urgent to focus on matters of tone. "Asha, I think I'm onto something. I need to go and check it out. I swear I will explain when I'm back."

"Go where? Back when?"

"It's honestly better if you don't know. Look in your own notes, though. You'll find it, too. I left the notebook on the table."

She didn't know it was possible for a day to start on such a high and to get so steadily worse with every hour. "Oh, come on."

Falk paused. "I know what it looks like, so I'll just say it, and it's going to come out a mess. Here goes. It's not cold feet. I'm not making shit up. Please trust me. Last night . . . this morning . . . I—I may be in love with you. Which is part of why I have to do this."

Tamaskar sat there searching for words, then realized she was actually searching for feelings. She had already prepared to be furious at Falk, knew *how* to be; at least it was a clear path forward. But now that that plan had been scuttled, nothing came in its place.

Finally she just did what he would do. "Is Krista there? Put her on the phone."

He laughed before hanging up, which, for the moment, was proof enough of his devotion, because it was an absolutely terrible joke.

■ ■ ■

Stammheim Prison, Stuttgart
April 27, 2024

Falk stared at the double doors at the meeting room's far end, reminding himself not to look smug, vengeful, or petty when they opened. It would be even better not to *feel* any of these things, of course. Yet Burnham wasn't even there, and a part of him already seethed.

Perhaps it was the room itself—clean, well-lit, and devoid of any character in a way that paradoxically also marked it as German. He knew better than to think of prisons as places where one should suffer, but what he'd seen of Stammheim so far looked like a Hampton Inn. He assumed that Burnham's private cell, too, was much nicer than the damp basement of an ancient brewery.

Or maybe it was the directly preceding interaction that had set him on edge. "Ah so," the officer who signed him in had said, toggling to English mid-sentence at the sight of his new passport. "Herr Falk, of Incarcerated Americans Abroad, here to see Philipp Brenner." Falk had opened his mouth to protest before realizing the Germans had Burnham booked under his original name. "Yes."

"You are lucky. He gets hundreds of visitation requests a day."

Gee. What an honor to be chosen.

It had taken Falk a couple of weeks to arrange his flimsy cover in a way that wouldn't immediately ping back to the Agency. He had incorporated IAA in Cyprus and remotely bribed a clerk to backdate its creation by a year. He had almost called it the Committee for Incarcerated Americans until he looked at the acronym.

Lost in mental preparations, he missed the moment the doors swung open and a guard brought in Burnham. Falk got up, not knowing the local procedure, but there was none: Burnham walked in, the guard left, and that was it.

Unless the Stammheim prison uniform was corduroy pants and an Aran sweater, he was wearing his own clothes. His famous hair had been cut shorter, though this wasn't required—Burnham's own choice, Falk surmised, to make himself look like more of a victim of a cruel state. Either way, the floppy forelock was gone, and he looked instantly older without it. The twitchy shoulder movements remained. Falk had never considered that they could be the onset of a neurological condition, not a mannerism.

Burnham took the free chair. The tabletop between them was a smooth expanse of pinewood. Just like during their first sit-down, Falk began by checking the corners for cameras. Amazingly, the German obsession with privacy extended to prisons.

"Did you know," Burnham said in lieu of a hello, "when the Red Army Faction were kept here, the entire place was covered with a steel net? They were afraid their followers would try to rescue them by helicopter. That's power."

"Yeah, well. Your followers are at home on their computers," Falk replied acidly.

"For now."

"And, from what I recall of Baader-Meinhof, it didn't work out so great for them."

"No, it did not. Might work out not so great for me, either." He noticed that Burnham's German accent had become more pronounced, even to the point of an occasional syntactic error. Perhaps it was the forced immersion into his native environment, with no Brits or Americans around. Or perhaps the man had simply stopped trying to sound like anyone other than himself.

"At least," he added, "if they kill me here, it will be known as the Felix Burnham Wing."

"I doubt that very much," Falk said. "I don't know if you follow the news, but Germany is recoiling from the likes of you as we speak. Reschke is the hero."

Burnham drummed his fingers on the table. "All right," he said, getting some of his old voice back. "Let's skip past the glaring irony of our changed circumstances. You won, I lost, et cetera. But there's a dignity in a clean loss that I intend to die preserving. You must be here to 'turn' me, in your vampiric parlance. Let me stop you right there, Mr. Falk. I'm not interested."

"I respect that," Falk said, "I do. But I also wonder if you realize exactly whom you are protecting by doing that."

Burnham sighed. "And the mediocre mind games begin. You're wasting your breath."

"Got it. You don't want to talk. That's fine, I'll talk for both of us." Falk got up, put his hands in his pockets, and since nothing appeared to preclude him doing so, began to pace the room. "Remember how defensive you got when I suggested that the plot to kill Reschke was Cormorant's, not yours?"

"Whose?"

"Sorry, I call our mutual friend that. What do you call him?"

"Nice try, Mr. Falk," Burnham said. "You can call him whatever you like."

"Anyway, I stand corrected. It was all you. Your plot, your pitch, your big idea. And that's what attracted him to your side."

Burnham shrugged. "Apology accepted, I suppose."

It was time to go in for the kill. Falk had been rehearsing the next part for over two weeks, ever since that morning he, driven by rage and revelation, bolted from Asha's house. He took a moment to check his logic one last time.

The prisoner was looking up at him, amused. "Is that it?"

"Wouldn't that be nice," Falk said. "Here's the problem. If Cormorant was the one who wanted Reschke dead, he would have done it himself. God knows he has enough blood on his hands. Your association makes perfect sense in one case, and one case only: if his goal was to *fail* at killing Reschke. Fail so badly, so embarrassingly, that it would wipe out you, your whole movement, and the Reichsbürger in the bargain."

Burnham did his best not to react, focusing his attention on the thriving fiddle-leaf fig in the corner instead. The hook was in. Falk sat back in the chair and made himself comfortable, half consciously parodying Burnham's own stance in his videos.

"The truth, *Felix*," he continued, "is that our friend is a classical liberal, in his outlook if not in his methods. So put yourself in his shoes two years ago. Cormorant looks at the world and sees signs of a rightward turn everywhere. Russia, the country he had spent decades trying to reshape in his image, goes mask-off fascist and starts a land war in Europe. Italy, Hungary, Greece all succumb to various degrees. Germany looks to be next. So he does what he does. Step one is to take a part of his fortune that's held in a friendly Russian bank and have a GRU agent move it West, in a way that leaves a subtle but visible trail. Step two is to start casting about for the *worst possible candidate* to carry out an assassination. It takes him a year, but he finds the perfect one. A preening blowhard with delusions of world-historic grandeur. You."

"You're trying to rile me up." Burnham pursed his lips. "Classic transference. I guess it must still hurt to realize I've used you as a patsy."

"Glad you brought up that word," Falk said. "Next, Cormorant arranges a sit-down between you and the Russians in St. Petersburg, and makes it rain on your whole idiotic operation like you've never dreamed. You are now sitting on tens of millions in dirty money, and hiring killers left and right. Best time of your life, I'm sure. Dom Pérignon for everyone. Let me guess, that's when you got the Rover and the Pagoda, too."

"And now you just sound envious," Burnham said, playing bored but a little too bored. "I am beginning to regret spending my visitation hour on this. I thought you'd be funnier."

"At that point," Falk continued, ignoring him, "Cormorant's job is basically done. A right-wing clown with a private army and provable GRU funding is already a good enough story to tell the world. So he uses Free Pen Foundation, his pet nonprofit, to bring Alan Keegan to Prague and hand him your head on a Czech crystal platter." He carefully watched Burnham's face as he went on. "The problem is, the puppet thinks he's a real boy now. You've got your own spies on the payroll, and desperate fans you've swindled out of their last dollar who will do anything to get it back. So you find out, and you murder Keegan."

This time Burnham didn't even try to play it cool. "No," he said, hitting the table for emphasis. "No! Absolutely not."

"Yes. Keegan dies, which brings *me* into the picture. And Cormorant and I, we have history, to put it mildly. But unlike you, Cormorant is a wholly rational actor. He doesn't do revenge. He plays the angles. So he vouches for me when you check, fully aware that I'm there to take you down. In a way, Felix, we're both his patsies. Keegan was plan A. I became plan B." Burnham raised his index finger to interject, then decided against it.

"Want to hear the saddest part?" Falk asked, to dead silence. "I think you knew all this, on some level. But you've been chugging your own Kool-Aid for so long, you *still* thought you were going to outsmart him."

"Are you done?" Burnham suddenly barked.

"I don't know. You tell me."

"I suspected," he said a little softer. "Is that what you want to hear? It was, I suppose, too good to be true. But I had the money, the staging grounds, the manpower. And he was just a frail little voice on the phone. I thought I'd get rid of him later."

"Tell me who he is."

"In a minute, once I hear your offer."

"There's no offer," Falk said. "Not after Keegan. The offer is to redeem one tiny piece of yourself before the rest of you rots in hell."

The last thing he expected Burnham to do was smile at this, but smile the man did, a wide, honest grin. "Oh, I think you will do better than that, Ari. Because, smart as you are, you haven't quite put it together yet. And I just have."

"I'm listening."

"Katya Lisichenko," Burnham said. "The little Ukrainian pebble in my shoe."

"What about her?"

"Well, based on what you just told me, one would have to assume Cormorant—I rather like the name now—had her under surveillance ever since using her double to move the money West. Which means he *knew* she recorded me at the Angleterre. He *knew* she tried to contact you. So ask yourself a simple question. If Cormorant's only goal was to set me up and ruin me, like you say, why not just let that poor woman get out and tell the world? Why did Keegan have to die the exact moment he had that video in his hands? Why did his killer have to be a fan of mine, not a hired pro?"

The room was cool, but Falk felt a trickle of sweat on his neck. He knew the answer, and it was already making him sick.

"Because otherwise," he said, "I would stay in hiding."

"Ta-da." Burnham raised his voice in something very close to triumph. "You said it yourself: The man plays the angles. Sorry, my boy, but there is only one reason your friend is dead and Lisichenko is rotting away in a Russian colony. I may be vain, yes, but you're far too modest. You've always been his plan A."

Falk sat thunderstruck, his mind refusing the implications so furiously that it spun out on a thousand tangents instead. It took him a minute to reel his thoughts back in. A minute more to see the outline of a response. Burnham got up, went to the door, and rapped on it, saying, "*Fast fertig.*"

All you've achieved was a slight hiccup in a plan that has more redundancies than you can possibly imagine.

The clarity, once it came, was unbearable. He knew what he had to do, he knew how to do it, he knew he would do it, and that it would be the end of him. And he saw no other way.

"I do have an offer," Falk said, his voice already someone else's. "It's conditional on something you just said."

Burnham turned his head. "Yes?"

"It won't be heaven. But I can get you limbo."

■ ■ ■

Sea Ranch, California
April 28, 2024

Tamaskar watched the dot on her phone as it neared. Above her head, ocean wind hissed through pine needles. The Pacific was steps away. She could hear it sigh and crash, though all she saw of it was the occasional glimpse of a whitecap in the dark.

She stood at the top of a country lane cut through the woods, leading to a single house at the end. It was a modest timber-frame cube, unremarkable but for the dramatic slash of its roof; as if in a bid for even more privacy, it sat away from the road, in a ravine spanned by a narrow gangway. On paper, the owner of the house was one Jane Smith, eighty-seven. Its one and only tenant for the last thirty years was a trust traceable, via four shell layers, to a dormant marketing firm with a single client: Free Pen Foundation.

Inside the house, invisible to her, an old man sat in his favorite fireside armchair, eyes trained on the entrance. It's been a few hours since he'd gotten the call. He had considered going down to the basement to get his commemorative Browning, the only gun he owned, out of storage, but the thought of bullets flying around the house filled him with revulsion. He clutched his favorite book instead, the first edition of Nabokov's *The Gift*. His wife sat facing him on a nearby ottoman, staring up with a mix of love and pity. Two small pills trembled in her withered palm, white in the dusk of the room.

Having followed Falk's hint down the rabbit hole of her own scribbled notes, Tamaskar now knew almost everything. She knew how, back in 1989, an act of Congress had created an enormous investment fund to bring mortgages and credit cards—the systems of debt supposedly synonymous with freedom—to the rapidly liberalizing Soviet Union. How, around 2003, when history didn't end and free Russia began arresting its first dissidents, it was told to fold. How no one knew what to do with the billions it had made and could no longer legally use, now strewn everywhere from the Art Deco towers of Manhattan to KhromBank's headquarters in Moscow. How the fund became a foundation.

And, crucially, how a veteran investor named Lloyd Oakfield, born in San Francisco in 1935, a onetime CIA officer and McNamara aide, spearheaded the transition, then immediately resigned from the board of directors and vanished with no digital trace.

But as it turned out, she didn't really need to learn any of it. She knew she was in the right place the moment she got out of the car, turned the corner, and saw the handmade street sign. It read *Cormorant Reach*.

The dot moved another tick closer. The light from the screen illuminated Tamaskar's face. She had no chance of seeing before being seen, but that was fine. That was the point.

"Asha?"

They had been together for two days and apart for twenty, and still her stupid heart somersaulted at the sound of the voice. She looked down the road, saw no one, turned around. Falk softly stepped out of the woods. He was wearing all black—a tactical fleece, ripstop pants with reinforced knees, and flat-soled Chucks. The phone light glinted off the barrel of a pistol. He held it in both hands, pointed down.

"There you are," Tamaskar said in as casual a tone as she could muster.

She dimmed the phone. He holstered the gun. "How did you find me?"

"Don't worry, I'm the only person who can. You're still using my burner."

Falk gestured for her to step off the road, into the brush, and led the way. Tamaskar warily followed. They walked in silence toward the sound of the surf.

"I've asked you to trust me," he said, turning around once the road was far enough behind. "I would have been back tomorrow, you know."

"Yes," she said. "You would have been back tomorrow a murderer."

Falk took a step toward her. "Asha. No. It's not—" He searched for words. "It's the only justice left. Did you know Spaleta, back at State, sat on the Free Pen Foundation board for seven years?"

"I do."

"This is why I've cut you out of this!" She saw his teeth in the dark, and it wasn't a smile. "Goddamn it, why couldn't you trust me?"

Tamaskar stepped forward, too, putting her hands on his rigid shoulders. "Honest answer? Because you're blind with rage, and you are undoing everything we've done. Did you stop to think, even for a second, what it took for you to get here? You cut a deal with Burnham. Burnham! You actually went into a room with the man I spent years trying to stop, the man who almost murdered you, and you *negotiated*." She shook her head. "Incarcerated Americans Abroad. Jesus Christ."

"Burnham hasn't actually killed anyone. Cormorant kills with impunity. Has, for decades. I don't know how to put it any plainer."

"He also keeps the world from sliding into fascism."

"He *is* fascism."

"No. His means are vile. But you can say the same about every power, including the one we work for. At least he is relatively surgical."

Falk shrugged her hands off and stepped aside, shuddering in disgust. "Are you hearing yourself?"

"The dead are dead. All you are doing is proposing to add one old man to the list."

He walked a wide circle in the woods to calm himself before coming back. When he did, he spoke so quietly she didn't hear him at first.

"He got to you. He got to you, didn't he."

"No! I have no idea who actually lives in that house. I followed your notes and your phone."

"He got to you. In person or not, it doesn't matter. You've accepted him as part of the system."

"And Burnham got to you!" she screamed, hurt by the kernel of truth in the accusation. "What did you give him in return for Cormorant's name? What did you give that Nazi? Huh?"

Falk stared away. "I, uh, started a process," he said with some difficulty.

"You started a *process*? Fuck does that mean?"

"All I can say is, if it works, Burnham will remain neutralized. I promise you that. And some objective good will come out of it, too, you'll see."

"And does Cormorant need to die for this deal to go through?"

"No," said Falk. "He needs to die for Alan Keegan. And Petra Lorencová. And Anton Basmanny and Inga Lace and Klaus Staubermann. And more names that will tell you nothing, and names even I don't know. But, Asha, this has to end. Enough of this enlightened-oligarch bullshit. People have to have a say in their destiny."

"Look at the world," Tamaskar said, felt tears well up in her eyes, and blinked them back. "When people have a say, they just say *burn it down*. Again and again and again."

This time they walked side by side until they were on an empty beach. Through a single tear in the cloud cover, the moon slid in and out of view. Tangles of wrack lay here and there like dead seals, and the air smelled of rotting kelp.

"All right," said Falk finally. He took the gun, pushed mag release, caught the clip, and clicked the cartridges out into her palm.

"I love you," said Tamaskar.

"I love you."

"But it no longer matters, because you don't trust me."

He slowly shook his head no. She poured the heavy handful of bullets into her pocket. "Let's keep it clean, then. No goodbyes. Go. I'll wait here for a bit."

Falk reached out and squeezed her hand for a millisecond. "Look, it wasn't meant to happen." He seemed to wrestle with the urge to say something else, then went for it. "I'm allergic to cats, and you don't know who Blixa Bargeld is."

The realization that this was the last dumb deflating Falk joke she'd ever hear hit Tamaskar harder than anything that had happened before.

By the time she got over it enough to look up again, he was walking away along the shore. After a few dozen yards, he raised his arm in what she thought was a farewell wave; but then a small object arced out of it and into the tide. A few seconds later, when she turned her phone back on, the dot had disappeared.

EPILOGUE

Today

The prison van slogged through the mud. It wasn't the usual *avtozak*—an armored bus with a cage protecting the driver from the cargo—to which Katya Lisichenko had grown accustomed. This one was a regular, borderline-cute UAZ, nicknamed *bukhanka* for its resemblance to a loaf of bread on wheels. The radio played some awful patriotic psyop earworm, but at least it was on. The steering wheel had a sheepskin cover, the gearshift a silly topper in the shape of a boxing glove: the personal, subtly bucking the institutional. All of it was grounds for hope.

She had no idea where they were taking her. She had stopped guessing long ago, having gradually succumbed to the very Russian idea that contemplating the future meant nothing more than tempting fate to smack you harder. The governing law of the land was *Tomorrow will be worse*, and Katya's lived experience bore out this maxim.

The first official charge leveled at her had been crossing a border without proper documents: the Russian border, that is, in the unmarked cargo plane that had brought her kicking and screaming from Tbilisi. Resisting arrest and hooliganism quickly followed. Weeks later, she had become a witness in the much-publicized Orlan Finans case: The bank stood accused of using crypto to move its dollar reserves West after the Kremlin made it illegal to do so. Some of those reserves must have made their way back and to the investigators, because, before Katya knew it, the bank's president had gotten off scot-free and she had gone from witness to codefendant. An ethnic Ukrainian in wartime Russia, she could already see the next charge looming on the horizon. Half a year later, there it was: treason.

All of this, needless to say, was happening with Katya already behind bars. Her term thus kept telescoping forward, pushing her release into progressively more sci-fi-sounding dates until it threatened to touch the next century. The only visible mileposts in the cold fog of her future were new trials and hearings. At some point, she stopped paying attention to those details. She knew she would never get out.

And now, inconveniently, hope was back.

Katya had detected the first pesky twinge of it several weeks earlier. It had visited her in the workshop as she sewed a police uniform—the ironic occupation for most inmates of the IK-14 women's correctional facility. There would be a phone call for her in thirty minutes; she was to take it in the head of the colony's office. That in itself was highly irregular, as was the jacket she ended up making before heading there.

On the call were her useless lawyer and an FSB agent who had once pelted her with vague questions about her old bosses at KhromBank. Katya was solemnly told to "stay put" and not to "do anything," redundant advice at best but remarkably easy to follow. By the time she got back to the shop, the rumor mill had outspun the sewing machines: the United States, a friend whispered, had put her on the political-prisoner list.

The second incident had occurred two days ago. A new, unfamiliar FSB agent, of higher rank and education if his suit and accent were anything to go by, had come to see her in person; IK-14 was a six-hour drive from Moscow. His questions were even stranger yet more encouraging than his colleague's gnomic counsel, because there was an implied finality to them. They sounded like an exit interview. Was she remorseful for her treasonous actions? Sure, why not. Did she feel she had, on the average, been treated fairly? Yes, yes.

The *bukhanka* took a shortcut through a small, ugly settlement at the base of a giant lumber mill, then wheeled onto a forest road that at least had traces of asphalt to go with the mud. A clearing ahead turned out to be an airstrip, with a corrugated shed for a terminal and a lone flapping wind sock for a tower. A turboprop An-32 stood at the strip's far end, an odd, misshapen thing with engines set above the wings like two humps.

Katya's heart raced. A cocktail of hope, fear, and remembered trauma flooded her senses. The last time someone had driven her onto a tarmac was in the middle of a drone attack followed directly by a kidnapping. She barely registered how she got out of the van and on board.

Apart from her and the pilot, the plane held four people, all there for her in some capacity or another. One was her useless lawyer. Two were the FSB agents she already knew: the one who had called and the sleeker one who had driven up. He now had a windbreaker and a Yankees cap on, as if playing some kind of American tough guy; all he needed to complete the look would be a toothpick in his mouth. Another man, older, with the blank face of a killer, sat in the back playing World of Tanks on his phone and didn't lift his head to look. The useless lawyer smiled and said something useless.

"Is this an exchange or a transfer?" Katya asked. "Please tell me something. Anything."

The two FSB men consulted in a whisper. "You'll be fine, citizen," the agent in the windbreaker finally said. Then he pulled the cap over his eyes and went to sleep.

She tried to figure out the direction of the flight by looking out of the window at first, but it got dark minutes after takeoff. The plane puttered over a great black plain, with threads and puddles of yellow light for roads and towns. At night, all of Europe looked the same. Perhaps the West would be brighter and colder, with more LED illumination and less sodium vapor.

The flight felt like ten hours, despite likely not lasting more than four. Katya didn't have a phone or a watch to check the time, and didn't feel like asking any more questions. After a while, she went into a kind of standby mode, not asleep but not fully awake, either, and snapped out of it only when the plane was already nuzzling the cloud cover. The nightscape below looked more dramatic: mountains, valleys. Germany? Norway?

They flew low above a midsize city and landed on its outskirts. The pilot came out and opened the door himself. She knew at once that all her guesses had been wrong: muggy, heavy air filled the cabin. They must have been traveling south the whole time.

"Where are we?"

"Georgia," the useless lawyer replied, after checking with the nearest FSB agent if it was okay to say.

Katya's reaction was immediate and involuntary. She screamed and lunged for the doors; the languid killer type, now shockingly fast, sprinted from the back to tackle her. The guy in the cap was closer and grabbed her first, restraining her arms in a bear hug while saying *shh* like she was a baby or a cat or a lover. "Come on, silly," he whispered once she went limp in his arms. "It's just to change planes."

After that, everything was a blur. They boarded another turboprop, this one a more traditional-looking Bombardier with seats in numbered rows, tray tables, and other luxuries. It had more people on it, some with video cameras. The second flight took about three more hours. By the time it came to a graceless stop on yet another tarmac, it was morning again, and hotter still. A line of watercolor pink ran along the flat desert horizon.

"Welcome to Abu Dhabi," the guy in the Yankees cap said. Her freak-out had made him a little more forthcoming.

"Who am I being exchanged for?" Katya asked, using the chance.

"A great man," the other FSB agent answered, startling her. It was the first thing he had said the whole night.

An American and a German in business suits came on board, a strange combo. They looked around for a bit, consulted quietly with each other in their respective accents, nodded to the FSB men, and left. The doors closed again and stayed shut for another ten minutes, the longest in Katya's life. The nerves, the exhaustion, and the rising temperature inside the plane were all conspiring to make her sleepy. The sun rose. Hot air quavered over the apron; through the ripples, Katya could see a sleek Gulfstream jet parked on the other end and some vague human movement around it.

"All right, let's go," the Yankees cap said, suddenly urgent, grabbing her by the elbow. "Go go go go!"

They stomped down metal stairs and formed a row along the body of the plane. More men joined from somewhere on the ground, swelling their ranks to about twenty; she couldn't see any faces, nor did she care. Something similar was happening by the Gulfstream across the tarmac. That group was also all men with a single woman at its center, making it look like a mirage reflection of hers. Katya almost lifted her hand to see if the other woman would do the same.

"Okay." The agent in the cap touched her shoulder. "Walk forward slowly. Good luck."

Katya took a step, sun in her eyes, still expecting some terrible twist. Another drone. Another gun in the face. Another civil servant politely telling her she had already done this two days ago.

She turned around, panicking. The cap guy waved to urge her on. The killer hung back with his hand inside his jacket. It was pretty obvious what his job would be if anything went wrong.

By the time she faced forward again, a figure had separated from the other group and was walking toward her through the heat shimmer. The Great Man. Her price, her counterpart. Her equivalent-value object.

Katya made her way across, regaining some of her composure in the simple act of walking alone. The stranger was now close enough to look familiar. Sixty or so, silver hair, bushy eyebrows.

The man from the Angleterre.

"Of *course*," he said, passing by. She could smell his cologne. "Clever fuck." Katya didn't understand what this meant.

Twenty paces behind her, an FSB agent said, "Welcome to Russia, Mr. Burnham," in ear-splittingly bad English.

"Now, now," Katya heard him reply in decent Russian. "Let's not get ahead of ourselves."

After that, she wasn't listening, because she was now close enough to the American jet to recognize her doppelgänger: Asha, the woman with whom she had survived the Tbilisi attack. At this distance, the two of them looked nothing alike, of course, but she still felt overwhelmed by the sight of a friendly face. Katya found herself breaking into a light run, despite the men in front of her gesturing not to. Asha stepped forward to embrace her.

"Well done," she whispered. Katya wasn't sure if this was meant for her.

"Congratulations, Ms. Lisichenko," someone behind Asha said loudly. "You're free."

The men were already crowding onto the jet. Katya withdrew from the hug first and was surprised to see Asha still looking, as if frozen, past her and into the middle distance.

She turned and followed her gaze back to the Russian side. There, too, one figure stood motionless and staring while a scrum of FSB agents escorted Burnham into the turboprop. It was a man with salt-and-pepper hair and a narrow frame, wearing jeans and a T-shirt. He must have been part of the latecomer group.

"Come on, ladies," a uniformed Marine said from the top of the steps, ushering both of them up. "Let's get out of here."

The cabin fizzed with nervous laughter. Asha and Katya took their seats next to each other, window and aisle, the same way they had once sat in the back of Merab's Benz. A champagne cork hit the bulkhead. "Honestly, this might be the first time in my career I am witnessing an actual win-win," a red-faced man violently loosening his tie said to Asha, and for some reason, it was that phrase that made Asha's face spasm and distort. She twisted toward the window, her glasses wobbling in one hand while the other covered her eyes. Katya couldn't think of anything to ask or say, so she lightly patted her shoulder. Someone shoved two foaming flutes at them, spilling some as the jet began to taxi.

ACKNOWLEDGMENTS

Thanks, as always, to Lily, this time for putting up with an increasingly feral cohabitant as the Difficult Second Novel took shape. An eternal debt of gratitude to Binky Urban for making sure Ari Falk got to return at least once, and to the Scribner and Simon & Schuster UK teams for letting him out into the world in the first place.

Thank you to the first readers of the first draft—Alex Kruglov, Anne Vithayathil, Dr. Daria V. Ezerova of Cambridge (whose characterization of Falk as "kind of a slut" made it into the text verbatim), and last but not least Sarah Gregory and Matt Wright, who made sure the British characters' dialogue never strayed into the *'ello, guv'ner* territory. As is fast becoming a tradition, Max Adelman consulted on some tech aspects, while Anna Kraft checked and corrected my barely B1 German.

Almost every event in *Cormorant Hunt* has a real-life source or reference, publicized or not: from a close friend's (successful) flight to Estonia through the Shumilkino checkpoint, which became the prologue, to the 2022 prisoner exchange in Abu Dhabi that forms the epilogue. Most of the underlying research came from a combination of public sources and personal interviews. The *New York Times* story "The Princess and the Justice," by Abbie VanSickle and Philip Kaleta, inspired some details of Burnham's compound. The description of the CIA's Operations

Support Branch was informed in part by Patrick Radden Keefe's reporting in *The New Yorker*. One sentence in chapter 9 is a nearly direct lift from the song "Pollo Rico" by the brilliant Billy Woods. (If you recognized it, we should be friends.)

Finally, my heartfelt thanks to every reader of *The Collaborators*. It was an honor, a challenge, and a blast to be able to inhabit that world again.

This book is dedicated to the memory of Alexei Navalny, and to everyone fighting to preserve democracy against strongmen of every stripe. Unlike Asha Tamaskar, I am still optimistic.

ABOUT THE AUTHOR

Michael Idov is a novelist, director, and screenwriter. A Latvian-born American raised in Riga under Soviet occupation, he moved to New York after graduating from the University of Michigan. Michael's writing career began at *New York* magazine, where his features won three National Magazine Awards, and he has served as the editor in chief of *GQ Russia.* He is also the author of *The Collaborators*, *Ground Up*, and *Dressed Up for a Riot.* Michael has worked on numerous film and TV projects, including *Londongrad*, *Deutschland 83*, *Leto*, and *The Humorist.* He and his wife and screenwriting partner, Lily, divide their time between Los Angeles, Berlin, and Portugal.